Project Hope

Project Hope

David L. Purcell

Published by Sabin Lake Publishing, St. Paul, MN

This is a work of fiction. Names, characters, and incidents are products of the author's imagination or are used fictitiously and are not to be construed as real. Any resemblance to actual events, locales, organizations, or persons, living or dead, is entirely coincidental.

Cover Design by Steve Kuhn

ISBN: 979-8-9857055-0-8 (paperback)
ISBN: 979-8-9857055-1-5 (ebook)

www.davidlpurcell.com

To Kirstin

1

At 6:15 on a Monday night in late March, Zin McGuire found herself on the balcony of St. Paul's Cathedral, looking down at the floor, some twenty feet below her. She didn't want to jump, but the idea had just appeared to her as she stood at the balcony railing, a whim, really, but it found traction somewhere in her uneven state of mind and sort of stuck there. It was an ugly thought; she tried to put it out of her mind.

Zin looked out into the dimly lit sanctuary below, noticing for the first time the tiny chapels tucked away in the corners of the cathedral, each one with a single row of pews, lit by a single overhead light. They looked intimate and peaceful; she wished she had headed to one of those chapels instead of choosing to explore the balcony, a spot that felt lonely and remote, amplifying those same feelings inside her. She knew she wasn't really considering jumping, but something was prodding her to test herself. Maybe she was tired of feeling helpless about her life. Maybe it was the three rum and Cokes still coursing through her body. Zin stepped forward and leaned out over the balcony railing until her feet began to lift off the ground, balancing just above her hips, pushing herself to the verge of losing control. She wasn't a thrill seeker, and so, when she crossed some invisible threshold with her center of gravity, the jolt of fear only confirmed that she wanted to keep her feet planted firmly on the ground.

Zin leaned over the railing, more careful now, and stared down at the floor twenty feet below her. The cold white marble was indifferent to her situation. *Fall on me or not, I don't care.* Even though there wasn't a body lying on the ground below her, she kept staring at the spot, as if wanting to be certain that it hadn't happened. She imagined her body contorted on the ground below her, arms splayed out, a leg bent at an impossible angle. She also imagined surviving that fall, and then, well, she knew that would be worse.

No, what she wanted was to disappear. She stood at the railing and closed her eyes, still puffy from all the crying, and tried to imagine what it would mean to disappear, walking away from her current life, starting over somewhere new. Was it possible? Can you do that? Just pick up and go somewhere far away, with no baggage, no history? Maybe. The idea floated with temporary possibility, but ultimately, it couldn't escape the gravity of her dark, little world, and she let it crash, another silly dream.

Zin took half a step back, only then realizing that she had a white-knuckle grip on the top rail. She was breathing hard. She wanted Rick to feel a measure of the pain that he was causing her and jumping off the cathedral's balcony and breaking her neck might have been a good way to scatter guilt around, to Rick and to everyone else who had been dumping on her. Make them feel an eternity of guilt. But what if, in the end, no one cared?

Zin fretted now, feeling angry at herself again. She had been punishing herself all evening and she didn't want it to continue, but it was hard to keep the waves of humiliation from crashing back on her, a constant tide of self-loathing, and now she had something else to be angry at herself for, this time for being too weak to do anything. She imagined Rick laughing at her for being too scared, and she immediately felt the urge to destroy something. Zin scanned the balcony, but all she could find was a small, ornate cross, maybe fifteen inches high, mounted on a wooden foundation and sitting in the corner of the balcony on a pew, something that must have been left over from a past ceremony or event. She walked over to it and picked it up, inspecting it. The cross was hollow, its shell comprised of brass circles of different sizes, each circle attached to others at its edge. It would do.

Zin brought it back to the railing and held it out over the edge, a sacrificial offering, a substitute for her not being the one to hit the ground. She was holding the cross out over the rail, imagining it dropping and shattering and causing a mess, when a distant movement caught her eye. Down on the altar on the opposite side of the church from her was a man wending his way toward the pulpit. Zin immediately ducked behind the cross. She held her breath as she spied on the man, but the more she watched him, the more she felt confident that he hadn't noticed her. The man was moving around the altar, inspecting one item after another with what looked like a spoon. Zin assumed he was staff or clergy, maybe closing things up for the night, but his dress seemed wrong—he wore a purple jacket, green pants, and what appeared to be black Converse high-tops—and he acted like a stranger who was looking for something, not like someone who knew what he was doing and wanted to finish his job and go home.

Eventually, the man left the altar and began to roam around the sanctuary, and as he got closer, Zin could see him better. He was not tall, maybe about five foot nine, and appeared to be in his early thirties or so, with blonde hair that seemed to have a mind of its own. The man didn't appear to be affiliated with the church, and after a bit, Zin got the sense that she had caught someone who didn't want to be observed.

The man was getting closer now and Zin panicked, ducking further down so only the top of her head protruded above the top rail. She continued to spy on the man as he wandered around the sanctuary for about five more minutes, inspecting windows, pews, candles, bibles—nearly anything that he came across. Zin stayed, squatting low, watching as the man worked his way toward the back entrance. Finally, he stood up abruptly and craned his neck to gaze at the frescos that circled the dome far above. He stood motionless for a long minute, his face calm as he absorbed the scenery above, and then without warning, snapped his head back down and marched straight out the main entrance.

Zin leaned over the railing to search for him, but she couldn't see much underneath the balcony. She wanted to follow him—it seemed like he was up to no good and it intrigued her—but given the evening she was having, she decided she didn't need to make things worse. She heard one of the big front doors close and then all was quiet.

The little diversion over, Zin's awareness returned to the cross she was still holding. Her lips twisted into a frown as she studied the cross for a long moment. She liked the little cross and didn't really want to break it, but she also didn't like the idea that she was chickening out again. The idea of destroying a cross seemed disturbing to her, as if tempting fate or, more specifically, thumbing her nose at God. But then she shook her head slightly. This was a silly inanimate object; she shouldn't be so superstitious. She always played by the rules. This time she would do something dangerous.

Moving quickly so she wouldn't lose her courage, she stepped forward and grabbed the cross with both hands. Zin leaned over the rail, eyed a spot on the ground as if it were a target, and let go of the cross. And as she did, a figure stepped out from under the balcony immediately underneath her. The cross dropped, perfectly upright, directly above the person. Zin screamed, and a fraction of a second later she heard a thud as the cross hit its target.

2

Father Jay O'Brian stared into the little white sink. Its age was showing; little grey scratches marked the entire bowl, culminating in a brown haze of a ring around the drain in which sat a hardened, cracked stopper missing a chain. Above, two handles, each a slightly different size and shape, sat at the corners of the sink. Jay turned one handle and waited for the slow trickle to turn warm. Then he rubbed his hands together and brought them up to his face, giving himself a slap. *Fool!*

Jay examined his tired features in the mirror above the little white sink, noticing the rusty trim that lined the mirror. He hated this dressing room. In fact, he wanted to get out of this church so badly that he started eyeing a window in the corner of the room. It didn't open upward; it could only be pulled outward slightly. *What good is a window that you can't crawl out of?* St. Andrew's Catholic Church was not an architectural gift to the state of Minnesota, a Twin Cities treasure, or even remarkable for the city of Coon Rapids. Built around 1960, it was a combination of beech wood, burnt orange bricks, and uninspiring shapes. Luckily, it wasn't Jay's church, and if the crowd would just dissipate, he could slip out the side entrance and get back to his home church in St. Paul, probably never to return.

Jay looked at his watch. It was 2:45 p.m., and having just finished the funeral service for one Mr. Harold Thompson, formerly of Anoka, Minnesota, Father Jay was now trying to forget the last 60 minutes. Rather, it was more of an attempt to will himself to another place. Another time would have been better; exactly one hour ago would have been just fine. Jay walked over to the window and tried to peer through it to the parking lot to see how many cars were there. His attempt at surveillance was broken by a small cough that came from outside the open doorway. Father Jay turned to notice the ten-year-old altar boy looking terribly uncomfortable and holding an envelope. Father Jay sighed a deep sigh of resignation and looked at the boy.

"Yes?"

"Umm, they gave this to me to give to you."

He handed the priest an envelope and then quickly wheeled away, bounding down the stairs to the back door. The priest looked quizzically at the white envelope until a pang of recognition hit him across the head. He grimaced as he opened the envelope, squinting his eyes as he peered in it. Just as he feared; a simple thank you card and a tip! No weapon of guilt could have stabbed deeper than this—a tip for performing a funeral service in which you insulted the deceased.

Father Jay looked around for his coat and headed toward the backdoor. It was times like this when he wished he had a change of clothes so he could sneak outside without anyone identifying him, but he knew that if he was caught changing, he would look like the weasel he was trying to be. Father Jay walked, close to a trot, to his little ten-year-old Toyota and slipped in. Normally, he would stick around to see how the family or helpers in the church basement were doing, but this was not a normal situation and, luckily, this was not his congregation. The deceased had been without church, and one of his sisters occasionally attended Father Jay's church in St. Paul, so the family had asked him to come out to some suburban church in the middle of nowhere on a Monday afternoon and perform a funeral service for a heartless, mean-spirited, soulless man. Well, that is the impression Jay got when he met with some of the family a couple of days ago. None seemed too sad to see Harold go.

Father Jay made his way to Highway 10, heading toward home. He gunned it as soon as he hit the highway, wanting to get as far away from the scene as he could. He always hated funerals. He never really knew what to say. Everything always sounded so shallow, so unconvincing or so useless. He often didn't know the deceased at all, and to try to summarize a person's life in front of those who knew him or her, at the most sensitive time for the family, seemed like a sadistic test at best. He hated to admit it, but he enjoyed the funerals best if he knew the person or knew that the person was a figure of some importance to the community. At those funerals he could throw himself into the emotion and come out charged, filling the congregation with real feeling. In those circumstances, it was clear that he was speaking with conviction, and even if he wasn't completely eloquent, he knew he could move people. But this Harold guy...when his siblings spoke of him there was no love lost for the man. They joked about him—his miserly ways, his grouchy attitude, his lack of drive. He never married, and you could understand why, with a personality like a toad that even his family wouldn't vouch for after he had gone. Father Jay knew that he wasn't going to say anything memorable. Or at least, that is what he was expecting, until he decided that this funeral warranted a little light-heartedness. He used the sermon to poke fun of Harold, and the first little joke he threw in got a few smiles. The second one didn't come off too well, and a good orator would have known to change course in time to avoid the collision, but Jay was never good at moving off script, and when he made the third comment, he could see in the faces in the pews that he had crossed a line, and Harold's sister in the front row frowned and crossed her arms in front of her chest. No one said anything, but the reception he got later wasn't warm thanks, but icy formality.

Jay turned on the radio and then remembered the envelope. He pulled the plain, white envelope out of his pocket as he drove and thumbed through the bills. He remembered that the envelope had been sealed when they handed it to him, or they would have probably pulled a few bills out. But one thing was for certain; they would have given him something. Jay had long ago learned that Minnesotans, and Minnesota Catholics in particular, were much too driven by the guilt of expectations to not have tipped him. He had been with people at restaurants who had received lousy, indifferent service, but they would still give the same tip, even against the protests of the others around. They would throw the tip on the table while stating the obvious, "they sure don't deserve this." Not that they were big tippers. They just always felt obliged to do the same thing, lest they be perceived as cheap.

Jay looked up in time to pull his swerving little car from the side of the road back into his lane, but quickly lost focus again, beginning to debate what he would do with the cash. He had never fully bought into the ascetic life of the priesthood. He was wrestling with the thought of saving this pittance for a new car or spending it on something more immediate. The priestly salary was such a pittance; he got it—they weren't supposed to have a lot of needs—but they should have a way to make money on the side, or something. What he really wanted was a big pickup, which was completely impractical for a city priest. As he was deliberating what to do with the money, he noticed a slow-moving car ahead of him and he jumped into the left lane, accelerating quickly to pass. The speed felt good. What he really felt like was just staying on the road and driving all night, driving somewhere new.

***

Deputy Jeff Zimmer of the Anoka County sheriff's department sat at the on ramp above the highway, sipping on a Mountain Dew and feeling a little bored on this quiet Monday afternoon. He was about to move his car to catch the speeders in the afternoon rush leaving the metro area for exurban homes when he noticed a little Toyota swerve over the line and then pull back. He put his car in gear and accelerated down the ramp—he had to move his car anyway, so he might as well watch this little car for a minute. When the Toyota accelerated suddenly and passed another car, he decided that the speeding, swerving car deserved more attention. Besides, it was one of those little Japanese cars, reason enough to pull the guy over. He pulled into the left lane and accelerated without his lights on until he was right behind the idiot. Officer Zimmer loved these types of pullovers. The guy didn't even notice that a squad car was ten feet behind his ass. He followed for about twenty seconds before hitting his lights. The guy in the speeding car snapped his neck slightly and made eye contact through the rear-view mirror, that familiar look of terror on the man's face. Officer Zimmer didn't need to be able to read lips to know what was said next.

***

Father Jay's stomach dropped as he glanced into the rearview mirror and issued a curse that you normally didn't hear from a priest. He slowed down, pulled into the right lane, and then over to the shoulder. Jay sat and waited, pulling his wallet out of his back pants pocket, and holding it in his lap. He knew that the collar was always the wildcard in these situations. Some people felt an immediate wave of reverence for the clergy and had a hard time scolding someone who is such a figure of authority. But the collar rubbed others the wrong way, and an opportunity to knock an authority figure, especially of the type that may have caused them anxiety in their childhood, was too good to let go. Father Jay could usually tell within seconds who was going to cause him grief. As he sat in his car, he looked back through the rear mirror and watched the officer, still sitting in the squad car, probably doing a license check. The officer eventually got out of the car and headed over, checking out Jay's car along the way. The officer was a big man with a bit of a paunch, a crew cut, and small, narrow eyes. As he bent down toward the window, Jay saw the slightest smile appear and then quickly vanish in the officer's face. This was not going to be pretty.

"License and proof of insurance, please," said the officer.

"Sorry officer," Father Jay said as he fumbled with the glove compartment. He offered a small prayer of thanks when he found his insurance card. "I was swerving, I know. Something fell out of my pocket, and I bent down to retrieve it. Stupid of me," he mumbled, with a mock 'I'm stupid, I should know better' shake of the head. A wave of guilt swept over him for lying, but he justified it by telling himself that he wouldn't be learning anything if he got the ticket, so why should he get one?

He handed the license and insurance card to the officer who didn't say anything at first, just studying both cards very thoroughly.

"Do you know how fast you were going?" Father Jay's eyeballs darted to the upper right in a panicked attempt to come up with a good answer. There never was one, which is why they always love asking the question.

"Umm, not sure," he finally answered.

"67. Do you know what the speed limit is here?"

"I thought it was 65 on the highway here," he pleaded. He looked around as if to prove his point, but it was obvious that the mix of farmland and occasional bait-n-ammo store of the early highway scene had changed over to the fast food, pawn shop, liquor store strip malls and more frequent gas stations indicating that he had crossed some urban threshold—one with lower speed limits.

"Nope. 55. Why don't you come have a seat in my car while I fill this out." Officer Zimmer was enjoying this immensely. Father Jay obliged, feeling like a fool. He sat down in the passenger seat while Officer Zimmer punched something into a little computer. Jay looked around at the equipment and then noticed something missing.

"So, where's the radar gun?" he asked, mostly curious. Officer Zimmer didn't look up.

"Don't have one," he answered. Father Jay thought about that statement, which didn't seem like the right answer.

"Then…how do you know how fast I was going?"

"I pulled up behind you and looked at my speedometer," answered Officer Zimmer. He kept writing, unperturbed. Jay mulled on this one for a minute before raising another question.

"But what if you were going faster than me to catch me. Your speedometer would read higher than mine because you had to go faster to catch up to me." He wasn't a physicist or anything, but surely this logic was reasonable. Father Jay gave the officer a look that he hoped would convey a benign thoughtfulness, someone who wasn't looking to insult the officer, and would accept the officer's apology with grace and dignity. A glance at the officer indicated that this wasn't going to help.

Officer Zimmer stopped writing and slowly turned his head toward the priest. "Listen, *Father*, I saw you swerving all over the road, pulled up behind you and rode your ass for a good ten seconds until I finally gave up on the notion that you might notice me and so I turned my lights on. I had p-l-e-n-t-y of time to check your speed."

"OOOOkaaay," whistled Jay, turning around to look out the window. He wanted to say a prayer for the officer to be smote down by a bolt of lightning but held himself back. The officer finished writing and handed him two pieces of paper.

"Why two pieces of paper?"

"You had two violations. Speeding and a seat belt violation. You need to send in a payment within 20 days or appear in court." He started opening a file case and added without looking up, "Have a nice day."

Jay drifted back to his car and sat deflated in the front seat, grumbling to himself about the pathetic state of the Anoka County Sheriff's department. He played through several scenes in his mind, first taking the officer out with a kung-fu move and lots of sound effects (POW – BLAM!). In the next scene, he had told the quaking officer to 'find something better to do than pulling over kindly priests for minor offenses. He imagined a soliloquy where he would ramble on about the state of crime in the area, shaming the officer into an apology. Finally, in the scene he liked best, as the officer was about to get out of the car he floored it, speeding off and losing the officer on back roads.

When Jay returned to reality, he realized that the police

officer wasn't going to leave until Jay did. So, to avoid another meeting with Officer Friendly, he pulled out carefully (with blinkers and all) and drove, much too slowly, back to his home church.

Jay swung into the church parking lot. It dawned on him that he couldn't remember any part of the drive home, his mind having been obsessed with thoughts of the botched funeral and the unforgiving police officer. He looked at the clock and figured he could get a little work done—his mood almost settled down now—only to see the big, new SUV that his church bookkeeper had just purchased sitting in the row next to the church garden. He had heard her talking about the SUV's features (pretty much everything one could want), and he knew how much money Miranda made (not much), and knew that she wasn't married, so this must have come from an inheritance. She hadn't said anything about how she had financed it, and he wasn't going to pry, but it just made Jay even more frustrated with his little car.

Jay walked into the office area and found Miranda sitting in the front desk instead of her usual office.

"Hi Father," she said, looking up from her computer screen which, from Jay's angle, appeared to be filled with a shoe shopping site. "How'd the funeral go?"

"Oh, just fine. I insulted the deceased and then got a ticket on the way home. You know, the usual." Jay stood at the mail slot and thumbed through the letters and papers that had been left for him.

"Oh. That sounds like a bad afternoon."

Jay closed his eyes and took a deep breath. "I just like to antagonize the mourners. Say, where's Barb?"

"She had to go pick up her grandson today. Had to leave early."

"Oh, yeah, I forgot. Thanks." Jay walked back to his office and plopped down at his desk. He started up his computer and started reading some emails. He was trying to read the minutes from the last regional clergy meeting (which he had skipped, again), but found himself rereading the first paragraph. He sat back in his chair and swiveled around to look out the window behind him. He stared out the window for a few minutes before deciding that maybe he'd work better from home, so he shut down his computer and headed out. Miranda had already left, so he didn't need to say goodbye.

Jay pulled into his driveway, just a couple houses down from the church, opened the garage door, and slid the car into the little detached garage, turning off the radio. He crossed to the side door of the house and let himself in, leaving his coat on a peg in the back stairwell and tromping up through the kitchen. He paused at the refrigerator and opened the door to see if a snack was handy, but he didn't see anything easy, and it seemed a little too early for dinner. He frowned and went around to his living room to turn on the TV, but after flipping through the channels, the late afternoon options were pretty thin. He sighed and decided he should try again to get a little work done.

Jay headed upstairs to his office and started working on his sermon for Sunday. He had a theme already picked out, so he thought he could just start fleshing out some details, but after about two paragraphs and half an hour of work, he found himself rereading the same sentence over and over and decided to give up. Seeing that it was past five o'clock, he determined it was now late enough to make an early dinner—something frozen would be good. Jay lumbered back downstairs and opened the freezer this time, finding a Jumbo Man frozen chicken dinner that gave him pause—he was starting to feel like a jumbo man around the waist—but he decided that tonight wouldn't be the night to worry about his weight. He turned on the oven, unwrapped the cardboard carton, and went to look for a bottle of wine.

Jay found the bottle, a malbec, made a mental note that this was the last bottle in the house, poured himself a glass and went to the living room where he sank his large body onto a lumpy couch and turned on a sports network. Baseball season openers would be in a couple days, and he wanted to hear some news about his Minnesota Twins. He was supposed to go to the worship committee meeting tonight, and he knew better than to show up to a meeting after drinking, but tonight the wine seemed more important. No one would notice one little drink. After half an hour and a couple glasses of wine, his phone buzzed to tell him his food was ready. He pushed himself off the couch to go get the meal, and returned with a hot tray, an oven mitt, and the bottle of wine, now half empty. He poured himself another glass and sat back down in front of the television, scarfing down the baked chicken and mashed potatoes. When he went for a refill on his glass, he looked at the bottle—now a bit more than a quarter left—and decided to hold off for the time being. He had a meeting at church in half an hour, after all, but he knew how to hold his alcohol and when to stop. He decided he'd have just a little splash more before he left. Twenty minutes later, Jay went down the back stairs to get his coat and headed out for the two-minute walk to church, the empty bottle of wine sitting alone on the kitchen counter.

3

Zin stared, frozen in horror, at the body lying face down on the ground below her. Her mind went blank—this couldn't be happening. After a moment, the body started to move, releasing Zin from her paralysis. She turned and ran downstairs, deathly afraid of what she might find.

When she reached the scene, she found the man who had been roaming around the church, now sitting up and rubbing his shoulder and back. She ran up to him and stopped at his feet, watching him with eyes wide before speaking.

"Are you okay?"

The man nodded slowly. "Yes, I believe so." He started to get up and swing his arm in a big circle, rolling his shoulder to test it out.

"Oh, I am so sorry. I...I was just..." Zin fell silent. The two looked at each other for several seconds before the man spoke.

"You were not trying to hit me." It wasn't a question.

"No, no, no, I wasn't. I was just, I don't know, fooling around. I thought you had left. I never meant to hurt you."

"I understand," he answered. He looked at the cross lying on the ground nearby and then up to the balcony above. "I am lucky I ducked. That would have hurt." Neither said anything, both considering the alternative outcomes, which were not very pretty. Then, abruptly changing tone from thoughtful to cheery, he turned back to Zin and smiled. "Well, I believe I should leave for real this time. Have a good night." He nodded and then turned and walked toward the front doors.

"Are you sure you're okay?" called Zin, bewildered.

"Yes," he said, stopping briefly to reply. "I will be sore tomorrow, but I am mostly okay. Thank you." He turned and walked out into the night. The doors closed, but Zin kept staring at them. *That's it?* She was confused and now very awake, the adrenaline of the incident bringing her to immediate sobriety. She sat in a nearby pew and closed her eyes, a ball of dread forming in the pit of her stomach. She was still shaking, and she felt a little weak.

Zin thought about the situation. She had entered the church, tried to destroy an object, and almost killed a man. She scanned the sanctuary, wondering if anyone had heard or seen the incident. Miraculously, no one had come by, but her luck wouldn't hold on for long. She spied the cross lying on the ground about ten feet away and walked over and picked it up. One of the arms of the cross had a dent in it, and there was a scratch on the wooden foundation, but it was intact. She held it and shook her head, issuing a small prayer of apology, and then, looking around, decided to place it on a small table that was set along a back wall. Having pressed her luck enough, Zin walked briskly to the big doors and left the church.

Outside, the sun had set, and she stood on the steps in the grey twilight and took a deep breath, the cool air feeling good in her lungs. *What a night!* She was lucky to come out of this unscathed. She wanted to probe her feelings, turn them around in her mind, examine them, try to understand what any of this meant for her, but she instinctively knew that she couldn't do this right now with the adrenaline still pumping. She would give it plenty of analysis later, probably during another sleepless night.

Zin started to head back toward the downtown area where she had parked, hoping to avoid the strange man from church. She had nearly crushed his skull, after all, and wanted to imagine that he was just fine. But as she started down the long flight of church steps, she noticed that the man was not far in front of her, and she couldn't help but wonder what the man's story was. Maybe he needed a hand. She owed him something.

Zin hopped down the steps a little faster so she could keep an eye on him. With her senses about her, she again noticed that he was dressed oddly—the purple winter jacket was threadbare, and his emerald green off-brand pants were a tad too short on him. After following him a bit, curiosity and loneliness teamed up again. She trotted to catch up.

"Umm, Sir?" she called. The man didn't pause or even acknowledge her. "Hey!" She called louder. He stopped in his tracks and waited. She jogged up to him, huffing slightly. "Umm, I wanted to apologize again," she said.

"Yes, you said that. Apology accepted," he replied. He smiled politely and turned back to his walk. Zin stopped and watched him go, confused at the disparity between the man's demeanor and appearance. The man was getting ahead of her, so she jogged a couple of steps to catch up.

"You're sure you're okay?"

"I believe so. Your scream probably saved me. I was able to see the object falling just before I was hit."

"Umm, yeah. I guess that's one small blessing. I thought I was alone."

"I returned to look at something. I guess my timing was bad," he replied. "It was a cross, correct? The object you threw at me?"

"Yes, it was a cross, and I didn't throw it at you." The man looked at her with narrowed eyes and the start of a wry smile and then turned away.

"So, if you don't mind me asking, what were you doing in the church?" asked Zin. "You seemed to be looking for something."

"I am doing a little...exploring," he said, not pausing or looking at her this time.

"Okay," answered Zin, her expression hardened with doubt. He certainly must have been looking for something to steal, but given what just transpired, she wasn't about to get him in trouble.

The man turned right onto Kellogg Boulevard and since they were on the route back to her car, Zin stayed with him. The man didn't appear to be bothered by Zin's proximity, seeming to not even notice her, and Zin didn't have anything better to do anyway, all that waited for her at home was her television and a bottle of wine. Besides, she was too curious about this strange man to let it go just yet. The traffic was light and there weren't any other pedestrians on their path, but as they approached a freeway overpass, she once again noticed a homeless encampment tucked behind a sound barrier, faded blue and orange tents packed densely in two rows, a few dark figures squatting in front of their tents.

"So, do you live around here?" Zin asked, but instantly felt like she had crossed a line, a potentially awkward one since they were approaching the homeless encampment, and Zin expected that he might turn and head into the mini tent city. She also realized that although he was certainly a little odd, it was she who had just vandalized church property, was nearly guilty of manslaughter, and was now basically stalking a stranger. Luckily, the man didn't seem to care.

"No. I am visiting this city and several parts of the United States of America, Canada, and Mexico," he answered. "I am examining the culturally relevant artifacts of the area." Zin raised her eyebrows and nodded slowly, as if waiting for something else to follow. It didn't. Zin tried to detect an accent, but he didn't seem to have one. Or maybe it was just hard to place. She wasn't sure.

"Well, that sounds like it could be a very long trip."

"Believe me, it is. It feels like an eternity, and I just got started."

"So, are you on vacation?"

"No. I am studying. I am a sort of..." he thought about it for a few seconds, "cultural anthropologist. I am particularly interested in religion," he replied, glancing briefly over his shoulder up at the face of the cathedral behind them. Zin looked up as well but kept the dialogue going. This was the most interesting person she had met in a while, and she didn't feel like being left alone with her thoughts and the guilt that would certainly accompany them right now. Plus, part of her wanted to trip him up on his story, which was obviously a bunch of baloney.

"So where have you been so far?"

"This is my first stop," he answered.

"You started your U.S. visit here?" Zin almost laughed but recovered when the visitor didn't appear to find it amusing.

"Why do you sound surprised? I find it to be a pleasant city."

"No, no, nothing wrong with Saint Paul, Minnesota. It's a nice city and all. It's just not the place most people start their tours of North America." Zin smiled. The man didn't.

"Yes, well I am trying to reach most of the large metropolitan areas of the continent, and I thought I'd start in the middle. This metropolitan area isn't the geographic center, but I can't visit every city—I must set a size limit. Winnipeg was closer to the center but was a little smaller than I wanted."

"Sure. That's a very...logical plan," replied Zin, nodding very slowly, squinting slightly at the man. Zin's nod turned side-to-side as the man turned and started walking away again as if she wasn't there. Zin walked with him.

"Where are you going next?" asked Zin, not giving up.

"Chicago, Illinois. I plan to stay here until your Easter Sunday. I understand that to be of religious significance here. Am I correct?"

"Yes. That surprises you? It's not exactly a secret."

"Is there some religious ceremony? I would be interested in seeing one."

"Easter Sunday? Well, since you were interested in religion, you could attend the mass back at the Cathedral that morning." Zin hooked her thumb to point back to the church on the hill. "It's pretty impressive. They have a beautiful service on Easter."

"Oh," he replied, seriously. "I might do that." Apparently tired of answering questions, he asked one of his own. "Where do people go in this city at this time of day?" he demanded, still walking.

"Well, it's after seven o'clock on a Monday evening. Most people are either at home or will be soon. But you can see all these people here going to the hockey game in this stadium tonight," she replied dutifully, stopping with the man at a stoplight. A short "Hmph" was the only response to Zin's answer, as if it was an unusual fact that he wasn't expecting.

"There are many people in this stadium, correct?" the man asked.

Zin rolled her eyes and sighed. "Yes, of course."

"I would like to go in and observe this event," he said, almost as an order. Zin stopped in her tracks, frustrated with the visitor's apparent lack of social graces.

"Well, it'll cost you quite a bit. Someone might sell you a ticket." Zin looked around and saw a man standing across the street, flashing a couple tickets at passersby. "That guy over there has tickets," she pointed. Zin's new friend immediately walked over to a tall, heavy man with a thick beard and a baseball cap. Zin shrugged her shoulders and followed, curious at what might play out next.

"I would like a ticket to the game," he said immediately to the side of a large man with a bald head and full, shaggy beard, holding a pair of tickets in his meaty fist. The scalper hadn't seen him coming and turned to face him.

"Sure bud. I got a pair in section 114, row N. Real good seats. Seventy-five bucks each.

"I only want one ticket, and I do not have 75 dollars."

"Ok, how much you got?"

"I do not have much money," he answered. He turned to Zin. "Do you have 75 dollars?" Zin glared at him. *Ahh, now the panhandling starts. Well, this is a new tack.*

"Umm, no, and I'm not planning on buying you a hockey ticket."

The scalper let out a gravelly laugh. "Well, that didn't go so well, did it now? Sorry bud, but it looks like your lady friend isn't going to help, and I don't blame her." Zin and the strange little man walked on away from the stadium. Zin thought she should have been offended by his behavior, but what she really felt was pity for this man, who seemed so clueless.

Zin and the man stood at a stoplight, waiting for the walk signal. Zin, her curiosity losing the battle against fatigue, was ready to part company with this strange man, but standing there she became aware that she was hungry and knew that there wasn't much at home. Surrounded by restaurants and having already paid for parking, she decided she'd like to pop in and grab something. She was about to say farewell to this man when she looked at his disheveled hair and old jacket and wondered if he might need a meal. She did nearly smash his head, after all. She probably owed him a meal. She sighed.

"Would you like to go to a restaurant and get something to eat?" asked Zin, and quickly added "my treat. I feel bad about what happened back there." But she immediately regretted making the offer. Here was a strange man, and although he looked harmless, this could go terribly wrong. The light turned and they started crossing the street.

"Oh, what was I thinking," she shook her head. "It's Monday night, I've got..."

"Yes," the man answered before Zin could finish her excuse.

"Oh. See, I wasn't thinking," she stammered, stopping in her tracks at the opposite street corner. "I forgot, I've got some errands to run tonight and I really should get going." Her voice trailed off lamely. He didn't seem to notice.

"I would like to go to a restaurant," he said, now with certainty. "Can you show me a good restaurant?" He looked at her expectantly. She stared back for a few seconds, her rational thought center and her subconscious both screaming loudly that this was not a good idea. She ignored them both.

"Well, I guess I've got some time on my hands tonight. What the hell." She didn't really know if she did or not—she couldn't remember what was on her calendar—but tonight she didn't care. Having nearly offed herself and then nearly killed a stranger, she figured that any time she spent on herself was bonus time. And if anyone asked, especially Rick, she could now say that, yes, she had been on a date with another man. At least technically.

"Yes, please show me a restaurant," answered the visitor, looking around, not at Zin.

"Okay. But before we go anywhere, maybe we can introduce ourselves? My name is Zin," she said, offering her hand to shake. The man shook her hand but didn't offer his name.

"Where will we go?" he asked. Zin looked at him for a moment, waiting for the introduction that didn't come. She sighed again.

"I was thinking of that Italian restaurant right over there," she pointed down the street. It was a popular place, very public, so although this would likely be a highly uncomfortable meal, there would be little chance of danger. And besides, she didn't feel that she could pull out now. The man nodded, turned, and started walking. She jogged a little to catch up with the man who continued to ask child-like questions as they walked. Zin frowned. This act, or whatever the man was putting on, was getting old.

Zin was really struggling with the man's story. He seemed to have lived under a rock all his life yet had obviously known about the U.S. and spoke with perfect English. It was seeming less likely that he was a thief, but instead was probably suffering from mental health issues, which made her more anxious about the dinner.

As they walked, she felt her phone buzzing in her pocket. She pulled it out to check it and saw that it was Kim, returning the call Zin had made just a short while ago when she desperately needed to talk. Kim was probably at a happy hour—she had heard Kim talking to Cheryl Lundquist about going to Lucky's after school today—and Zin obviously hadn't been included. *Screw her.* She put her phone back in her pocket.

She was glad when they made it to the door of the restaurant. She stepped aside as a couple in their 50s made their way out the door, the man with a toothpick in his mouth and his coat open to let his substantial belly roam free. Inside, Zin had to adjust her eyes for the darkness, but she could see that the place had largely emptied out. She could smell onion and tomato sauce, one of the features she always loved about the place. A young woman dressed in all black was talking to a waiter and peeled away to greet them.

"Two for dinner?"

"Yep," answered Zin. The hostess took them to a corner booth and laid out some menus for them.

"What are you hungry for?" asked Zin. "I'm hungry. Kinda ravenous, actually." The visitor looked concerned as he examined the menu.

"I do not know. What will you be having?"

"Probably the lasagna. I've been dieting forever. A lotta good that's done me. So, I don't care tonight." The waitress appeared and Zin ordered lasagna and a glass of wine. The waitress turned to the man.

"I will have the lasagna as well," he answered, looking at Zin for approval. Zin nodded in encouragement.

"How about something to drink?" asked the waitress. The man seemed to struggle with a decision. He turned to Zin.

"How bad is drinking wine? Will I get in trouble if I drink it?" he asked in a voice barely above a whisper.

"If I got into trouble every time I had a glass of wine, I'd be locked up in prison for the rest of my life." Zin snorted.

"So, it is not bad? I had been told to watch out for the alcoholic drinks."

"Told by who? What, have you never had a glass of wine before?"

"No."

Zin gave the man a hard look—substance abuse often went hand-in-hand with homelessness, and his story was not adding up. But something about the child-like look on his face made her relax. "Well, there's a first time for everything," said Zin, looking up at the waitress. "Make it a bottle."

The waitress left and the man's gaze followed her across the room. Once she was out of sight, he turned to examine the entire room, his gaze moving quickly from one table to the next, trying to take everything in like a house cat let outside for the first time. As he did, he put his opposite hand on his sore shoulder and massaged it. Zin grimaced.

After examining every corner of the room, the man's gaze stopped at a nearby table. He was staring too intently and had been noticed by an older woman who frowned and said something to her dining partner. Zin was about to distract the man, but at that moment, the waitress arrived, and, after opening a bottle and allowing Zin a taste, she poured a glass for both of them. The man grimaced when he took a sip and Zin laughed a little.

"So," Zin started, "you were saying you were here…"

"Why were you in the church?" interrupted the man, his head swinging to face Zin. Zin, caught by surprise, involuntarily pushed back from the table.

"Ummm, I don't know. It was cold. I needed a place to sit down for a few minutes, I guess."

"You were upset."

"Uh, yeah, I suppose. Wait—you were watching me?"

"Yes."

"Huh." Zin scrutinized the man. She wanted to scold him for watching her, but after all, wasn't it she who had been spying on him?

"I saw you lean your body way over the railing. It appeared you were contemplating jumping."

"Me, no, no," she answered, shaking her head vigorously. "I was…I don't know. It was stupid and…I didn't really mean it. I just wanted to…I don't know." Her voice trailed off. "I'm fine, really." The man didn't say anything, just watched Zin. Zin, uncomfortable now, suddenly found her wine interesting, spinning the liquid in the glass and taking a couple sips.

"Do you live near the church?" he asked.

"No. I live a few miles away."

"Where do you live?" The question made Zin uncomfortable, and she remembered again why this was a bad idea all around.

"A few miles west of here," she answered. Zin craned her neck to search for the waitress, who appeared as if on cue out of a doorway and looked to be carrying a large tray and heading their way. Zin took a long drink and downed her glass of wine. The man followed her lead. *Yes, definitely nuts.* The waitress brought out their food and poured another glass of wine for each of them. The man eyed his lasagna suspiciously, but taking his lead from Zin, took a bite and smiled, quickly diving in for more.

The two ate in silence for a couple of minutes before the man started another round of questions.

"How do you spend your time? Do you have an occupation?"

"I'm a middle school teacher. Social studies." The man nodded, as if that explained something.

"Do you enjoy being a teacher?"

Zin poured the rest of the bottle into her glass, sat back, and looked at her glass, turning it slowly in her right hand. After a long pause, she answered.

"Oh, I guess so. I enjoy working with people. It's a tough job, though. Thankless at times." Zin caught herself slurring a little. She kept staring at her glass, shaking her head now. The man didn't interrupt. Zin continued, talking to her glass. "I mean, I try to make a difference in my little corner of the world, but sometimes I wonder what good it really does?" Zin's voice trailed off as she stared at the glass in front of her, swirling the burgundy liquid around and around. The two sat in silence for a moment, the man continuing to eat. Zin pushed her plate away and brought her phone out of her purse. Out of habit, she started scrolling through posts, shaking her head and frowning.

"You look...annoyed," offered the man. Zin popped her head up, quickly putting her phone in her lap.

"Oh, sorry. It's just some bonehead on social media. Doesn't know jack but seems to think he needs to tell everyone his opinions. So tired of it." Zin's voice regained some energy. "So, you haven't told me anything about yourself."

"I told you everything. I am traveling and studying," he answered, slurring a little bit as well. He took another sip of wine and avoided Zin's gaze, looking instead at a nearby TV screen which was showing the hockey game.

"Well, for starters, how about a name?" The man sighed and ignored her for a moment before answering.

"Henry."

"Henry? Just Henry?"

"Yes." Henry focused on his lasagna.

"All right, where are you from, *Henry*?" Henry didn't look up but giggled a little.

"What's so funny?"

"I should not," answered Henry to himself, shaking his head and helping himself to another bite.

"Shouldn't what?"

"Nothing.

"You can't do that. You have to tell me now," ordered Zin. Henry seemed to take the order seriously and looked around uncomfortably at the tables near them. "What?" demanded Zin. "What's the big deal?" Henry didn't say anything for a few moments, and then looked around the room cautiously.

"I don't know," said Henry, looking down. Zin nodded and leaned in, her eyes widening with interest.

"So, what is it? Why can't you tell me?" Zin dropped her voice. "Are you here illegally? I could help you with that. You don't have to worry about me, I won't tell. I have a friend whose wife is an immigration lawyer. I could ask them if she could help."

"Oh, I am not too worried about that," answered Henry. "You see, I am...not from here."

"I know, that's what you said," replied Zin.

"I think we should forget about it," said Henry, focusing again on the lasagna. "Did I mention that I love the taste of this dish?"

"Now hold on. You won't even tell me where you are from?"

"I really must come back here for more food of this type. It is truly delicious."

"Stop changing the subject!" Henry sat back in his seat, seeming a little smaller. "So, you won't tell me where you are from, but you are visiting America, studying something... culture and religion or something like that?"

"Yes?" answered Henry quietly. Zin raised one eyebrow, sat back, and took a sip of wine, remembering that she was dealing with a crazy guy off the street.

"Oh really," she answered slowly, the slightest smirk appearing on the corners of her mouth.

"That is correct."

"Studying what, exactly?" Zin took another sip of wine. She knew she should be worried about hanging out with a clearly delusional stranger, but the more time she spent with the silly little man, the more he seemed ridiculous instead of threatening. The wine wasn't helping.

"How shall I put it?" he asked no one in particular, staring down at his plate. After a moment's pause, he continued. "I am trying to answer the question *is it good that humans came into existence, or would the universe have been better off without them?*" He looked up and gave Zin a weak smile.

Zin just looked at him blankly. *Yup. Crazy sauce.* But having crossed some sort of imaginary line, Henry was suddenly eager to talk.

"Humans are certainly special. But think of it this way. There are some special species on this planet that get displaced by human activity. So, my...study...boils down to trying to quantify the benefits versus the cost associated with humans."

"Well, that sounds like a pretty big project," Zin replied, stuck somewhere between nervous and amused.

"It is. It is much more difficult than I expected it to be," he answered.

"Really? Who'd a thunk it? Judging the value of all of humanity's achievements and then weighing them against the loss of the dodo and the wooly mammoth. Sounds straightforward to me."

"I did not say judge. I am simply trying to identify some objective criteria. There are infinite ways that one could measure the benefits and costs of humanity. I cannot be that comprehensive."

"No, of course not," Zin, nodded, smirking. "So, you are going to, say, give a certain score to humans for creating sonnets and figuring out calculus, but then take off points for every species we wipe out?"

Henry shrugged. "That is a simple way of describing it. There is inherent value in human ingenuity and creativity, but there is also the opportunity cost for other species.

"Opportunity cost?"

"Yes, what could other species have achieved if humans were not stunting their growth."

Zin closed her eyes and took a breath. The food and wine were combining to make her sleepy again. She kind of wanted to drop the conversation, but she decided to just see where it might be going. "Okay, now we are really going into the fantasy world here. First of all, these aren't creatures that are about to compose a sonnet or work out calculus."

Henry frowned and looked up at the ceiling for a moment before answering. "Hmmm. I am not as sure as you are about that. In terms of human lifetimes, maybe. But on a larger scale, humans are not so much farther along than some of these creatures."

"I'm well aware that we humans can be pretty crummy. That's about all I know these days. But we're the only game in town when it comes to an animal that can create, build, communicate...anything, at least at a high level of, umm, sophistication." She sat back in her chair; arms crossed. *Wait, why am I bothering to argue with this guy?*

"Humans are definitely the most evolved species. But I was talking about loss of potential for other species that are not so far from humans as you might think. From an objective point of view, is a sonnet more beautiful than the call of a blue whale? Can people really communicate better than that of a wolf pack that can work together soundlessly to make a kill? Is the average human morality more advanced than an ant colony whose members work tirelessly for the greater good, willing to sacrifice their lives for others?"

"I would say, yes," answered Zin, frowning slightly. Quiet followed for a few seconds. Zin had gotten engrossed in his fantasy world view for a few minutes, but now remembered that yes, here was a man who had serious delusions. She took a deep breath and managed a tired smile. "So, what is the verdict so far? You think we are worth it?" She took another drink from her glass.

"I am not certain yet, as I only recently started my evaluation."

"Hmm," Zin said, finally making eye contact with the waitress and signaling for the check with a motion that looked like a conductor trying to shake a fly off her wrist. They both sat quietly with their thoughts for a moment before Henry glanced up at the TV near them, an expression of concern on his face. Zin turned to see what was holding Henry's attention. News of a shooting at a convenience store in Texas was scrolling across the bottom of the screen. After a minute, Henry spoke up.

"That is a tragedy."

Zin shook her head. "Nothing ever changes. There are so damn many evil people out there."

"Do you think so?"

"Yes," she replied adamantly. "No doubt."

"Do you think people are inherently evil?"

"Umm, no. I don't know. Maybe not evil. But selfish. Taking care of number one. If things don't go right, we devolve pretty quickly." She thought about it for a moment. "Sometimes just plain mean. And yes, sometimes evil."

"Do you think people have always been this way? Do you not think people were worse in the past?"

"I don't think we've changed," answered Zin. "We've always been this way."

"So, humans are not likely to improve."

"Probably not."

Henry considered this. "Maybe mankind will wipe itself out? It seems to be destroying the planet rather quickly."

"Maybe we will. We probably deserve it."

"I do not think that humanity is as bad as you make it out to be."

"You need to get out more."

The waitress brought the check and placed it in the middle

of the table. Zin glanced at Henry, who only looked at it curiously. Zin shook her head—no sense asking Henry to split the check—and brought out a credit card. She paid and they walked out the front door in a silence fueled by Zin's sudden foul mood. They stepped into the brisk night air and Henry turned to her.

"Zin, although you defended humanity's achievements, you seem indifferent about humanity. Maybe worse than indifferent. Do you see no redeeming value in humankind?"

Zin smiled sadly. "I guess you caught me on a bad day. I'm not feeling so warm and fuzzy about our species right now."

"I am sorry," Henry replied. I cannot help you with that." He stood for a moment in thought, but then his eyes brightened. "Or maybe I can. What if we performed a small experiment?"

"What kind of experiment?" asked Zin.

Henry trotted back to the restaurant entrance and tore a piece of paper off a flyer before returning to Zin. "Do you have something to write with?" Zin fumbled in her purse and produced a pen. Henry scribbled quickly. "Here."

Zin stared at the paper with confusion. "What is this?"

"I wrote down ten random times, one per day, starting tomorrow. You and I will meet at those times and observe."

"Observe? Observe what?"

"Humanity. We will watch other humans."

"And do what?"

"Score them."

"What do you mean, 'score them'?"

"Decide if mankind was good, bad, or neither at that very moment."

She glanced again at the paper. "Huh? You want us to judge mankind at these exact times? I don't get it?"

"We will sit for a period of time making observations. Let us say one minute. And then we will confer and decide if mankind was good or not. We will keep score."

"We're judging all of mankind in a minute?"

"Only what we observe during that minute."

"What if it's just a guy walking down the street?"

"Then that will be what you will evaluate."

"Hmmmf. Sounds crazy," answered Zin. "Why am I not surprised? Sure. Why not. Okay. Then what?"

"If mankind seems to be good more often than not, maybe my conclusions will be different. Or at least you might think better of your fellow man."

Zin stuffed the paper into her pocket. She remembered that the man was crazy, and despite the haze of alcohol, she knew it was best not to make plans to meet with him. It was time to escape before it got awkward.

"Um, sure. I'm betting the score will be four for humanity, six for a big mistake. Well, thanks for the company, Henry, but I need to head out now."

"Okay, Zin. Thank you for providing me with dinner and introducing me to wine. I will tell everyone I meet to avoid it at all costs." He looked serious, and Zin had to smile.

"Goodbye, Henry. And I'm sorry about the shoulder. I hope it doesn't hurt too much tomorrow." She turned to go.

"Zin, wait," said Henry, approaching her, digging in his pocket for something. Zin realized they were alone on a dark street, and she felt a sudden surge of panic. But before she could do anything about it, Henry had found the item he was looking for and was handing it to Zin.

"I forgot. If I am to find you, you will need this." He held out his hand, palm up. On it was a small, orange ball that looked like the super bouncy balls Zin had seen so many times in toy stores and vending machines. Zin took it gingerly and examined it. It felt like a simple metal ball.

"Okay," she said, smiling in relief. Goodbye now." Henry turned to walk away, and Zin watched him go, making sure he wasn't going to follow her. As she did, it dawned on her that the crazy man probably had nowhere to stay that evening. Reluctantly, Zin called after him.

"Say, Henry. Do you have a place to go tonight? Do you have a place to stay?"

"Oh yes. I have a nice place to stay. Thank you for asking." Henry turned and sauntered away. Zin wondered if the nice place was a hotel, the floor of a homeless shelter, or a cardboard box under the bridge. She decided her inquiry was enough for tonight and headed home.

4

The worship committee of St. Stephen's Church met on Monday, which was all the more reason Jay hated Mondays. He didn't need to attend all committee meetings, but he pretty much had to attend this one, the agenda of which was basically for the organist and choir director to figure out what they would be playing and singing, based on a theme for the service that they had hoped Father Jay would be able to establish several weeks in advance. At least, that is the way things were run by their previous priest, a fact which the choir director would bring up as often as possible. The problem with this approach boiled down to the fact that Jay had no idea what he was planning on doing several weeks in advance and didn't really want to be that constrained—he wanted to go where the spirit led him on a weekly basis. And the musicians were not happy with this. Tonight's meeting was no exception.

"So, for the second week of May, have you established a theme yet?" asked Marjorie, the choir director.

"Umm, I haven't quite nailed that down yet," responded Jay, which was basically the same response he gave every week.

"Ok. Well, looking at the readings for that day, we have Luke 9, the story of Jesus traveling and some people on the road saying they would follow him. What if we performed hymn

532—*I Will Follow Thee*?" Marjorie had obviously already done her homework. Marjorie looked over at Bonnie, the organist, who folded her knobby, wrinkled hands in her lap and nodded her head of white hair in approval. As long as it was in the hymnal, Bonnie wouldn't object. She'd been playing at the church for 28 years and through seven choir directors now. She was not interested in expanding her musical repertoire.

"That sounds good," answered Jay. When he had first joined St. Stephens, he had come to the first few meetings with a bunch of ideas about different types of music that they could pursue, such as a guitar choir or a band, but the committee, namely Marjorie, had made it clear that unless it was written many years ago and required an organ, it was pretty much blasphemous to suggest something else. Jay had since accepted that he didn't really have a strong opinion about the music and, like Bonnie, he had come to realize that suggesting an alternative to Marjorie would just get you into a long discussion in which you would be asked in a smiling, professional way, what your reasoning was for choosing a particular song, which, it turned out, was never as good as hers.

The meeting, as usual, made Jay feel like a student who hadn't completed his homework, and he was relieved when the meeting wrapped up. He went upstairs to his office, checked a few emails, grabbed a notebook and his coat, and since it was the last meeting of the evening, walked around the building to make sure everything was locked up.

Jay headed home, deep in thought. He walked to the parish house and then kept going down the block, making his way to the busy parkway, four blocks away. He crossed at the stoplight and walked to the little neighborhood park, now silent and empty. Jay sat down on a short wall next to the playground, hands in his coat pockets, head down, staring at his feet. He thought that the walk and the cool air might help him think through the issues that had been bothering him, but he soon discovered that mental brute force wasn't really a way to explore his feelings.

As Jay was about ready to leave, a couple walked by with two young children. Jay intuited that a priest stalking a playground wasn't a good vibe and looked up and smiled at them. The couple gave an awkward smile and nod of their heads and walked past. Jay shook his head, stood up, and meandered toward home.

As Jay rounded the corner to his street, he eyed a funny little man with dark, greasy hair, a plain, tan jacket, and thick-rimmed glasses walking quickly down the sidewalk, staring straight ahead. It was Patrick. Jay liked Patrick enough, but tonight he just wanted to get home. He was hoping Patrick would let him off with a simple hello. It was not to be.

Patrick looked up and called out loudly from thirty feet away. "Well, hello!" Patrick had stopped, meaning that Father Jay couldn't just walk past him. Jay walked up to the funny little man who barely came to Jay's chin.

"Hi, Patrick, how are you doing tonight?" Patrick was not one for a segue.

"Say, the Twins look like they might be pretty good this year, don't you think?" Baseball. Patrick's favorite and pretty much only topic of conversation.

"I think so," replied Jay, trying to keep things short.

"Yeah, their pitching staff looks good. Ortega looks like he'll be a good pitcher. He has a really strong arm. He has that thick mustache. Lots of players have mustaches these days. They didn't use to. They used to be clean cut or have beards. I remember Aguilera had a beard. Remember him? He was really good. I don't like mustaches. I like to be clean cut. I see you do, too?" Patrick's flurry of observations somehow always led in a stream-of-consciousness to facial hair. Baseball and facial hair—strange obsessions. Jay nodded patiently.

"Yup. Don't like the beard. I can't really grow a good one, too thin," he replied, rubbing his face as if to demonstrate his problems with facial hair.

"Yeah," said Patrick with a look of serious contemplation. He looked down and rubbed his own chin, then brightened up as he found his footing with a new discussion topic. "How is the church? I don't really go to church. My mother never did, so I didn't. She said it wasn't something she was very interested in. Did your mom go to church?"

"Ummm, the church is fine," answered Jay. "My mom did go to church. They were pretty serious about it, I guess."

"Is that why you're a priest?"

Jay frowned. "No. I don't think so, anyway. It's complicated."

"The weather is kind of grey, isn't it? I wish it were sunnier. Don't you wish it was sunnier?"

"Yes, grey and cold." Jay did his best to transition. It sounded forced, but he wasn't sure how much nuance Patrick would follow. "So, I'm getting chilled. I think I'd better head home. You have a good night, Patrick." Jay started walking and Patrick didn't move, just turned in place to watch Jay as he walked past.

"Good night," he called to Jay's back.

When he got home, Jay headed to the refrigerator and snooped around a bit, pulling out a block of cheese and a bottle of beer. He grabbed a box of crackers and headed to the living room. A movie was playing on TV, one that he had seen about five times but still liked, so he sat and watched it until there were three empty bottles on the coffee table in front of him and his head kept bobbing, which was his signal to turn off the lights and the TV and make his way upstairs.

Sleep came quickly to Jay, but it didn't last. He woke up thinking about the funeral, the worship committee, and then how he was universally disliked by the parish council. Realizing that a little bout of insomnia was upon him, Jay tapped his phone to check the time, expecting it to be relatively close to morning. The clock mocked him as it snapped to 3:07 a.m. He had already been awake for a while and was nowhere near sleeping. He tried the usual remedies—relaxing, trying to clear his mind, even reading for a while. Still, sleep evaded him. Jay turned to the defenses that his ego usually relied on: *it wasn't that bad*, and, *it was going to get better*. All his problems rolled through his mind in an endless loop, but instead of his psychological armor appearing, he noticed that two different truths had seemed to materialize after a time and then began to solidify. As they became more and more apparent, he couldn't help but recognize them: *nothing he did was making a difference to anyone*, and *nothing was ever really going to change.*

Jay had always hated his phone alarm's ringtone. It was an annoying bell melody, but he had tried every other alarm sound his phone offered and hated them all as well. When the alarm went off at its usual 6:15 a.m., it did so without pity for the man who last looked at the clock at about 5:20 a.m. before his brain finally surrendered and let him sleep. Given the circumstances, the phone didn't really stand a chance. Jay swiped his arm across his nightstand, knocking off a glass of water and sending his phone tumbling under the dresser, a little gremlin still playing an annoying melody on the bells. Jay rolled on his back and closed his eyes, focusing on the wonderful feeling of near sleep, while trying to keep himself awake because he knew that if he didn't, he would miss the morning mass.

After ten minutes, Jay grimaced and sat up. He crawled over to the dresser and stuck his thick paw under until he found the phone, turned off the alarm, and stood up. Guilt, more than anything, made him shower and shave. It was a cold morning, and he took his time getting himself dressed and making some coffee. By the time he got over to church, it was 7:15 a.m. Thankfully, none of the rosary-clutching ladies were waiting for him. On a morning like this there were probably only going to be about six people in church, the rest being scared off by the cold, damp weather. Jay had hinted at ending the morning mass schedule early in his tenure at St. Stephen's, but a small but vocal group raised a protest that seemed to suggest it was important for tradition's sake and because other churches weren't offering it anymore, or something to that effect, so Jay let the matter die. But now was maybe time to bring it up again—there was a reason other churches were dropping this; it was because no one came.

Jay went upstairs and turned on the lights, and then changed into his robe and sat in the darkness trying to enjoy the sleepy feeling. He could hear the call of the rosary from the sanctuary, the single voice of the leader and the monotone murmur of half a dozen respondents. Jay waited until they finished and then got up and straightened his robe and his hair. He looked out the window and saw a car with three teenagers in it heading toward the nearby school. They looked carefree, and Jay sighed audibly, thinking about his life of twenty years ago. He tried to imagine telling the teenage Jay what his life would be like as he neared 40. Jay knew what his response would have been. *Are you kidding?*

5

Zin's brain had become accustomed to this task: assessing a situation that was about to become an incident. In about half a second, she would have to react to a student in a proper way that balanced the often-conflicting needs of keeping the class in line and on task, making sure the boy wouldn't make the incident into something bigger than it was and get him into trouble, and letting the boy know that his action was inappropriate. To do this, she had to know how her class would react, understand the motivations and background of the person involved, and know techniques that would diffuse the situation. She was tasked with keeping nearly 200 young teens a day, 30 or more at a time, occupied, engaged, on-task and in order. It was like herding snakes with nothing but a stick and your voice. She had to talk for hours a day but know when to stop talking and assign a task or a group activity. She had to understand their interests, capabilities, motivations, and perspectives.

And understanding these students was not so easy. These were young adolescents—puberty-charged, post-child, pre-adult creatures that had raging hormones and constantly shifting emotions. She was at different times during the day part counselor, part parent, part friend, and yes, part teacher. None of these are skills you are born with. It took a couple of years to understand how to avoid being railroaded by a rambunctious class, or how to avoid bursting into tears after fighting with a student, or how to recognize a student who was stoned, or who hadn't eaten in two days.

So now, Zin had to react to this kid, a kid who was a head smarter than the rest of the class but who usually didn't choose to apply those smarts in the best way. And she wasn't in a good mood.

"What Corey is referring to is that Amsterdam, the largest city of The Netherlands, and no, not its capital, that's The Hague by the way, has adopted some rather liberal laws that include legalized prostitution. But no, sex is not one of the main exports of the Netherlands. Corey is just reading too many National Geographic magazines." The class laughed at this. Situation diffused, or so it seemed.

"Does anyone else know one of the main exports of The Netherlands, or some of its main industries or resources." Silence ensued, as usual. "I don't suppose anyone remembers reading about it last night like I asked?" Zin's shoulders slumped.

"Sex is probably a main industry then, if not an export." It was Corey again from the back, sitting in a serious pose, his short, straight hair looking a bit unwashed, and his black t-shirt faded. He had only the slightest smile on his face. His eyes, however, looked ready for a fight. The class laughed again, anything to do with sex would usually get an outburst of giggles, and their eyes widened in anticipation of the teacher's reaction.

Miss McGuire, as they called her, didn't waste any time. She shot the briefest of glares at Corey. *God, these kids' brains are just soaked with thoughts of sex.*

"Enough Corey." Even though she was several inches shorter than Corey, Zin McGuire's demeanor conveyed a definite sense of someone who was not to be messed with. Most kids weren't after trouble and knew that they had hit the boundary. Some kids, however, needed the attention more than they needed to be on the good side of a teacher.

"What? It's true. My dad says it's a big tourist draw. That's gotta be a lot of money for their economy. It's a huge business. And business travelers probably go there just for that reason, which probably helps the business economy."

"Corey," Zin responded firmly. "I don't want to hear any more about that topic. Understood?" Corey gave the slightest of nods, trying to keep a straight face. *His Dad? Sounds like a winner. They don't fall far from the tree.*

Zin sighed and turned back to the class, her eyes slow to leave Corey. "Tourism is not really a major industry in The Netherlands. But the Dutch have chemical and petroleum processing and natural gas reserves. They also happen to produce most of the flowers that you see in flower shops. Holland is known for its flowers." Some of the girls nodded appreciatively. Zin turned back to the map of Europe on the whiteboard and was about to move on when she heard Corey whispering loudly.

"Owen has large natural gas reserves as well." A couple of guys gave little huck-huck snickers.

"Corey!" Zin whipped around. The class immediately ceased all chatter, shocked by the unexpected loss of control. Zin's nostrils flared, her breathing heavy, the bags under her eyes clearly visible. She steadied her voice. "You will see me after class," she said in a sharp, matter of fact tone. She turned around so the class couldn't see her and started talking about Brussels, her eyes closed, hoping to avoid tears. The class remained quiet after that. The students, including Corey, knew that if any further disturbance ensued, two things could occur: either Corey would make the stupid mistake of opening his mouth again and get detention, or someone else would start something, and the entire class would get a huge assignment. They could sense that today was not a day to push it.

Zin continued with her brief introduction to northern Europe until the bell rang. As the students rose to leave, she called out, "Hold on, hold on. You have a reading assignment. Chapter twelve, the first three sections. Okay? It's on the board." She tried to get some eye contact from the kids who mostly just scrambled out. She headed back to her seat but happened to catch Corey trying to sneak out of the classroom with the other students.

"Um, Corey?" she called as Corey reached the door. Corey turned around, rolling his eyes as he approached Zin's desk. Zin was sitting and Corey looked down at her, trying to convey a tough shell that wouldn't be broken. Zin looked at Adrian, a tall, gangly boy with a mop of curly hair, who was waiting to take a make-up test.

"Adrian, can you wait outside for just one minute?" Zin waited until Adrian ambled out, pulled up the sleeves of her black sweater, and then turned to Corey with a hard glare.

"Corey, I don't need you disrupting class. You know that. And I am especially bothered by your comments about prostitution." She waited for a reply, but Corey just stood there, doing his best to portray indifference.

"Do you understand?" She grilled him. Corey frowned and nodded, maintaining eye contact.

"Here's the deal, then," she explained. "You will write a one-page essay by next week on why it is important to respect women and not treat them like dirt." She paused, realizing she was letting her emotions affect her choice of words. "I want it typed or written neatly. By next Friday." It was a touchy subject, assigning a paper about respecting women to an eighth grader, but she didn't feel like asking permission today, and if the school administration dug into it, she was itching to fight. Besides, topics like prostitution were usually seen by the administration as something to avoid at all costs, so they probably wouldn't push it too far with her.

"What? That's not fair!" he protested.

"Corey, you are about to lose all of your classroom conduct points, and it will drop you an entire letter grade, which, from what I remember, you can't really afford right now."

"I gotta go," he said in a flustered voice, stomping out of the room. Zin leaned back in her chair with her arms crossed, glaring at the empty door. *Corey, Corey, Corey. How long will it take you to learn that being smart doesn't give you the right to be a jerk?* Zin lamented the fact that Corey probably would never learn this lesson. Kids like Corey were typically beyond her reach at this point.

Zin remembered Adrian and poked her head out into the hall and called him in. Although the classroom was empty now, he still headed to his normal seat and slipped into his chair, his long legs sticking well past his desk. Zin handed him his quiz and told him he had fifteen minutes, and then returned to her desk and logged onto her computer to check her email. She first checked her work email: two students requesting information about missed assignments because they were absent, a parent who wouldn't be at the upcoming parent-teacher conference who wanted an update, and another helicopter mom wanting to talk about her son's recent test scores. She dealt with each of them and then checked her personal email: ads, neighborhood news, social media teasers—the usual. She was about to log out when she noticed an email from Cindy Erickson who chaired the social justice committee at her church. It was an agenda for tomorrow's meeting: updates on service projects, fundraisers, and something called Project Hope.

Zin frowned and gazed off into the distance, not seeing the maps on the white block walls in front of her, lost in her thoughts. She had been drifting from church for a while now and didn't want to have to explain her marriage situation to anyone. But she felt like being with people.

The sound of someone shifting in a chair snapped Zin back to reality. She glanced over at the young man seated in front of her, scribbling away, his forehead scrunched in concentration.

"Five minutes," she said softly. The young man glanced up, frowned, and then put his head down and scribbled some more. Zin started grading a stack of papers. She was usually annoyed at having to work around a kid's absence by providing make-up tests, but she liked Adrian, and he seemed to need a break, so she didn't begrudge him this extra time. After a few minutes, she checked the clock and put her papers away. "Time's up." Adrian put his pencil down and sat back with a sigh. He untangled his lanky frame from his desk and walked up to hand in his paper.

"Thanks Adrian," she said and watched the boy collect his things. "You feeling better?" He had missed three days last week

43

and his attendance over the last couple of months had started to become a concern.

"Huh? Oh. Yeah. I'm good. Thanks," he muttered as he made his way out the door, not looking back. Zin sighed and was packing her bag with a folder full of papers to grade tonight, when her classroom phone rang. She looked at the number and picked up the phone.

"Hello?"

"Zin, Carol at the front desk. There is a man up front for you." The voice on the other end dropped to a low, conspiratorial voice. "He said you are supposed to meet with him in precisely 5 minutes. His words."

"Really? I don't remember scheduling anything today after school. Who is it?"

"He said his name is Henry."

"You've got to be kidding!" Zin exclaimed.

"No, I'm not. What do you mean?"

Zin groaned. "Oh, nothing. Never mind."

"Should I send him up, or do you want to come down here and get him?"

"Do not send him up here. I'll be down in a second."

"He says you have four minutes."

Oh Lord.

Zin marched down to the front office and opened the door to survey the reception area. Henry was sitting in a chair in the corner, hands folded in his lap, looking eager but not worried. Zin mustered the most reasonable voice she could produce.

"Henry, can you come here?" She beckoned with her finger for him to follow, and he immediately stood and followed her out the door. Zin was relieved to see that he wasn't wearing the same clothes as the previous day, but instead was donning a pair of black pants, a lime green shirt, and the same sneakers. She walked down the hall until they were alone except for a few kids who were still making their way outside. Zin rounded on Henry as he approached.

"What are you doing here?" She demanded, eyes narrowed

and arms crossed.

"It is our time to meet," answered Henry, as if the answer was obvious.

"How did you find me?"

"I gave you the tracking device," he said, confused at the question. "I told you it would lead me to you."

"Bullshit!" She glanced around to see if any kid had heard the outburst. She was about to continue, but Henry interrupted.

"Okay, our minute starts right...now." Henry started looking around at the students near him.

"What?" Zin practically yelled. "Are you talking about that stupid idea you had outside the restaurant?" Henry looked back to her and nodded, a look that implied that she was the crazy one, not him. "You've got to be kidding! I can't believe you followed me here." A couple students were now looking at them, heads huddled together, whispering.

Henry leaned into Zin, his voice soft with concern. "Zin, we are supposed to be observers of our surroundings. However, you are affecting your surroundings by drawing attention to us." Henry went back to observing students who were hanging out on the steps outside the front door. Zin sighed audibly, her shoulders slumping. This guy was too much. They stood silently for a long minute before Henry ended it.

"Okay. That was our first minute. What did you observe? Was it a negative, positive, or neutral experience in your mind?"

"Negative. Definitely negative," answered Zin, glaring at Henry.

"Interesting," he replied, seeming oblivious to Zin's body language. "What did you observe that made you feel this was a negative experience?"

"Well, first of all, a guy I hardly know followed me to my work," she answered, still breathing hard."

"I am sorry you forgot about our appointment," answered Henry.

Zin kept going. "And see that kid over there, having a good chuckle with a couple of his buddies?" Zin motioned with her head toward three boys who were standing about 50 feet away at the entrance to the gym. Henry turned to look straight at them.

"Yes, I…"

"Don't stare," Zin demanded. "He was being extremely rude in class today, showing disrespect for women and disrupting my class. Now he's laughing at me. You made me look stupid."

"That is unfortunate," answered Henry, this time finally seeming to be affected by Zin's news. "I guess that we will call this first experience a negative one. That is too bad," he said, looking past Zin as in thought, a frown twisting his mouth. After several seconds, a wave seemed to pass over him, leaving him almost cheerful.

"Okay. Well, maybe next time it will be better. Our next observation will take place tomorrow night at 8:07 p.m." He looked to Zin for acknowledgement. Zin glared at him with a tight frown. He really did look like a misfit, and he seemed earnest and, truth be told, harmless. She knew that was a naïve impression, but in her current miserable state, he seemed to be the odd little lifeline that was being thrown her way. She took a deep breath of resignation.

"So, you want to observe people again? Like this. This is what you had planned?"

"Yes. I thought we agreed on this."

"What else do you want?" Henry looked confused again.

"Want? I don't want anything." Zin stood for a few moments, arms folded, a look of doubt on her face.

"You're leaving now, right?"

"Yes."

"All right. Goodbye," she replied, leaving no question that he should be going. Henry nodded and without another word marched out the front doors. Zin watched to see where he was heading, but he walked to the sidewalk and then around the building, out of sight.

"What an odd little man."

6

Zin maneuvered through the rush-hour traffic and made her way to a strip mall where she pulled into a parking lot. She peered up at the nondescript office building: four floors, red brick and concrete, a plain, brown sign standing near the street that listed about a dozen businesses that were housed in the building, including Riverside Therapy and Counseling. She found a parking spot and dug her phone out of her purse, pulling up the clinic's website, wanting to check the picture of the therapist again so she would recognize him when she got to the clinic. He seemed decent enough from his picture and bio—his credentials were fine, and he looked friendly, albeit maybe a little smug. Zin had wanted a woman therapist, but it had seemed imperative that she see someone as soon as possible, so she didn't feel she could be choosy. A friend had recommended this clinic, which happened to be in her insurance network, and he seemed to be one of the few therapists she could find that had openings. She reached over and grabbed the rear-view mirror, adjusting it to check her appearance; the woman staring back at her looked tired, with dark circles under her listless eyes. She frowned, chewed her thumbnail until just a couple minutes before the appointment, and finally got out of the car.

Zin made her way up to the fourth floor and found the room

of the clinic, a small waiting room covered in tan wallpaper with thin blue stripes. Zin checked in at the reception area and took a seat underneath a dusty watercolor painting of a rainbow. She reached for a magazine, but everything appeared to be about two years old, so she gave up on that and pulled out her phone to see what her social media feed was saying. She knew what she would find—too many pictures of beautiful families returning from glorious spring break trips, but once she had started scrolling, she had a hard time stopping. It felt like pulling the arm on a slot machine—that next pull will make it worthwhile. After scrolling for a couple minutes, she sighed and stuffed her phone into her purse.

When the door opened and a man called her name, she was initially confused; the man in the doorway didn't look like she had expected him to look. The man before her was probably fifteen years older than his profile picture on the clinic's website, with thinning hair, a mustache, and a bit of a paunch hiding behind a sweater vest. He gave a courteous, if not warm, smile, and opened the door wide, gesturing for Zin to come his way. Zin rose from her chair slowly and approached him

"Chaz Pearson," he introduced himself, sticking out his hand. Zin shook it.

"Zin McGuire. Glad to meet you."

"Well then, Zin, let's head down to my office. Zin followed him down a dark hallway, finally arriving in an office at the end of the hall.

"Have a seat," he said, pointing to a chair opposite him. The room had two comfortable chairs facing each other and a small loveseat placed against a nearby wall. Prints of sailboats were scattered on the walls. Zin took off her thin black coat and laid it over the arm of the chair. "There's water and coffee on that table over there," he pointed to the back of the room, next to a window. Help yourself anytime you want."

"Thanks. Nothing right now," she answered, sitting down, adjusting her jeans. Zin noticed the sound of fans coming from a couple corners of the room. "What's with the fans?"

"Not fans," he corrected. "White noise makers. Sometimes

the walls can be a little thin, and although we never can hear anything that anyone says, it just makes everyone more comfortable if we block it. It was my idea," he added, chest puffing out a bit.

"Makes sense," answered Zin. *A good room to put a baby to sleep in.* "So, I just want to start by telling you that I haven't done this before."

"No worries, no worries. You are in capable hands. Maybe I should start by giving you my background. I have a master's degree in counseling psychology, I'm a licensed marriage and family therapist, and I have almost twenty-five years of experience as a therapist and counselor." Chaz finished and looked expectantly at Zin, who didn't say anything at first.

"Umm, great," she finally offered. Chaz gave a satisfied smile.

"Well, good. So, I hope that makes you feel better about this process. And it is a process. One we start today. Let's begin. Tell me why you wanted to meet."

"Well, I guess I'm having a bad couple of months. You see, I caught my husband cheating on me."

***

When Zin was a child, she talked and talked, happily gabbing without a second thought. She could even be a little goofy at times, and she certainly wasn't afraid to say anything. She wasn't a showboat—she never really craved attention—but she was direct, and because she was a little girl it came across as cute instead of irritating. But something changed as Zin reached middle school. Zin no longer was her ebullient self, prone to chatting away at the dinner table until her parents had to use awkward segues to change the subject. Instead, she clammed up, not wanting to share anything with anyone. She kept a diary that she locked up in a desk drawer and she would consign her thoughts to those pages—the transgressions, the hurts, the misunderstandings of her tween life. And for a long time after that, the idea of sharing her deepest feelings with another person was unimaginable.

Zin thought about that private part of her, the one reluctant to open up, as Chaz continued to pry those feelings out of her.

"So, how long have you been feeling…down?" asked Chaz, glancing down to check his watch. It had been over a half an hour of venting and revealing and it felt good to share, but now she wasn't sure that she wanted to be doing so with this man. She rolled her eyes, tilted her head back at the ceiling, gave a sigh of resignation, and plowed ahead.

"I don't know. Probably for months." Pause. "Maybe years." Another pause. "I mean, I haven't felt excited about anything since…I guess I can't remember. Maybe the trip to Sedona last year? I was really happy that he wanted to go on a spring break trip—he usually can't get away from work, or he is traveling for work—so it felt special that he planned it." Zin cracked her knuckles, took a breath, and looked at the ceiling again. "I usually had to plan all our trips, you know, and he never was very excited about them. Never enough golf in the itinerary. Anyway, I was excited for Sedona. I did enjoy it, but it didn't play out as I had hoped; he pretty much just drank and played golf that entire week, but at least I got to go to the spa and do some shopping and even a little hiking and enjoy myself. But other than that, I don't know. When I think about it, I guess I've kind of been in a funk for a few years."

Zin paused at that, tugged on her shirt collar, and fanned herself. She got up out of her chair and walked over to the table, pouring water from a dispenser into a Styrofoam cup. She took a sip and closed her eyes, her voice taking on a distinctly chillier tone. "I guess it turns out the scumbag had been screwing his assistant that whole time."

She thought about it—cause and effect. Did he cheat because she had started sinking, or was her sinking the result of him abandoning her for something new? She knew what he would say. In fact, he had essentially said it.

"He thinks it's my fault that he strayed, by the way." Zin looked over to Chaz and caught his head snapping up, his sleepy eyes blinking a couple times.

"Are you okay?" asked Zin, eyes narrowed.

"Umm, sorry, I missed that last bit," he replied. "You were saying?"

Zin's voice took on an edge. "I was saying that my husband blamed me for his cheating." She returned to her seat but was glaring at Chaz now.

Chaz's expression hardened. "I apologize," he replied, slowly, and though his face was neutral, Zin didn't detect any apology in his eyes. "So, you think he blames you?" He looked at Zin with a professional veneer, prodding her to move past this awkward moment, as if it was beneath her to be upset by this triviality. Zin shook her head but decided to push through it.

"I know he blames me. Or tried to. He claims it's my fault he strayed. Apparently, I wasn't doing enough to bring a spark to our relationship. He actually said that. I mean, I don't know what came first, my...I don't know what to call it, I guess I'll say depression...or his cheating, but what kind of guy comes up with an excuse like that? I mean, really? He's been such a jerk since I caught him. He blamed me for not trusting him. He seems pissed that his little world is getting inconvenienced."

Zin thought about Rick and closed her eyes and clenched her fists into balls. It had been a couple months now, but every time she pictured him with C.J. she wanted to scream. And kick. No, not kick, punch? No, not quite right. Drag him down the street by his hair, drop him on the cement, and jump on him.

"Yes, that is a terrible thing to say," replied Chaz, shaking his head. "He obviously doesn't want to take any responsibility for his actions."

"No, he doesn't. He's embarrassed and just striking out."

"That's right. It's hard to admit mistakes. It takes a big person to admit they messed up and ask for forgiveness. Has he asked for any kind of forgiveness?"

"At first, but when it became clear that I didn't want to just sweep it under the rug, he got mean."

"Hmmm, that's not okay," said Chaz, thoughtfully, tapping the fingers of his hands together. "So, have you thought about your role in all of this?"

"What do you mean?"

"Well, marriage is a two-way street. I think we know what Chaz could have done better. Have you thought about your role in how your marriage started dissolving?"

Zin furrowed her eyebrows and gave Chaz a hard look.

"I'm not sure what you're getting at? Are you saying that I'm somehow responsible for the fact that my husband was screwing his assistant?"

"No, no, no. Nothing like that. No. But like we said, it's hard to admit mistakes. I'm just wondering if you've examined that at all?"

Zin sat in silence, looking at Chaz, her nostrils flaring with each deep breath. After a long moment, she stood up and grabbed her coat.

"I think we're done here," she said, and headed toward the door.

"Ms. McGuire?" Chaz called out, a small concession in his voice. "Zin, I'm sorry," he stood up now. "Please come back. I think you were getting into some important feelings that we need to explore." Zin ignored him and kept walking. "We are making progress. Why don't we sit back down, I'll get us each a cup of coffee, and we can continue? I've got a little time on my calendar—we could extend the session a bit." Zin turned to look at Chaz. It was clear to her now that this had been a bad move.

"Yeah, I don't think so," she said, looking straight at him. "Goodbye Chaz." She turned and walked out the door, Chaz shaking his head behind her.

Zin made her way to her car where she crawled in and banged her fists against the steering wheel. She wanted to cry but didn't want to give into that right now. The last thing she wanted was for Chaz to come out of the building and see her crying in her car. For the second day in a row, she wished she could just disappear.

7

Jay pulled into the parking lot of the Lakeview Senior Living Retirement Center, turned off the car, and sat for a moment with his eyes closed. He was tired and didn't want to have to go in. He looked up at the building's sign and smirked; this place was miles from the nearest lake, and there certainly wasn't any view. After another minute of enjoying the peace of his car, Jay finally bowed to the inevitable, hefted his considerable mass out of the little car, and ambled to the front door, where security buzzed him in. It was Tuesday at 10:00 a.m., so that meant his weekly visit to Mabel Jorgenson, one of the long-time members of St. Stephens, and possibly the crankiest. She had become a shut-in ever since she fell six months ago.

Jay took the elevator to the second floor and wandered the halls of the complex, getting some appreciative nods from a few folks, mostly wispy little ladies on their way to lunch, already queuing up for the 10:45 a.m. meal. Jay pulled up to apartment C-122 and knocked on the door.

"Who is it?" barked a voice from somewhere inside, not near, but he could still hear it clearly. Somehow Mabel still had a stronger voice than anyone he knew, even if she wasn't getting around much anymore.

"It's Father Jay," he called.

"Well, you know I don't lock it. Come on in." Jay rolled his eyes to the ceiling, took a deep breath, and forced a weak smile onto his face as he opened the door. He entered a living room where a white-haired lady sat watching a talk show, a crocheted blanket sitting on her lap. She wore a heavy blue sweater and thick glasses and her straight hair fell all around her except for the bangs that were cut across her forehead, giving the impression that she was wearing a white helmet. She tilted her head, furrowed her brow, and frowned at him, as if someone had presented her with an unusual gift not to her liking.

"Good morning, Mabel, how are you today?" asked Jay, a little on the loud side.

"Still alive," she croaked. "Don't know why, but that's the way the good Lord wants it, I guess. He must have some purpose for me yet."

Yeah, to test me. "Well, we never can know his plans, can we?"

"Hmmmpf," she muttered. Jay wasn't expecting an invite to sit, so he made his way to an old, green couch and settled in.

"So, how are things? Has anyone seen you about that leaky faucet yet?"

"No. I've called about four or five times. Every night I lie in bed and listen to that stupid faucet. It's driving me bananas. They used to take care of things around here. I don't know what is going on—they're driving this place into the ground, I say."

"Oh, I don't think it's that bad, is it? I see they are replacing the gazebo out back. Looks like it will be nice."

"What a waste! No one ever goes there. The only ones who go there are snotty little kids who are tired of visiting their grandma and grandpa and need to run around. They should be putting up new wallpaper in the dining room, that's what they should do. That dining room wallpaper looks like they spread some glue on a newspaper and threw it at the wall."

Jay pictured the dining room. He had eaten there previously on visits and had to admit she was mostly right about that.

"Speaking of dining, what time is your lunch? I don't want to keep you from it."

"Oh, don't worry. I don't usually do lunch upstairs. I do

breakfast and dinner." She looked at Jay. "You didn't bring donuts, did you?"

Jay took a deep breath and summoned his inner Zen. He'd heard this many times before.

"No, I didn't," he answered, trying very hard to keep a neutral expression on his face.

"Father Harvey always brought me doughnuts. I'm big on the maple long johns. He'd get the chocolate ones with custard filling and get me a maple long john. I haven't had a maple long john in a long time."

Jay nodded. Every time he heard this, he told himself he would get her one next time. But by the end of their meetings, he usually changed his mind.

"What do you have going today?" asked Jay, trying to change the subject. "Doesn't your daughter come on Tuesdays? Or was it Thursdays?"

"She comes whenever she wants, which is not too often. But it's more than my son. Haven't seen him in about three months."

"He lives up by Alexandria, right? That's a bit of a drive?"

"Yeah, well he's just about retired. He should have the time to get down here." She paused and was quiet for a moment, but then seemed to pick up a train of thought, her voice a degree softer. "But for today, probably nothing. Watch TV. That damn therapist will probably come by and try to get me to walk around. She says I should be up on my own, but my hip hurts too much." Jay looked at Mabel and wondered if maybe the reason she was dragging the therapy along was that she liked the visits from the therapist. She did a good job of hiding her loneliness behind a hard shell. He almost started feeling a little empathy for her situation when she piped up again.

"Speaking of therapy, looks like someone here needs some exercise. You're packing an extra tire these days, Father. Gotta get out and play some tennis or something. Father Harvey used to play tennis. He was in great shape. Older than you, by quite a bit, but trim. Good lookin' young man." Jay gave her a weak, benign smile and then got up and walked to the kitchen.

"Excuse me for a second, I'm just going to get a glass of

water."

"Glasses to the right of the fridge," she called. Jay knew where they were, of course, but first he reached above the fridge, pulled out a bottle of Jim Beam that someone had placed there, likely when she had moved in a year ago, got a glass from the cupboard to the right of the fridge, and poured himself a shot. He downed it quickly, then put the bottle back up in its spot, rubbed his eyes, and filled the glass with water, returning to the living room.

Jay hated Tuesday mornings.

***

Tuesday night found Jay sitting at home, watching the Minnesota Twins baseball game. He eyed the clock and saw that it was 6:50 p.m., which meant that he had better get over to the church for the parish council meeting. He had come to dread the affairs and wanted to avoid the small talk before the meeting, so he had learned to leave the house at the precise time that would bring him to the meeting exactly when it started. Jay turned off the television with some reluctance, threw on his coat, and sloshed through the puddles on his sidewalk for the half block walk to the church. At least it was done snowing now. He hated shoveling the sidewalk in front of his house, especially since the church wouldn't pay for it, which he thought was just another cheap way that the parish council was trying to get back at him. They paid to have the church sidewalks and parking lot shoveled, but the parish house, practically next door, was the responsibility of the priest. The previous priest had insisted on doing it himself for the exercise and to save the church money, so there wasn't a line item in the budget for it, and Jay refused to beg for it. Jay hated them for it and refused to shovel unless the snow was deep enough to cause trouble.

Jay arrived a minute before seven and went downstairs to the parish library, a sitting room with chairs and a couple of small tables where the parish council met. A few little wrinkled, blue-haired ladies sat chatting against one wall. A few older men were sitting in folding chairs, a couple of them talking about the weather. Only two of the people in the room were younger than Father Jay, a fact that always made him feel inadequate. William Leland, the parish council chairman, watched Father Jay arrive and hang up his coat. He was a tall man with white hair and trimmed gray beard and was always neatly, though conservatively dressed, tonight in tan dress pants, white cotton shirt, plaid, sleeveless vest, and penny loafers. Staring at the nearly tardy Father Jay, he spoke up.

"It appears that we can begin now," he said, crossing his legs, his penny loafers pointing to the rest of the attendees. Father Jay closed his eyes and took a deep breath before sitting down.

The meeting was mostly uneventful. The committee chairs each talked about projects they were involved in. Cindy from the Social Justice committee reminded everyone that they would soon be a host church for Project Hope, the homeless shelter project that provided temporary housing in church basements for a month. Barb, the church administrator, gave her standard report. Barb was the same age as Jay's mother, which endeared her to him, and was always kind and in good spirits. He enjoyed her company and her solidarity against an otherwise uncooperative parish council. It sounded like more boiler work would be needed. Miranda, the church bookkeeper, volunteered to get estimates. Jay never could understand why Miranda kept volunteering when committee members were willing to make these calls, but since she didn't seem to overextend herself in any other area of her job, Jay was fine with it.

The final part of tonight's meeting was the part that Jay was dreading. The diocese had come up with a new salary schedule and the parish council would be reviewing it as part of the budget, including salary adjustments for the other staff members. The worst part was that they would be able to ask all about his earnings as if it wasn't a confidential matter and he wasn't there. Jay already knew that the diocese was having budget problems and the salary adjustment would be tiny, so it was doubly embarrassing for him. Marvin Schneider cleared his throat, put on his glasses, and looked at his papers. A small, stern-looking man with a grey goatee and glasses, wearing a brown V-necked sweater over a white shirt, he was an auditor at a government agency and was always complaining about meager government salaries. Consequently, he was never sympathetic to proposals for staff salary increases. Jay found him to be one of the most judgmental people in the entire church. Strolling around the church basement after mass on Sundays, he looked as if he was a principal trying to find a student getting into trouble. He always was offering advice to people on any variety of subjects, and he always had a critique for Father Jay.

"The parish staff committee has met with the budget committee to review finances and salaries for the parish staff. In addition, we've received the adjusted salary schedule for Father Jay. We review staff performance based on the objectives they set at the beginning of the year, and review our church finances to see what, if any, compensation adjustments can be made." A few necks craned to make sure they could hear the next part.

"Given the current state of the church finances and increasing cost of health care, we are recommending a two percent increase for staff, other than Father Jay. The compensation package for Father O'Brian remains basically constant, which is good for the budget, except for the increase in health care costs. You see the numbers on the sheet I provided. There is a base salary, insurance benefits, and retirement benefits, along with a training budget. We need to approve the staff salary and other expenses as part of our budgeting process." William Leland rubbed his grey beard and asked if there was any discussion. A plump white-haired woman in a brown corduroy coat asked the obvious question.

"So, what is the total compensation package for Father Jay?" Marvin told her. Everyone tried to remain expressionless when the number was given, but Jay noticed a couple of little old ladies raise their eyebrows. To them it was a large amount of money, but everyone forgot that the package included all health care costs, the retirement savings that the church provided, and because of accounting reasons, it included all household utilities. The true salary was meager.

"So, Father Jay is not getting a raise this year?" asked Julie Moyer, a soft-spoken woman who always came across to Jay as the picture of kindness.

"No. Not at this time." Marvin replied.

"Not even a cost-of-living adjustment?" Julie looked like she was fishing for a possible modification, but she didn't push it.

"No. I expect that this is because of the current financial troubles at the archdiocese and the large increase in health care costs for his medical coverage." The room was silent for a few seconds. Father Jay sat cross-legged with an unattached look on his face, trying to appear as if the discussion was about the color of the bulletin board at the front of the church instead of his private business. William, noticing in the silence that the mood had turned ever-so-slightly sympathetic for the young priest, called for a motion.

"So, do we have a motion on the floor?" The plump woman responded with an appropriate motion.

"Do we have a second?" Someone muttered 'second'.

"Okay. Any discussion?" William glanced around quickly, then proceeded. "All in favor say 'Aye'." The attendees uttered a general murmur of acceptance.

"All opposed?" A second of silence followed.

"Then the motion passes. Next on the agenda, the church bazaar that is coming up." Father Jay sat silently throughout the rest of the meeting. He was too distracted to contribute much to the conversation. The meeting seemed to drag on forever, but after two hours, everyone was antsy and wanted to get going. Jay said his goodbyes and made his way up to his office, listened to a phone message from a parishioner whose father was now in the hospital, and walked out into the night, locking the church behind him. The last of the council members was leaving the parking lot as he made his way down the sidewalk. It was a cold, damp, early spring evening, and he dug his hands deep into his coat pocket and picked up his pace. Spring seemed to have a hard time getting its traction.

Jay headed home with a plan on making a couple of calls. One of his ideas was to do outreach to members who seemed to have stopped coming to church. He had proposed his idea to the parish council, and it had received a luke-warm reception. Rather than push the idea, he decided to do the calling himself. It seemed like a good idea at the time, but in practice, it almost never happened that anyone wanted to discuss this topic with the priest of their former church, and Jay was thinking of dropping the process altogether. If he was being honest with himself, half the time he didn't blame them for leaving the church. He had enough misgivings of his own.

Jay didn't waste any time when he got home. He knew there wasn't anything to eat in the house, so he immediately called for a pizza delivery. While he waited, he opened a bottle of wine and headed to the couch. The plan was to make some phone calls while he snacked and watched ESPN. After a bit, there was a knock on the door and a large pepperoni pizza in his hands.

Jay poured himself a glass of wine and started going through the list. There were only four names on it; this should go quickly. People rarely answered, which made everyone feel better. Jay could leave them a voicemail, knowing that they weren't likely to call back and he had done his duty. He had gotten to the point where he really didn't want them to answer; in the rare case when they answered the phone, it was always an awkward conversation, sounding more like a telemarketing call than anything.

Jay made it through the first three names on the list with little concern, leaving two voicemails and finding that he didn't have a good number for the other. The next name on the list was Rick and Zin McGuire. He hadn't seen them for several months. Rumor had it they were getting a divorce, and both had stopped attending church. Well, Zin had stopped—Rick had rarely shown up in the last several years and would bolt immediately afterwards. He had seemed like a bit of a jerk if Jay remembered correctly. Zin had been a little more active, sitting on a committee occasionally and helping with some events. He looked at the phone number. He sure hoped it was Zin's, and not Rick's, but odds are, Rick wouldn't have given the church his number, anyway. Jay frowned and made the call.

"Hello," came an impatient voice from the other end.

"Hello. Is this Zin?" Jay asked. He didn't know why this made him nervous.

"Yes, who's this?"

"Zin, this is Father O'Brian from St. Stephen's church. How are you?"

"Umm, hi, Father. I'm doing okay, I guess." She sounded surprised. They all were.

"That's good." It was awkward already. Jay took a breath. "I was just checking in. Do you have a minute to chat? Is this an okay time?"

"Sure, I suppose. I don't have anything going on that the pause button can't handle."

"Umm, great. So, I'm calling because, well, we just haven't seen you for a while at church. We're just wondering how you are doing, or if you need anything."

"I'm doing okay," she answered, guardedly. "I'd like a winning lottery ticket, but I don't need anything, thanks."

"Okay, umm, great. Well, again, just checking in. Seeing how you're doing. If you want to meet to discuss anything, I can always do that. If you need anything, or, well, whatever." Jay trailed off. *Well, that sounded extremely stupid.*

"Oh," replied Zin. She sounded a bit surprised. There was a long pause.

"So, that's about all I..."

"Sure, I'll meet," blurted Zin.

"You will?"

"Yeah, why not? I've got a lot on my mind and you're probably cheaper than my shrink." She laughed, a little too loud. Jay wondered if he wasn't the only one with a bottle next to him.

"Ummm, okay then," answered Jay. "Sure. Well, ummm, what day works for you?"

"Not tomorrow. Maybe Thursday?" answered Zin.

"Sure," replied Jay. "I suppose after work would be best." They finalized a time and Jay got her address before he hung up. He sat back in his chair and took a drink of his wine. He wasn't sure what that was, but he felt like he had just asked a girl to a high school dance. And just like then, he was surprised to have gotten a yes.

*****

Zin hung up the phone. It wasn't every day that a priest called her, and she wasn't sure why she had agreed to this desperate plea for attendance, other than because she was in a 'what the hell' sort of mood today. Now that she thought about it, it most likely was just going to be a pitch for donations or something. She thought about calling Father O'Brian back and making up some excuse to not meet but decided not to. It seemed that this was the week of bad decisions. She had already agreed to meet that strange man again, which, she realized, was probably the second dumbest thing she'd done that week. When she thought about it, agreeing to meet a priest wasn't even in the top five of her week's mistakes. And it was only Tuesday.

The phone call reminded Zin that her mother had left her a message earlier in the day, asking her if she had Easter dinner plans. Zin had tried to coach them in texting for little things like that, but it never seemed to have stuck, and she decided that talking to her parents on the phone was probably a child's obligation, anyway, so she let it go. Well, talking to her mom, anyway. She almost never talked to her dad.

As if to confirm the thought, Zin dialed her parent's home number and her father answered.

"Zin, how're you doing?"

Zin almost laughed at the distance between her reality and the answer she was about to give.

"Fine, Dad. Just fine."

"Good, good to hear. Let me get your mother for you." Zin closed her eyes and shook her head. Her father rarely got farther than a cursory check-in before jumping off the call. Zin used to take offense to it, but in recent years, she had come to a more nuanced realization; he feared their conversations.

Zin could hear her father call for her mother, and after a few seconds, Judy Meyer picked up the phone, her coarse alto sounding as business-like as ever.

"Elizabeth. Thanks for calling back. You got my message about Easter dinner?

"Yes, and I'm free."

"Good. We're having ham, as usual, and I'm making my goat cheese scalloped potatoes."

"Love those. What can I bring?"

"Oh, don't bother. I have everything covered."

"How about a bottle of wine then?"

Judy hesitated. "Yes, that would be great," she answered, less than enthusiastic. "Just FYI, your dad likes a chardonnay."

"Sure, I can do that."

"Okay, what time?"

"You know, I don't have much going on. I could come any time."

"How about one o'clock?"

"Sure."

"Okay, we're all good then." Judy paused and Zin sensed something else was coming.

"Ummm, one more thing. What are you doing on Friday night?"

"This Friday night?"

"Yes."

"Let me check my calendar. Oh, wow! I'm free. Isn't that strange?" Judy didn't laugh and Zin got suspicious. "Why?"

"We're just having a couple of people over from the club and thought maybe you would join us?" Now Zin was the one pausing. This didn't sound interesting at all, and it smacked of pity.

"I don't know, Mom. That doesn't sound like my thing."

"Are you busy?"

"No, but..."

"It'll be fun. Just a little dinner and a few drinks. I promise we won't keep you out late." Zin didn't understand her mom's insistence, and at most other times of her life she would have just told her no without a second thought, but maybe they were worried about her. She sighed.

"Oh, all right. But it seems like I'll be a third wheel or something."

"Nonsense. It'll be fun. We'll see you then."

They hung up and Zin rubbed her forehead, massaging away the slight headache that was starting to take hold. She thought about her week. She felt like at every turn she wasn't really in control, that others were pushing her to do things she normally wouldn't do. Or maybe she was letting people do it. Whether she was agreeing because she was interested, or because she was too tired to resist, she wasn't sure.

8

Wednesday nights often found Jay attending the finance meeting with the prickly Marvin Schneider. Given that he had sat through the humiliating salary discussion the night before, he was all too glad to have an excuse to skip the finance committee tonight. Instead, the Spring Fling event committee had called a special, emergency meeting to discuss their situation. Florence Nelson, co-chair of the committee, a venerable matriarch of the church, was very anxious about the fundraiser. It was the big annual event for the church that was held in late spring and provided a generous share of the church's annual budget. Father Jay walked downstairs into the meeting room and found a room full of people chattering anxiously and looking over lists. Upon his arrival, the group assembled in a circle of folding chairs and started in. They told Jay of the current predicament.

"I don't know what we're gonna do," Florence professed, shaking her head. "We usually have live music, but we don't have anyone booked yet. Two groups already cancelled on us. Plus, we are way behind on donations." She looked over at Margaret Sheilburg who nodded in agreement as she knitted furiously on a sweater that was taking shape in her lap, a pink candy-striped cross adorned the front of the green garment. Jay said a small prayer for whomever was the intended recipient of that sweater.

Father Jay listened with forced earnestness to reports about the pies and cakes (they had very few volunteers), the fact that they couldn't use the same venue as last year (the high school gym wasn't available), and the fact that they were short on volunteers in general. It was, as far as everyone could see, the worst situation any of them had ever seen.

"It's almost as bad as the year the van rolled into the bazaar," Jim Miller pointed out, not cracking a smile. Several of the older ladies nodded, remembering the fiasco of twenty years ago when the van from the rental company slipped out of gear, backing over the table of the desserts, and then knocking over a table of canned goods. Of course, that year was one of their best fund-raising years ever, as everyone assumed that there would be lost revenue and donated twice what they normally would have. Donations kept rolling in for three weeks after the event from guilt-ridden church members who had heard about the disaster but weren't there to witness it.

In truth, the volunteers had been drying up slowly over the years, which was more apparent to the few, hardy, gray-haired volunteers than to the younger, newer church attendees, who had only known things the way they currently were. But the committee members remembered the days when practically the entire church participated in the event. All that remained was a small group of dedicated folks who had been driving it for years.

Father Jay listened to the worries and the complaints, watching the clock as they ran well past the hour meeting time. He didn't want to seem rude, but tonight he just didn't want to be there, and he felt like doing something for himself. Janelle Magnuson was still in the middle of a diatribe about the difficulty in getting good rental equipment when Father Jay finally interrupted, having found no room for even the slightest segue.

"Folks, I hate to interrupt you, but I'll probably have to be leaving here shortly. I'm sorry for that. I know this is a tough situation. Is there something I can do?" he asked. Janelle Magnuson stopped her story and looked at Father Jay.

"Well, Father," Florence answered. "We wanted you to

know. We're thinking about calling off the Spring Fling." The room went quiet. Jay sat back, digesting this one. The Spring Fling brought in nearly a quarter of the church budget. They couldn't not do it.

"Umm, yeah. That wouldn't be good," said Jay, his face contorting in his newfound concern.

"No, it wouldn't," replied Florence. "But we are stretched thin. Each year we get fewer volunteers, and with the school backing out on us, we now have a venue cost we didn't expect."

Jay walked back through the discussion points with the committee members, brainstorming options. They discussed a plan for a scaled back version of the event that seemed doable in the time they had. By the time the meeting ended, Jay found himself with a throbbing headache.

Jay headed upstairs. As he walked to his office, he noticed the door of the church bookkeeper was open and a light was on. He popped his head in. A heavy, middle-aged woman was sitting in front of a computer and practically jumped out of her chair.

"Oh! Father Jay! I...I thought your meeting was over an hour ago," she said, eyes wide. "You scared me."

"Oh, sorry Miranda. Didn't mean to scare you. I got asked to attend the Spring Fling's committee meeting. Got big problems for the Spring Fling. What's got you here so late?"

"Oh, I just wanted to catch up on the first quarter budget numbers. For the finance committee," she added quickly.

"They're asking too much of you," replied Jay.

"Oh, no. They're not bothering. No worries," she smiled, a little too much, Jay thought. His throbbing forehead reminded him it was time to go.

"Okay, well, don't stay too late. Good night." Jay headed back downstairs to see if the church was now empty, thinking about the fiasco that was the Spring Fling. Marvin Schneider would not like to hear about the budget deficit. Marvin didn't seem to like Jay much, and Jay would say the feeling was mutual, but he had to admit that Marvin seemed to have gotten the budget and accounting in order since he started leading the finance committee and seemed to be working with Miranda a lot. If only the church had more money, all of this would be easier.

***

Zin pushed the button, waiting to be buzzed into the back of the church, watching her breath flare into wispy white clouds in the cool evening air. She waited for over a minute. *What am I doing here?* She straightened her clothes and realized she had spilled ketchup on her simple grey blouse and even on her faded blue jeans. *Ugggh.* She zipped her coat up a few inches to hide the stain. She waited for another half a minute and had just turned to walk away when the buzzer sounded, and she reluctantly pulled the door open. Inside, she stopped for a second, looked around, and took a deep breath. She trudged downstairs to the parish library, a sitting room with mismatched lounge chairs and two small, worn tables where the church committees usually met. A few older ladies sat chatting against one wall, a paper cup of coffee in hand and a few middle-aged men were sitting in folding chairs talking about the snow still clinging to their yards and water that had made its annual journey into their basements. Zin walked over to the table where Cindy Erickson was unpacking a handbag. Cindy, wearing a thick blue sweater, large glasses, and short, brown hair was in her mid-fifties, which made her one of the younger committee members.

"Well, hi Zin," said Cindy as she noticed Zin, mild surprise appearing on her face for an instant before disappearing into a warm smile.

"Hi Cindy."

"Good to see you, Zin. How are you?"

"Oh, I could complain, but then you wouldn't want me around, so I'll keep that to myself." Zin gave Cindy a weak smile and took the folding chair a couple seats away from Cindy, plopping a notepad and folder on the table in front of her. She kept her coat on.

"Oh, you can complain around me, I don't care," replied

Cindy. "Are you here for the committee meeting?" Zin sensed that she wanted to dig for more information. Or maybe she was paranoid.

"Yeah, it's been a while," Zin half sighed. "I guess I just got busy last year. Didn't seem to have the time for much." she answered, offering a polite smile. She liked Cindy well enough, she just wanted to skip over the last, well...year if possible.

"Well, you didn't miss much. You know us, same old, same old."

Zin nodded. It was probably true. The social justice committee was a steady group of people who kept at it, year after year, getting little attention or thanks: fundraising for missions, serving meals to the homeless, tutoring, collecting school supplies.

Zin made pleasantries with the other committee members as they wandered in and took their seats. The meeting consisted mostly of updates on recent initiatives to tutor at the neighborhood school, the fundraising event they had conducted with a local electronics recycler, and plans to participate in a construction project that summer to help with homeless housing. Each activity needed participants, and Zin's mood soured as the evening went on. She was the one who needed help—why should she be wasting her time on this? Plus, every interaction was a risk, every conversation a minefield where she might be forced to divulge embarrassing personal details about her life. She decided to avoid any commitment to participate in any volunteer opportunities, telling herself that she wasn't sure that she wanted to commit to being around the church or mingling with church members for a while. She had come here because she didn't want to be alone tonight and this idea had popped into her head, but now, after passing on a few opportunities to volunteer, she felt like her reluctance to volunteer was becoming awkward, and she began to feel that this had been a mistake. She sat quietly, hoping things would wrap up. Cindy had a last agenda item.

"We are in pretty good shape for hosting Project Hope next week, but we still have several slots to fill. So, if you can shake the tree and try to find another volunteer or two, it would help a lot. We still have eight slots to fill, including Easter Eve."

"Project Hope?" asked Zin.

"Oh, sorry," answered Cindy, turning to Zin. "It's a program that provides homeless shelters for the county. They rotate hosting at different churches every month. Families are bussed to a church in the evening, we feed them a meal, play games with kids, or help with homework, and two volunteers stay overnight. We get them breakfast and help them on their way in the morning."

"We're hosting this month for the first time," Arlene Porter chimed in. She was a thin woman with glasses, her greying hair pulled back in a loose ponytail.

"Here?" Zin asked confused. "I don't get it. Are families sleeping on the floor of the church basement?"

"No," Arlene answered. "The program brings cots and blankets and sheets and little portable walls to make a private little room or corner for the family. But it isn't the Ritz by any means."

"What about their belongings and such?"

"That depends," answered Cindy again. "For some of them, the bags they are packing are all they have. There's also storage at the center where they go during the day. More likely, they leave their stuff with family or friends for a while. Some put their stuff in storage lockers, but that's risky. If you miss your payments, they can sell your stuff."

"Hmm," noted Zin, pausing to reflect on the notion of literally living in a suitcase.

"So, yes," continued Cindy, turning back to the others. "We still need volunteers. If you think you can take another shift, let me know. Easter weekend shifts are obviously going to be the hardest to fill."

Zin listened as the group started discussing what to do with the upcoming special Easter offering, but she started to drift off, imagining what she would do if she had to pack her life into a few suitcases. The things to leave with neighbors or relatives. A storage unit. Zin had always thought of herself as independent, but when it came down to it, she knew her parents could bail her out of any potential problem. It would be the last thing she would want to do, but knowing she had a safety net was a luxury she had always taken for granted. What if she didn't have that safety net? She realized that her current situation scared her, but she would never know the true fear of desperation.

A brief pause in the conversation snapped Zin back to the meeting at hand, and when Zin glanced at the clock, she panicked. 8:03 p.m. The time had triggered the memory of Henry telling her about their next meeting. She figured it would be impossible for him to find her here, but somehow, he had found her yesterday, and the thought of Henry knocking on the door with the entire committee staring at Zin made her nearly nauseous. She hopped up immediately.

"So sorry," she interrupted, quickly gathering her things and stuffing them into a bag. "I forgot...I have an appointment. Tonight. Gotta run. I'll see you later. Thanks so much." Zin backed out of the room, waving at the others, the rest of the committee uttering their goodbyes and waving back. Zin turned and jogged down the hall where she ran into Father Jay.

"Zin?" exclaimed Father Jay, a pleased look of surprise on his face.

"Uh, hi, Father," she stammered, also surprised. She felt like she was caught, but she didn't know why.

"Boy, what a coincidence! What brings you here tonight?"

"Well, after we talked last night, I got the meeting reminder in my email. For the Social Justice Committee. I haven't attended for about a year, and I, I don't know. I just decided to come for some reason." She shrugged, glancing around him.

"That's great!" said Jay, ignoring her body language. "That's a great group of people. I wish I could be more involved in their work." The conversational ball fell into Zin's court, but she didn't pick it up. She tried to make her expression blank, not wanting to encourage conversation, but not wanting to be rude. They stood for an awkward moment half smiling at each other until Zin heard footsteps behind her. Coming down the hall was a stern looking man wearing tan slacks and polo shirt. The man eyed them curiously as he passed them.

"Goodnight, Marvin," said Jay, nodding at Marvin. Marvin nodded back.

"Night," he offered, but as he turned toward the stairs, he slowed down and stopped to tie his perfectly tied shoe, within earshot of Zin and Jay.

"Well, I should be off as well," offered Jay, glad that the awkward stalemate had been broken. "But we're on for tomorrow, 6:30, right?

"Right," answered Zin, tersely. "See you then." She walked quickly past Father Jay and almost ran into Marvin, who was now standing around the corner, looking at a paper in his hand.

"Oh, sorry about that," she said.

"Marvin Schneider," Marvin said extending his hand. "I know you've been attending here for a while, but I don't feel like we've met." He eyed Zin as they shook hands. "I think we have. But it's been a while. Zin McGuire. Glad to meet you."

"Oh, yes, yes. Of course. Now I remember. You and your husband have been members for a while."

"Well, yes. My husband and I were members. Or are, I guess." Zin decided on the spot that she was tired of dodging the issue. "We're separated, actually." At this, Marvin's eyebrows lifted.

"Oh? I'm sorry to hear."

"Don't be. He's a schmuck." Marvin attempted an awkward laugh, but Zin didn't. "Anyway, nice meeting you. Gotta run." Zin walked briskly past Marvin, who turned to watch her go, the faintest of smiles on his lips.

Zin flew up the stairs and out the door. She hustled down the sidewalk and was rounding the corner of the church when she almost knocked over Henry, who was standing still, staring at the cold, clear sky.

"Henry!" exclaimed Zin, bouncing backwards. "What are you doing here?" she asked, confused and angry. She knew the answer, but she couldn't believe it would really happen. Zin suddenly felt her stomach drop out from under her; she felt vulnerable and more than a little afraid. She backed up half a step and looked around, but only saw an empty parking lot and a couple houses on the corner that had dark windows—a bad spot to be cornered by a crazy homeless man. She started wondering when the committee would wrap up but knew that they often dragged it out until close to nine o'clock. She thought about turning around and running back to the church, but Henry found his voice, which seemed more silly than threatening.

"Did we not discuss the time of our meeting?" replied Henry, once again looking at Zin as if she might need psychiatric care.

"No. I mean, yes," she answered, flustered. "But I didn't…"

"Shhhhh," interrupted Henry, holding up his hand to hush Zin and looking around, listening intently. Zin stood, arms crossed, tapping her toe, waiting for Henry's hiatus from civilization to be finished. She noted that today he was wearing brown pants, a pink button-down cotton shirt with a green V-neck sweater, and a pair of what looked like work boots. Zin shook her head.

"Okay," he said, finally relinquishing his hold on the moment. "I am sorry, but you were late, and we missed part of our minute. But I do not think…" he paused. "Well, I do not want to influence your perspective. What was your experience during the last minute?" He noticed the look on Zin's face and quickly added, "Your observations about humanity, that is. Remember, I am not part of that observational scope." Zin closed her eyes in disbelief. *No, you don't seem to be part of humanity, as far as I can see.*

"Aside from the fact that a stranger keeps tracking me down," she replied, arms still crossed, "I don't think I noticed anything during that minute. It's pretty quiet."

"Okay. Well, that was my observation…"

"What the Hell are you doing here?" pounced Zin, hands on her hips. "Really. How did you find me? Are you following me? Because I'm going to start yelling at the top of my lungs. My committee meeting is just getting out and they'll all be right behind me. Someone will hear me."

Henry started to talk, but stopped, rubbed his chin, and then continued. "Zin, I do not understand why you are surprised. I gave you a location device."

"No, that's baloney," yelled Zin. "You're scaring me, Henry." Henry's face collapsed. He looked like a child who had just learned that no one wanted him on the team. Zin softened. "Henry, you can't keep doing this."

Henry scratched the back of his head and looked around, a pained expression on his face. "Do you not want to keep our bargain? About meeting ten times and keeping score?"

"No," answered Zin, but added, "at least not like this. Not in places like this, at times like this." Relief seemed to flood Henry's face.

"So, maybe tomorrow's time would be better, anyway," he offered. "It was supposed to be at 6:52 p.m." He looked at Zin with a dash of trepidation. "Would you be able to meet then? Just for our one minute?" Zin stared at Henry without saying anything. The funny blond hair, the odd clothing, the glint of the spoon under his shirt. She didn't know what to make of him. He didn't come across as having chemical dependency issues or a debilitating mental illness, other than the fact that he believed he could get a doctorate in the economics of humanity. Zin knew that it wasn't smart to agree to meet him again, but she also felt oddly liberated by her own circumstances, and she couldn't help but feel a sense of compassion while standing under the stained-glass windows of the church. She gritted her teeth and nodded.

"Yes, Henry, I could. Just for our minute. But I am going to specify the location," she added.

"That would be fine," answered Henry, eagerly.

"Well, how about somewhere we'll see people. How about the lake? Do you know where Como Lake is?"

"I believe I do."

"Can you be at the main pavilion? At—what time did you say?"

"6:52 p.m."

"Sure. 6:52 at the Como Lake Pavilion tomorrow."

"That sounds great, Zin."

"You just get home now, okay?" She made a shooing motion with her hands. Henry backed away.

"Thank you, Zin," he said, then turned and walked along the side of the church, reaching the sidewalk and turning out of sight. Zin watched for another minute to make sure he didn't return, and then glanced behind her. She could hear the doors opening and decided to leave before she was spotted – she did not want to explain this to anyone from church. She couldn't even explain it to herself.

9

Zin ducked out of school as soon as she could on Thursday afternoon and raced home. Kim had stopped by Zin's classroom to check in with her, and on a whim, Zin had asked her if she wanted to pop over for a drink after work. Now, standing in her kitchen, looking at dirty dishes, a frozen pizza box, and piles of mail sitting on the table, Zin wished she would have just suggested going to Lucky's or somewhere close to work for that drink.

Zin scrambled, picking up dirty plates and bowls off the table, throwing them quickly into the dishwasher. She ran into the living room, grabbed the pillow and blanket off the couch, and jogged up the stairs to her bedroom and threw them back on her bed. Back downstairs, she took a quick peek at the half bath on the main floor to see how bad it looked. It wasn't terrible—she didn't use it much—and balled up some toilet paper, wet it, and wiped down some surfaces. There were still piles of papers on the dining room table and a bunch of glasses and several pots and pans on the counter when the doorbell rang.

"Dammit." She threw a few pots into the sink, brushed off her old grey blouse, and headed to the door. Outside, a tall, thin woman with shoulder-length straight blonde hair and a sky-blue jacket stood on her porch. Zin made herself smile as she opened the door.

"Hi Kim. Come on in." Kim entered holding a tall, thin brown paper bag.

"I thought we could use this today," she said, and pulled out a bottle of cabernet and held it in front of Zin.

"You have amazing powers of intuition. Leave the shoes. Come on in." Zin took the bottle, set it on a little counter peninsula, and turned to the cupboards behind her to pull down a couple of long-stemmed glasses. She set one down on the opposite side of the counter in front of a stool, and Kim followed suit and took to the stool. Zin dug in a drawer looking for a wine opener, not finding it. "Now, where did that opener go?" she said to herself before realizing it was on the countertop behind her, a cork still in it from the night before.

"Did you see the email about the construction delays on the new wing? We're never going to get that thing built," said Kim, a little too eagerly. Zin sensed that she was trying a little too hard to appear casual. Or maybe Zin was just overly self-conscious. Zin agreed, finally getting the bottle open and reaching across the gray granite to pour Kim a glass before pouring herself a drink.

Zin remained standing, opposite of Kim. "I can't see how they are going to get the science department in there before the fall." They both took a sip of the wine and a silence fell between them. Zin picked up the conversation. "So, how are Tom and the kids?" She realized that the family updates might lead to the subject of Rick, but she needed to go there sooner than later.

"Oh, Tom's doing fine. Been busy at work lately—some big project that is winding up in the next couple of months. He's had to be online late at night, talking to his offshore team, so that's been annoying. Sophie is doing spring soccer on a club team now, so that's like four nights a week. Liam is playing baseball in the rec league, so that's not as intense."

"How has Sophie liked seventh grade? I remember she had a hard time in sixth."

"Yeah, their school had switched from a junior high to a

middle school, so it was the first year that the sixth graders were in the same school. The school definitely wasn't ready for it. Everything was chaos. You know how it goes. It takes a while to get things squared away after a change like that, and they had some turn-over, and a couple of teachers changed the grade they were teaching."

"Uggh. I can imagine. God, I would hate that," Zin said, rolling her eyes.

"Yeah. This year is a lot better. Teachers know what they are doing, and Sophie's a lot happier."

"Middle school is so hard on kids. Especially girls. Do you ever wish she was in the same school as you?"

Kim scrunched her face a bit and rocked it back and forth in thought. "Sometimes. Maybe. I dunno, kids need their space, and some fear any form of being different, any way that they might stand out, and parents can be a big embarrassment. So, no," she laughed. "I don't think so."

"Makes sense," said Zin. "Middle school is a terrible time for kids. They can be so rotten to each other. Don't need to make things harder."

Kim tilted her head back and forth, as if trying to see Zin's point of view. "I'm not sure middle school is a terrible time," she answered, diplomatically. "I think it can be a challenging time for a lot of kids, and a few can be mean, but I think it is also an exciting and fun time for a lot of them, too." Zin looked away and frowned, emitting a tiny huff of doubt, but didn't say anything. They both took another sip and avoided eye contact. Zin broke the silence.

"So, today is the home opener for the Twins. Don't you two have some type of ticket package? I thought you sometimes went to the opening games?"

"We do. We've got a package with about twenty games in it. Tom loves it; I'm a fair-weather fan. He took Liam today, so I have to pick up Sophie when her practice is over." Kim glanced at the fitness watch on her wrist. "You're a big fan, though. Are you going to any games?" A look of fear flash across Kim's face as she recognized her faux pas.

"Yeah, those were Rick's work tickets. The company had season tickets and we went to quite a few games," she answered, and added, "but not anymore," and gave a little shrug with a 'what can you do?' kind of expression.

"So, how are you doing?" Kim asked. "We haven't really talked since a couple weeks ago when you told me that you two were separated."

Zin took a sip to buy herself a moment to think. Kim was a good friend, but she also didn't want the entire school to know about the sordid details of what had happened, or, necessarily, what was happening now. Still, she needed to deal with it. She looked away again.

"Ummm, I'm doing okay. I don't know. I'm still processing it." Then added, "It's been a rough week." Kim didn't move, just keeping her focus on Zin. Zin sighed and tackled the issue, turning back to Kim. "I caught him cheating."

"Oh, Zin," Kim replied, looking horrified. I'm so sorry."

"Yeah, the dirtbag was screwing his assistant at work. I think it's been going on for years from what I can tell."

"Oh, Zin.".

"Yeah, it sucks." Zin took another drink of wine and looked away. She hadn't told anyone the details behind their separation yet, and although she hadn't divulged many details to Kim, it was a relief to have told a friend about some of it. Another moment of silence ensued.

Kim prodded cautiously. "And now what are you going to do?"

Zin reached across the gray granite countertop to grab the bottle that was in front of her friend. She poured a little more into Kim's glass, and even more into her own and took a drink.

"Oh, I'm going to divorce him," she added matter-of-factly. "I've hired an attorney." Kim nodded her head, looking like she was imagining that she was in Zin's shoes.

"What does he say?"

"Oh, he's been a jerk. First, he denied it. Then he minimized it and told me I was making too big of a deal of it. Then he basically threatened me, telling me I'm making a big mistake.

Now he won't cooperate with the lawyers."

"Uggh," groaned Kim.

"And, of course, he controls all our finances. That's the scary part. I was stupid all these years. I had no idea about most of our finances—I had always let him handle money stuff. What a mistake." Zin shook her head and stepped away to reach into one of the white cupboards behind her. She pulled out a small bowl and then moved to another cupboard and reached up to pull out a jar of mixed nuts. She poured them into the bowl and set them in the middle of the counter, grabbing a handful. She looked up at the ceiling while she popped a few into her mouth. "He knew what he was doing. He grabbed half of the files from our file cabinet. Probably figured out his action plan the night I caught him. Who knows what he's done now? My lawyer says he won't be able to hide anything, but it won't be easy getting the information." She rubbed her forehead. Zin stayed quiet. She thought about telling Kim about the last few days, but instinctively decided that she didn't want to talk about the events of Monday night, or the strange man who kept popping up. Instead, she just closed her eyes and groaned. "God, what a week."

Kim leaned forward, her blue eyes earnest with compassion. "Zin, I'm so sorry. You didn't deserve this."

"It happens," she said, forcing a sad smile. She looked at her friend, who, unlike most of her other friends, had never complained about her husband. "Well, not to everyone." Kim stayed quiet and looked away out a big window onto a small brick backyard patio. Zin followed her gaze.

"It really makes you feel lousy," Zin said after a moment. Kim glanced back at Zin, but Zin kept gazing out the window at something that wasn't there. "How could he treat anyone with such...indifference? Especially his wife." She shook her head and kept her eyes fixed outside, her jaw clenching and unclenching. "I'm so angry at him." She took another drink. "You know, I'm the one who wanted kids. He didn't. First, he said we should just wait a bit, focus on careers, whatever. We were in our late twenties when we got married, but it didn't seem to be an unreasonable idea. Then he avoided the subject. And after a while, he said he didn't want to be starting a family so late. I don't know how I let it happen." She turned to Kim. "It's crazy how you can just get in a rut, doing your thing day after day, and you wake up and a dozen years have gone by." She looked away again. "God, I just threw away my life for that bastard."

Kim looked helpless. "Zin, I just want you to know that I'm here for you. And if you need anything, please, just let me know. I can't imagine how hard this is."

"Thanks, Kim. That means a lot."

"And listen. About Monday. I just wanted you to know that wasn't an ordinary detention we had. Penny announced that she was retiring at the end of the year and a few of us math and science teachers decided to take her out at the spur of the moment. I saw you and I thought you might have heard us talking about it but wasn't sure. It would have totally been fine if you had joined us. I should have just said something."

"Oh, don't worry about it. I'm not that close with Penny. It's not a big deal."

"None of us are, really. She doesn't get involved with much. But she was surprised and pretty pleased that someone did something."

"Good for her," said Zin. She took a sip from her glass. They made small talk for a few more minutes before Kim looked at her watch again and got up to go, apologizing for leaving Zin and promising to be more available. Zin watched her get into her car and had just closed the front door when she heard the Bang of the back door being slammed. She stopped in her and held her breath for a moment. There was only one person who would do that, and she was in no mood to see him.

10

Jay stood in front of the mirror and frowned. He turned to the side, puffed out his chest and sucked in his gut. Then he let it collapse, returning the belly to its original shape. He was wearing his black clerical garb as usual, and on this warm spring day it felt like such a nuisance. For the thousandth time, he wished he could wear whatever he wanted instead of his black uniform. He'd gotten more relaxed as the years went by, ditching the black shirt and collar if attending truly personal activities when he shouldn't have to represent the church. When he was younger, he was much more reluctant to wear civilian clothes, and on a few occasions, he would go out somewhere—a baseball game, a movie—and on the way, pull into a parking lot, dig clothes out of a duffel bag and change in the car (no small feat for someone his size), and enjoy the day in the anonymity of a lay person. But it was too stressful; everywhere he went, he was paranoid that he'd meet a parishioner or someone who knew him, which would be an agonizingly embarrassing situation.

Jay messed with his hair, but there wasn't anything to be done with it. He pulled out a small spray bottle of cologne and spritzed the air, then stepped into the mist. He brushed his teeth and took one last look in the mirror before heading out of the house.

Jay had forgotten that Zin lived in the neighborhood, so when he went online to look up the address, he was surprised to find it only about eight blocks away. It was chilly and overcast, so he grabbed his coat and started to walk. Jay strolled down the street for a few blocks and turned left to go a few more, playing through different conversational scenarios in his head. So, he was quite unprepared when, half a block before Zin's street, a black Lexus with tinted windows roared straight at him out of an alley. Jay hopped back as the Lexus tore out onto the street without bothering to slow down and squealed down the road. He glared at the car but couldn't read the license plate.

"Idiot."

Jay got to the corner of Buchanan Street and Maple Avenue and turned right on Maple, where he walked to the second house, stopping in front of a green craftsman. He verified the house number then looked up and down the street. A grey Volvo drove down Buchanan and Jay waited until it was out of sight, then he marched up onto the porch, where he was surprised to find Zin hunched over on a wicker loveseat. Zin's face was red and puffy from crying.

"Oh," said Jay. He paused for a moment. "Umm, sorry. Looks like a bad time."

"Yeah," said Zin. She stood up, hugging herself.

"You okay?" asked Jay.

"I guess," answered Zin, shaking her head. "My asshole husband. Oops," she sniffed, "I'm not supposed to swear in front of the priest."

"I won't tell anyone," Jay said.

"Well, then, he's my asshole soon-to-be ex-husband," said Zin. She headed to the door. "Come on in, it's cold out," she offered, not looking back. "Sorry for the mess," she said as she walked through the house to the kitchen, Jay trailing behind like a scared child. "Been...busy." She corrected herself. "Aww, hell, that's not true." She half laughed as she walked to a cupboard, pulled a glass down, and grabbed an opened bottle of red wine off the counter. Holding the glass in one hand and the bottle in the other, she pulled the cork out with her teeth, spit it out on the counter, and poured herself a glass. She drank a big gulp before looking at Jay, who was standing next to the counter stool and watching the scene, half afraid, half wanting to laugh at Zin.

"Wanna drink?" she asked, already pulling another glass from the cupboard, practically daring him to comment on what he was watching. She didn't wait for an answer but headed to the dining room table with glasses and bottle in hand and collapsed into a chair.

Jay shrugged behind her back and got up and followed. "Umm, sure," he said. Zin pushed a pile of mail and dirty plates aside to make room at the table. Jay sat down, not letting his eyes leave her, as if she was a wild animal on a tenuous leash. "You know, I don't have to be here right now if you'd like to be alone." But after he thought about it for a moment, he added, "but if you want to talk…" his voice fell off into a question that sat between them for a moment.

Zin took a deep breath and poured Jay a glass, not looking at him. "Sorry, I actually forgot we were meeting. Honestly, I might not be the best audience right now," she said, raising a toast, and downed the rest of her glass. Jay took a sip.

"I take it he was just here," Jay said.

"Good guess."

"He doesn't drive a black Lexus, does he?" asked Jay.

"Why?" Zin looked at him curiously.

"He just about ran me over on the way here," said Jay. "He was in a bit of a hurry."

"Asshole," Zin said, pouring the rest of the bottle into her glass. "Oops, sorry Father. This is turning into a drinking game."

"Don't worry, that's what I thought when he just about ran me down." Jay sat quietly for a moment. "So, you and Rick aren't doing so well."

"That's the understatement of the year."

"So sorry to hear that," he said.

"That's what everyone says. Yeah, we're in the middle of divorce proceedings right now, and it's a bit ugly."

"Oh, that's rough. I'm sorry."

"It's not your fault. You don't need to apologize." Zin took a gentler tone. "Listen Father," she slurred. "I know we had an appointment and all, but I don't think I'm in the mood to deal with your recruitment speech right now. Plus, I was a good girl and was at church last night. Do you think we can have a raincheck on this meeting? I need to clear my head a bit. And I've got to meet a guy in about half an hour." Jay raised his eyebrows, then stood up.

"Yeah, no problem, I totally understand. You've got a lot on your mind. We'll just connect another time."

"Good. Thanks."

Jay turned and walked out of the kitchen and through to the porch. Zin followed him.

On the porch, Jay turned to face Zin, looking at her intently. "Are you sure you're okay?"

"Yeah, Father, I'll be okay now," she said, a little more solemn now. "Thanks for coming. I appreciate it." She gave him a quick pat hug and walked back into the house. Jay stood for a moment watching her. Then he shook himself and walked down to the sidewalk and headed home, his steps a little lighter than before.

Several houses down, a gray Volvo started up. It waited for about a minute before creeping past Zin's house, then turned the opposite direction from Jay and sped away.

11

Zin pulled into the lot near Como Lake and slipped into a parking spot. Just a couple of weeks ago it was snowing, and although the snow was mostly gone from the landscape, the cold and gray weather kept most everyone away; only a handful of hearty souls were walking around the lake today in groups of twos and threes. A couple of strollers headed down a trail with kids buried below a mound of blankets. Zin parked and walked over to the pavilion to find Henry. It didn't take long to spot him—he was the one on his knees, leaning over the dock and staring at the water through what appeared to be a spoon. Zin shook her head and moseyed over to him, stopping a few feet behind him, watching him for a moment before smiling at her strange friend. Tonight, he was wearing greenish khakis and what looked to be a shirt of course, brown material with orange stripes. Over the shirt he wore a jean jacket and a blue stocking cap with a red tassel. For some reason, the outfit worked for him.

"Looking for more creatures with a beef against humanity?" she asked, standing above Henry, her hands in her coat packet. He turned to look up at her, confusion etched on his face.

"The creature on that man's hook will attest to lost opportunity," he answered, pointing to a short, heavy-set

Hmong man at the end of the dock, reeling in a smallmouth bass.

Zin nodded. "Yes, I'm guessing you are correct on that account. Between him and my ex, I don't think humanity has a chance." Henry stood up and looked at her, frowning. "Come on, let's get this over with." She started to walk away down the path and around the lake. Henry jogged to catch up.

"You seem upset," said Henry, as he pulled up alongside Zin. She didn't look at him, but just kept walking. Zin knew she looked rough, her eyes still puffy from crying. Zin paused for a second before answering.

"It's my ex-husband. Or soon to be ex. Not soon enough, that's for sure."

"What did he do to make you upset?"

"He came over and started chewing me out." She looked over at Henry. "You know, I don't really want to talk about him right now. He just puts me in a foul mood, and I'd rather get my mind in another place. How much time do we have?"

"About five minutes until it is time for us to do our observation."

"Okay." They walked for a bit before Zin broke the silence.

"So, Henry. I gotta ask. You've inserted yourself into my life, but I don't know anything about you. So, tell me again, where are you from?"

"Far away from here."

"What? Wisconsin? Nepal? What does 'far away' mean?"

"It is not important."

"That's pretty silly. Of course it's important."

"I am not supposed to be part of the observation. I am interfering with my surroundings, and I should not be."

"Well, it's kind of hard to have a conversation with someone without observing them. Should I pretend you aren't here?"

"That would be best."

"Okay, that makes for an awkward relationship. But I guess that's what my life has become—walking with someone who wants me to pretend he's not there. Somehow, it's still better than walking with my ex-husband, so I guess it's a step up."

"Are you angry at your husband?"

"You don't get to ask me questions if you aren't going to answer any. And as I said, I don't want to talk about my ex."

"Okay, you can ask me a question."

"Fine," Zin thought for a moment. "Why are you studying humanity?"

Henry stopped walking for a moment and scrunched his face in thought before looking up. "Humans are fascinating."

"Yeah? How so?"

"They have so many dichotomies. They can fight a war and work for peace. They can be full of hate and very loving. They can be predictable and then can surprise you. They can be terribly selfish and incredibly generous. And these differences are not just across countries or societies, they are within individuals as well. It is funny and strange how you can hold two contradictory ideas in your head at the same time. Watching people justify their actions, which often go against their stated beliefs, is...entertaining."

"Yeah, I guess we lie to ourselves a lot. It keeps our heads from exploding. But entertaining? You must be really bored."

Henry looked curiously at Zin and was about to ask a question when he suddenly snapped to attention. Zin studied Henry.

"What is it?"

"Our minute starts now." Zin and Henry paused in the middle of the walking path and glanced around. The area was mostly quiet. A heavy man with a close-cut beard in black sweatpants and rings of sweat under the armpit of his sweatshirt trudged by, grunting as he went, and they stepped off the path to let him pass. Up ahead, a little girl on a small bike and big pink helmet was trying to keep upright as her father jogged alongside her. Several mallards landed on the lake near a patch of cattails that were being guarded by a red-winged blackbird. A couple of middle-aged women in spandex and hooded sweatshirts walked past them at a fast clip, one of them talking non-stop as they chugged by. An older, Asian-American man walked by slowly and serenely, smiling and nodding at them as he passed.

"The minute is up," said Henry, not looking anywhere in particular.

"How do you know that? You didn't look at a watch or a phone or anything." Henry ignored her.

"Did you have any thoughts about your experience?"

"Pretty quiet," answered Zin. "I don't think mankind wanted to play along with us tonight."

"Hmmm," frowned Henry. He studied Zin for a few seconds, but then shook his head and turned to walk back. "I should go now."

"Okay," answered Zin, now following the strange man. "And where are you going?"

"I have a place I go."

"That's it? That's all? You have a place to go?" Zin called, slightly agitated. "Is this place a house? Or an apartment? Or under a bridge?"

"You seem concerned. I appreciate your concern. But I am fine." Zin grabbed Henry's arm lightly and he stopped and turned to her.

"Listen, Henry. It's okay to ask for help. If you need something, just ask me," she said, staring straight at Henry. Henry looked at her curiously.

"Thank you, Zin," replied Henry after a few moments. "Maybe I will another time."

12

Zin sat on the couch, watching a TV series she had seen a dozen times. Comfort food, she thought. It was Friday afternoon and she had to meet Henry in about ten minutes. She wanted to skip her meeting with Henry—she was tired, busy, and she didn't want to have to deal with it today. But she also recognized that she was looking forward to these meetings in some way. The sessions were intriguing. Was she also nervous? Henry had a way of confusing her, making her feel both positive and guilty at the same time. She also felt indebted to him. She justified her continued involvement with Henry by thinking of it as a sort of repayment for the cross incident, as she liked to think of it, although the longer this kept going on, the less that justification seemed necessary. Still, she couldn't quite get a handle on her feelings.

Her phone was sitting next to her on the couch when it started buzzing, and she eyed it suspiciously. She let it buzz for a few seconds, but for some reason the number looked familiar, so she decided to answer. "Hello?"

"Hello, Zin?" Father Jay asked, sounding nervous.

"Hi. Who's this?" answered Zin, rather shortly.

"Umm, it's Father O'Brian. Sorry to bother you, Zin."

"Oh, not a bother, Father."

"Okay, good. I was just calling to check in. You were a little upset last night. Just wanted to make sure everything is okay."

"Oh, thanks Father. No, I'm okay. Nothing that a few more tears and a glass of wine couldn't fix."

"You sure? Do you need to talk to anyone?"

"No, but thanks for asking, Father. I've got to get going. I have to go to my parents' house for dinner tonight. I still owe you a raincheck, though. I know you probably work all the time…no worries." She drifted off, hoping that it might die there, but Father Jay didn't pick up on those cues.

"Maybe tomorrow afternoon? I have a church service in the evening but would be available most of the afternoon before that. Say, three o'clock?" The specificity of the request and her open schedule colluded in trapping her. She paused for a moment to think about it but found no good excuse to reject the offer.

"Yeah. That works."

"Okay, great," replied Father Jay, sounding cheered by the answer. "See you then." But before Zin could hang up, he added. "Oh, Zin?"

"Yeah?"

"Did I leave my gloves at your house yesterday?" Zin got up and walked to the dining room where they had been sitting.

"Yeah, right here on the table. I'm on my way out right now but could drop them off on my way. Any chance you could meet me in five minutes at the church parking lot? I can bring them with."

"Uhh, yeah. I can do that."

"Okay. See you in five."

Zin hung up the phone. She thought about Father Jay calling her again. He certainly seemed to be concerned about her. At least someone was, she thought. She looked at her phone, realized she was running late, and hurried out back to the garage. She opened the side door with her key, got in her little Ford, and headed to Church.

Zin arrived at the church parking lot to find it was empty

except for a large SUV parked near the back door. She found Father Jay already waiting for her, hands in pockets, his big body swinging to and fro slightly, as if he was listening to music. He walked up the car and she rolled down the window.

"Here you go," she said, handing him the gloves. "Have a good night." She smiled and made a little wave as she quickly rolled up the window. She didn't want to have Father Jay run into Henry.

"Uh, thanks," he said, looking confused as the window rolled up to cut off their conversation. "Bye." Zin waved again and busied herself with her phone. Father Jay waved and walked away, looking back once with a troubled expression.

After a minute, Zin checked the surroundings to make sure that Father Jay had left. She hoped Henry would show up soon, although she knew it didn't matter—their meeting time was carved in stone and being early wouldn't help. It was approaching 5:00 p.m. on a Friday, and she had to hit the road to get to her parents' house for dinner out in the western suburbs. She knew it would take a good hour in tonight's traffic. She still didn't know why they wanted to have dinner with her when she knew they would have her over again for Easter next week, but given that she didn't have a social life, she had accepted the offer. She was meeting Henry at the church because she still didn't feel comfortable giving him her address, and she didn't have time to drive to a destination outside of her neighborhood. Besides, she didn't know what Henry's transportation constraints were. Church was safe enough for now.

Zin sat in her car and checked her phone, seeing postings from a bunch of people who were certainly happier than she was—kids in sports tournaments, smiling families in sunny vacation spots, dinner at the latest restaurant—and decided to put her phone away, not needing any more reason to be down. She was alone, meeting a stranger in an empty parking lot, before having dinner with her mom and dad. Probably not something she would post about. The afternoon had cleared up and the sun was wrapping her in a warm blanket. She hadn't slept well last night, and it was the end of a long week. She leaned her head back and closed her eyes.

Rap Rap Rap. Zin bolted upright, seizing the steering wheel and looking wildly about. Henry knocked on the window again.

"Zin. Are you okay?" Zin shook her head to wake up. She looked over at Henry. He appeared to be wearing a large, camouflaged hoodie and black pants that were too big for him. His hair was its normal, wild blonde mess.

"You scared me," she complained. She opened the car door and pushed herself out of the car. She felt sluggish.

"You were sleeping," said Henry.

"Amazing powers of observation."

"No, it was quite simple."

"Sarcasm, dear Henry." She looked at Henry, who was holding a small, brown bag. "What's in the bag?"

"My favorite food," answered Henry, proudly.

"Really, what is it?" He lifted a white box out of the bag, smiling. Zin laughed.

"Little Debbie Cakes?"

"They are fabulous," answered Henry, eyeing the box.

"Well, I guess so." She popped her trunk and walked over to the trunk, depositing her purse. Henry gave her a questioning look. "I don't like to leave anything in my car," she answered. "People break in, and I don't want our one minute today to be me filling out a police report." She looked at Henry's bag. "Do you want to carry that or leave it in my car?"

Henry handed Zin the bag and Zin closed the trunk. "Let's walk around the block," she suggested, starting out. Henry caught up and they walked along together.

"I think we should meet where we can see more people," said Henry as they started to walk around the block. "This is a very quiet time and place."

"I agree. It just didn't work out tonight," she said, ambling along. "How much time do we have?"

"Four minutes and twenty seconds," answered Henry immediately without any sign of mischief. Zin shook her head.

A walking clock. "Where should we go?" he asked.

"Let's walk down to the parkway. It's busier. We might see something interesting." They walked in silence for a minute before Zin started up.

"So, tell me again, Henry. How does this work? You're going to check out a few cities and then come up with some formula that rates everything? Why don't you just get statistics off the Internet. That would pretty much tell you everything you need to know."

"Yes, I can gather information discreetly," he answered. "But I want to hear the stories of real people. Humanity is more than the sum of the facts and statistics."

"Makes sense," replied Zin, shrugging. He always had an answer, although she still didn't understand this man. They arrived at the busy street, standing at a corner next to a convenience store. Zin thought about the fact that in her pathetic world, standing on a corner next to a virtual stranger was the highlight of her social life.

"So, what is this thing we have going on here, Henry? You know, technically, I'm still married." Zin winked. Henry just gave her a confused look.

"I…I am not…"

"I'm just teasing, Henry."

"It is time," he said with a little jump, looking relieved. They both stood on the sidewalk at the corner of the intersection, gazing around at what humanity could throw their way. Traffic was busy, stop and go, cars racing between stop lights. A woman stood at a nearby crosswalk, but no one seemed to slow down to let her cross. A young black man on a bicycle rode down the sidewalk wearing headphones and carrying a backpack, swerving slightly to go around Henry and Zin. A petite, older lady waddled out of a Korean restaurant across the street. A woman pushed a stroller across the street opposite them. A couple blocks down the street, a ragged-looking man stood in the median, holding a cardboard sign that he was waving at cars that stopped at the lights.

"Okay," said Henry with a note of finality. They looked at

each other. Zin shrugged.

"Well, that's humanity on a Friday night at rush hour," she said. "Don't really know what to say." They walked back to the car.

"What was that man doing in the middle of the road with the sign?" asked Henry.

"I dunno. Probably homeless or something."

"And no one helps him?"

"He's probably trying to dig up some money for a bottle. Or something worse."

"Or he may need help," offered Henry.

"Sure," replied Zin.

"You do not sound like you believe it."

"Well, I don't."

"Why not?"

"Oh, I don't know. I get the feeling that most of these guys are trying to scam you," replied Zin. "I've been burned too many times." Henry contemplated this for a moment.

"And what if you are wrong?"

"Then I guess I feel bad," answered Zin. They walked in silence for a bit. Zin thought about Henry, how he seemed to be surprised at Zin's perspective after their sessions. From what she guessed, his life was much harder than hers. Why was he the one who seemed to think that everything was so great, when it obviously wasn't?

They approached Zin's car. "Can I give you a lift somewhere?" asked Zin, reluctantly.

"No, thank you. I meet lots of interesting people on the train."

"You have money for a ticket?"

"I did not know you needed a ticket," answered Henry. "The doors open, and people just get on. I assumed it was free." Zin shook her head for what seemed to be the hundredth time, dug out her purse, and handed Henry a couple of bills.

"Just buy a ticket this time. I don't want to hear that you got picked up by the police." She got in her car and backed out. Henry stood, holding the cash, then stuffed it in his pocket and waved goodbye.

***

Miranda stared at her computer, the screen showing a wedge sandal with brown suede straps. She then clicked on another browser tab, showing a similar sandal. She clicked back and forth one more time before adding the first sandal to a shopping cart and clicking through to buy it. Reaching under her desk, she grabbed her purse and dug out a wallet. When she finished the purchase, she looked outside to the mostly empty parking lot. She never worked even half a day on a Friday, so being here until nearly 5:00 p.m. was painful.

She shut down her computer and was standing up to go, when she noticed movement in the parking lot. To her surprise, Father Jay had come back. Miranda panicked; she knew she didn't have a good reason for being there, but before she could think of an excuse, he seemed to stop in his tracks. About thirty seconds later, a little car pulled up into the parking lot next to him. The driver rolled down the window and Miranda saw that Zin McGuire was in the front seat. She handed Father Jay something, and then Father Jay left.

Miranda was now more than curious and sat back down to watch and see if anything else might happen. Nothing did for a few minutes, but Zin didn't move, so Miranda kept watching. She was about to give up when a rough looking man appeared out of the blue and approached Zin's car. A panhandler, she thought, and began to worry that Zin might not be safe all alone in this empty parking lot. But Zin got out of the car to talk to him, and then took something from him and placed it in her trunk.

Even more surprising, Zin and the man walked away together. Miranda, confused and curious, left the office and moved around the church, spying on them from various windows as they first walked past the east side of the church and then the north side, eventually moving out of sight down the street. Miranda stayed at the last window for a while, but when they didn't return, she headed back to the office to close up. The two were gone for nearly fifteen minutes, and Miranda was about to leave, when she noticed that they had returned. Miranda watched as Zin took her purse from the trunk, chatted with the man for a moment, and then handed the man some money.

Miranda watched them leave, and then took her phone out of her purse and made a call.

"Hey, it's me. You'll never guess what I just saw."

13

George Meyer was gritting his teeth. He had just pulled back the curtains to his bedroom window and saw a little red Ford pull into the yard below him, a scar from a brush with a parking ramp pylon visible on the front passenger-side bumper. Always a BMW guy, the Ford was an annoying thorn in his side and a constant reminder that his youngest daughter didn't want or need his advice.

Elizabeth McGuire parked on one side of the expansive brick driveway and wiggled out of her car, looking suspiciously around her. She was carrying a bottle of wine and wearing black jeans and a white blouse with a plain, grey sweater. George clicked his tongue. *She never was one for fashion*, he thought. This was true. Elizabeth, or Zin, as she had come to be known since junior high, never cared a lot about what she was wearing. Her mom could rarely get her to dress up and never could get her to wear skirts or a dress. "It's just not me," she would tell her mom. Zin headed to the front door and George stepped back from the window lest she see him and think that he was watching her.

George sighed. He wasn't looking forward to tonight. He had always seemed to miss the mark with Zin, a problem that went all the way back to middle school, when his in-charge parenting style suddenly clashed with his daughter's need for space. He hadn't been emotionally equipped to deal with the ups and downs of her youth, the irrational fears of his moody, teenage daughter. He was logical, a fixer, someone to give orders. It made sense to him that when she had a problem, he wanted to fix it, but that was never what Zin seemed to need, and he was slow to learn it. Years ago, after she had graduated from college and seemed to barely be keeping her head above water, he had taken her to a BMW dealership and shown her around. He knew she was broke. She had gotten it into her head that she wanted to pay for college herself, so had endured the lean years of crappy apartments and too many meals of ramen. At the time, she didn't have a car and he wanted to give her a big present, but when she realized that he was going to buy the car for her and not one for himself, she put her foot down, right in the middle of the showroom floor. "No. I don't need a hand-out. I am NOT going to drive THAT kind of car. If I need something, I'll ask for it." She walked out of the building with an angry and embarrassed father in her footsteps. They fought in the car and drove in silence the rest of the way home. She never did ask for anything again.

George could hear the front door open and hear her daughter call out "helloooooo. Anyone home?" George heard Judy making her way to the front door, her high heels clicking quickly across the white tiled entryway floor. He could hear the pleasantries being exchanged; his wife's was voice elevated from excitement. George frowned. Zin didn't know it, but her mother was once again trying to play cupid, this time with the son of one of their acquaintances from the club.

George fiddled around upstairs as long as he could, changing shirts three times before settling on one, then straightening up the bedroom, even though he knew the guests would never come upstairs, and then organizing his cabinet of colognes and aftershaves. Finally, George sighed and made his way downstairs. In the hall near the kitchen, Zin was busy chatting with Anna, the cleaning lady and cook. Zin always had a good rapport with the help, and Anna had been around for years.

"Zin?" George said as he walked past. "How are you?"

"Hello Dad," Zin replied softly as George walked by. He squeezed her shoulders, checking discretely to see if she flinched (she hadn't). George walked to the kitchen to see how his wife was doing.

"How's dinner coming?" he asked as he stood in the kitchen, arms on his hips, assessing the situation as if he were about to take control and give orders.

"Fine, dear," replied Judy, smiling as she looked up. Anna had left everything clean and nearly finished, with a couple of pots just simmering on the cooktop in the center island for Judy to attend to. Zin and Anna filed into the kitchen.

"Do you need anything else, Mrs. Meyer?"

"No, Anna. It all smells wonderful. Thanks so much."

"No worries. See you later." They all said their goodbyes and Zin gave Anna a hug before she headed out.

"Can I help with anything?" Zin asked.

"Ummm. Let me see," said Judy, as she poked her head into the dining room where the table was almost set. "We could use some wine glasses on the table."

Zin made her way into the dining room and opened the china hutch, pulling the Waterford glasses out one by one.

"Who's coming tonight?" she called from the dining room. George eyed Judy, who hesitated, glancing at George before her eyes darted away.

"Oh, just some people from the club. The Andersons and their son," she responded as nonchalantly as she could. George watched her daughter freeze for a moment and then shake her head. She didn't say anything. Then she marched into the kitchen and grabbed the wine bottle that George had started to open.

"I think I'll need a glass of that," she said, frowning. George glanced at his wife, who refused to display any form of concern. She didn't seem to want to concede that this was a bad idea. George knew better.

***

Zin sipped her wine and set the table. She debated whether to ask her mom more about this dinner and the likelihood that she was being set up but decided that she'd rather not get into a fight just as guests arrived.

Jim and Donna Anderson arrived ten minutes later, heaping generous praise for how lovely the house was and how glad they were to be invited. Their son Todd, a tall, athletic man with curly hair, stepped around his mother who was trying to take her coat off, took his own coat off, and handed it to Judy. He stood in the hallway, hands in his pockets, looking at the photographs along the hallway wall, already bored. Zin assessed the situation, sighed deeply, and went back to the kitchen to refill her wine glass.

George took Jim and Todd into the den to have a drink. Judy and Donna headed to the kitchen, where Judy putzed around with the chicken and salads. Zin didn't want to be stuck with the ladies, but didn't know what else to do, so she followed them to the kitchen, standing quietly off to the side, sipping her wine and offering either silence or polite agreement as Donna asserted her opinions on all manner of subjects, including people who were too big (anyone size 8 and above, judging from Donna's twig-like figure) and the fashion they shouldn't be wearing (at which, Zin unconsciously tried to smooth out her blouse). Luckily, the conversation turned to Donna's new hot tub and all the different jets you could choose from, which gave Zin a chance to pretend to be busy and drift away. She stood in the hallway, looking at pictures of their family hanging artfully at intervals along the hall, listening to the men in the den. They assumed they were among like-minded fellows, so the conversation had turned to politics, where they were berating certain politicians and their priorities during the current state legislative session. Zin shook her head and wandered back to dinner. Fortunately, it was time to eat, and Zin was sent to fetch 'the boys'.

At dinner, Zin was seated across from Todd at one end of the table, an arrangement that Zin had been hoping to avoid, but could find no way out of. The dinner conversation started with a discussion about the club, which Zin couldn't care less about. Luckily, the wine was good company, so she chuckled for no reason when everyone else did. Donna wanted to know more about this prospect.

"Tell us a little about yourself, Zin," prodded Donna.

Zin took a sip of wine and looked around the table at the faces now focused on her. "Oh, there's not much to tell."

"What do you do for a living?" insisted Donna.

"I'm a teacher. Junior high social sciences."

"That's nice," Donna answered. Zin didn't get the impression that she was really impressed but assumed that it might be acceptable to have a teacher as a corporate wife. It would be easier for her to quit teaching and become a housewife than if she were trying to climb some corporate ladder of her own. Zin imagined Donna as a mother-in-law and almost laughed out loud.

"Where are you teaching?" continued Donna.

"At Roosevelt Middle School in St. Paul."

"Wow," chimed in Todd. "You must have quite a time. That's in a pretty rough neighborhood, isn't it?" Zin knew what he meant. 'Rough' was always a code word for any urban area with a large non-white population.

"Oh, it's a good school. There is a bit of poverty in my neighborhood, but the kids are good…when they come to class."

Jim Anderson was shaking his head. "Schools these days. They can't figure out how to make it work. It shouldn't be that tough—they just need to be run more like a business."

Todd was nodding. Jim continued. "They could use a little competition, is what they need. They keep trying to get more money. They wouldn't need the money if they could figure out how to do things and if they had a decent teacher or two." Jim realized his faux pas and quickly added, "like Zin here." George and Judy exchanged nervous glances and focused on their salads.

Zin stopped chewing and bit her lip but didn't look up. She was afraid she was growling. She wanted to rail into him about how it wasn't a business. They were educating complex children, and you can't mass manufacture them. And she wanted to point out that lots of good teachers do leave because they become demoralized by low pay, no respect from society, and no support from parents who demand that it is always the teacher's fault that their son or daughter isn't getting an A.

But she didn't. Instead, she took another sip of wine and a deep breath and looked over at the clock. 7:45 p.m.

Getting antsy with the lack of chatter between the 'young' people, Judy abruptly changed the direction of the conversation.

"So, Todd, tell us a little about yourself," she asked, pointedly. "What do you do for fun?"

"Well, I guess I enjoy my music a little," he answered with apparent fake modesty. "Playing guitar and such. And I play a little softball and basketball."

"Todd's a softball star," Donna chimed in, oozing pride. "His team went to nationals this fall. Placed fifth, right?"

"Yeah," answered Todd. "We should've gone farther, too, but we had a bad game that night."

"You should have pulled Ted off the mound," said Jim. "He was killing you guys all night long."

"Yeah, I know," answered Todd.

"And what do you do for a living, Todd?" asked Judy, seeming to Zin that it was almost a scripted question. "You work at the same company as your father, right?" Zin gave her mom a funny look. It seemed like a polite way to say, 'Your father got you a job at the company he runs, didn't he?'

"Yes, I'm in charge of client solutions. We have to go out to the potential clients, do a complete audit of their current systems and come up with a plan for their work."

"He's *Director* of Client Solutions," inserted his mother again. "He's following in his father's footsteps." Zin looked up from her plate, gave a benign smile, and went back to work on her chicken Kiev. She felt the gaze of all the parents at the table on her, waiting to see if she registered some sort of impression regarding this young man.

Todd seemed to enjoy the spotlight, however, and was oblivious to Zin's indifference. He continued. "It's a small department, maybe 20, 25 employees," he said, again with false modesty. "But we know what we're doing, and we do it well." He could have left it at that, but he didn't. "We've managed to beat our budget this year, even though the company as a whole didn't fare as well. I just had to trim our payroll here and there to find some dollars." Todd was preaching to the table now. "Obviously, that's what schools need. You need to be able to cut the fat, instead of protecting all those old chumps that aren't working any more. That's the only way to make money these days. Schools just need to hire a few managers. I get real tired of hearing about how schools constantly need more money. They just need to figure out what to do with what they have."

Todd went back to eating, with both sets of parents now exchanging glances with their spouses before focusing on their chicken. Jim and George both commented on how juicy and tender it was. A brief silence had ensued and, like an animal sensing an impending storm, Zin's mother instinctively looked up and noticed that Zin was studying Todd as if he was a curiosity, an unexpected creature that had appeared at the table. The whites of Judy's eyes started to show in fear. She was trying to pluck a new piece of conversation from the air when Zin spoke up. Judy reflexively cringed.

"It must be tough for you," she said to Todd.

Todd turned to her, confused. "How's that?"

"Following in your father's footsteps. I'm sure everyone at the company figures that you got your job because of your father, when in fact you probably had to work extra hard just so you wouldn't ever be accused of that."

"Oh, it hasn't been a problem, really," answered Todd, a little less confidently than before. He looked down at the table. "I'll take some more rice, please. It's delicious."

Zin wasn't done. Judy looked at George with thinly veiled desperation; Zin had the predatory look of a snake approaching a victim.

"That must be a testament to your skill and hard work," continued Zin. "You probably had to be overqualified to get the job and work twice as hard as the rest to not give any appearance of nepotism. What's your average work week? 60 hours?" Zin played it straight, not smiling, an air of sympathy for someone who undoubtedly had to overcome prejudice. She took another long sip of wine. She had now finished her third glass and was reaching for the bottle at the end of the table.

"Umm, something like that. It's not too bad, really," answered Todd. "This chicken Kiev is terrific, by the way," he added, addressing Judy. "Where did you get the recipe?"

"Oh, something I found online…" started Judy, but Zin interrupted.

"Where did you go for your M.B.A.?" she asked, taking a chance. It paid off.

"Well, I started at the Carlson School of Management," Todd answered, "but I haven't finished yet." Zin nodded, deciding she had had enough fun with Todd. Unfortunately, her mom made it worse.

"Zin knows how that goes," she replied. "What do you have now? Two master's degrees." Zin closed her eyes and took a deep breath. She didn't need this.

"Something like that," she replied, not filling in any more details, hoping to let it die.

"What ambitious kids," beamed Donna, her teeth appearing to be clenched a little too tightly inside the big smile. "They make me tired just talking about it."

Zin managed to dodge any more awkward conversation the rest of the meal and during the drinks that followed. As they got up from the table, Donna took one last chance.

"Todd, don't you have an extra ticket to the Timberwolves game tomorrow night? Maybe Zin would like to go?" Todd hesitated, smiling, but with a strained, panicked look in his eyes as he met Donna's gaze. Zin saved him the trouble.

"Oh, thanks for thinking of me. But I already have plans." Zin decided that her walk with Henry counted, maybe not as a date, but at least as having plans. George, Judy, and Zin walked the Andersons to the door and said their pleasantries. When the door closed, Zin turned on her parents.

"Please don't do that again," she said, glaring at her mom.

"What?" asked Judy. She glanced at George, who was

keeping his distance, trying to avoid collateral damage.

"I'm not even divorced yet. I don't need you playing matchmaker."

"Oh, don't be silly," answered Judy, waving a jeweled hand dismissively and heading to the kitchen. "We just had friends over and thought you'd like someone your age to chat with, rather than just us old fogies."

"Whatever," replied Zin. She followed them to the kitchen, and they cleaned up, Judy making idle chit-chat to defuse Zin. After a bit, Zin made motions to leave, and George and Judy decided it was an opportunity to press Zin about her current situation. Zin assured them that she was doing fine.

"I'm getting used to having my own time. And space. Plus, I get to watch whatever movies I want, and I don't feel guilty eating chocolate ice cream. So, it's not that bad." She gave a sad half smile and pulled her coat off a rack.

"Well, it's important that you keep people in your life," answered Judy. She looked at Zin. "Listen, you don't have to do this all alone. Please let us help if we can."

George jumped in. "You doing okay with money? I know that lawyers can be expensive, and it can drag on for a while." Zin answered, a little less confidently.

"Yeah. I'm fine. I'm going to be okay there." George eyed her but left it at that.

When all was done, Zin walked out to her car, small and lonely in a driveway that was big enough for ten cars. She looked back on the house, taking it in. She didn't grow up in this house—their house growing up was very nice, but when their parents built this house five years ago, they went bigger, not smaller, which surprised her at the time, but in retrospect, she realized it was about staying on par with their peers. The three-car garage, huge front door, perfect lawn, gorgeous architecture—it was impressive, and Zin suddenly found herself deflated. Everything in her life was miserable and falling apart compared to this. She was sitting on the doorstep of 40, no children, staring at a divorce, and working for peanuts as a teacher. There was no way she was interested in this Todd character, but truth be told, he clearly wasn't interested in her, either. As for her parents, by the time they were her age, her dad was buying his second company, her mom was chair of every board or committee in their town, and they were definitely successful. Of course, her dad was never around, and as a high schooler, she resented him plenty for it. Maybe she still did.

Zin slid into her car and took a deep breath. She didn't feel like crying. She didn't feel much. She just felt numb.

14

Jay rounded the block and headed home. Once there, he made his way to the cupboard above the fridge—a whiskey sour sounded good right then—but the cupboard was pretty bare, a tall bottle of vodka with only an inch at the bottom was keeping guard over a bottle of Kahlua, a small bottle of brandy, and a mostly empty bottle of a Caribbean rum. Jay checked the clock on the microwave; plenty of time to go shopping. He paused for a moment, then went upstairs and changed into jeans and a plaid shirt. He was off the clock and not on church business, so why not dress like a regular guy? He grabbed his coat and headed back out to his car.

Jay preferred Gary's, the little hole-in-the-wall neighborhood liquor store near his house, but he rarely shopped at Gary's to avoid being seen picking up booze in the local dive, choosing instead to shop in a large, popular suburban wine shop where there were fewer members of his congregation and a little more anonymity. Wine Warehouse was the opposite of Gary's—immense, with rows and rows of wines, crates full of beer, and every type of liquor known to man.

Jay roamed the aisles of Wine Warehouse until he found an aisle of whiskeys and pulled down a large bottle. As long as he was shopping, he might as well replace that nearly empty bottle of vodka, so he wandered around some more until he found the vodka aisle. Sometimes he liked rum and Coke, so he turned into another aisle and picked up another bottle. Sometimes he liked to have a beer, so he went into the beer section where a young man was pulling a flat cart with multiple cases of cheap light beer, escorted by a Wine Warehouse employee. The young man was looking for more, telling the employee about the upcoming guys' weekend where ten of them were staying in a cabin. Jay thought about his evening plans—something frozen for dinner and a baseball game on the couch. He picked up a twelve-pack of his favorite local brew but found his basket was too full, so he walked to the front and exchanged it for a shopping cart. While he was here, he might as well pick up a couple bottles of wine—the prices were too good not to. Jay tried to find a label he had recently liked, but got overwhelmed in row two of the merlots, so he grabbed a bottle that looked attractive and wasn't too expensive, then found the rows of cabs and picked out another good-looking bottle, adding it to his cart.

Jay was rounding the corner, heading to the checkout, when he nearly ran straight into James and Lori Taubert who were huddled together, inspecting a bottle of wine. James and Lori were a pair of opposites that seemed to have no reason to be together. James, tall, thin, and scholarly-looking, serious and quiet, always attended church, but never appeared at any volunteer or other extra-curricular church activities or functions. Lori was the opposite: short, round, chatty and loud, and was highly engaged with the women's groups at church, often seen at bake or craft sales. Both of their heads turned to see Jay, whose expression was one of a child caught sneaking out of the house with a cookie. Or maybe a handful of cookies.

"Father Jay! How are you?" beamed Lori. Both James and Lori looked at Jay, then down to Jay's cart, which was now impressively full. Jay glanced down at his load, too, before looking back and responding.

"Oh, James, Lori. Hi. I'm doing well. How about you?" Jay's voice strained to project nonchalance.

"Oh, good. Yah. Just picking out a bottle of wine for dinner tonight." She glanced down at the cart. "Big plans for the weekend?"

"Uh, no. No. Just...doing a little shopping tonight. Making the rounds at all the stores. You know. Nothing much."

"Well, that's nice." Both parties stood in silence for a moment before Jay started moving again.

"Well, have a nice dinner."

"You, too," Lori replied, all smiles. Jay nodded and the couple's heads turned to follow him as he left. Jay turned the corner, let out a silent groan and closed his eyes. Lori was probably the last person he'd want to meet in this circumstance. He almost abandoned his cart for fear of running into anyone else, but instead, walked straight to the cashier, checked out quickly, and made a beeline for his car.

Jay pulled into the single car garage attached to the rectory and slid out carefully, his body a little too large to easily escape in this cramped garage. He popped open the trunk, balanced a box of bottles on top of the box of beer, and trudged into the house. He hung up his coat, put away the booze, and made himself the drink he wanted an hour earlier. He meandered over to the couch and collapsed onto it, causing an audible creaking noise. He turned on a sports channel to see if he could catch any baseball scores.

Jay sat for about twenty minutes and then decided he should find some dinner. The trouble was, he didn't feel like cooking tonight. He was feeling down after the encounter with the Tauberts and enduring the meeting at the central office where they were warned about upcoming financial problems. He was also bummed about his encounter with Zin. He had been looking forward to a chance to talk to her, but she seemed to want to get rid of him. She had been on his mind during today's meeting, which had made him feel guilty.

Jay finally pushed himself off the couch, walked to the kitchen and rifled through the cupboards, the fridge, and the freezer. A package of ground beef, half a box of spaghetti noodles, chicken lunch meat, a frozen dinner, and a frozen pizza. None of it sounded good. He'd rather go out, but he hated having dinner alone, especially where people recognized him— he always felt that he was being watched. Jay thought about it and knew what he wanted to do. He wanted to sit in the back booth of a dive somewhere with a burger, basket of fries, and a tall beer. And when he thought of doing that, a name came to mind.

Jay dialed a number and after a few rings, he heard a gravelly but cheerful voice on the other end of the phone. "Well, if it isn't Jay O'Brian."

"Hello, Father Casey."

"Dammit, Jay. You better call me Tom."

"Sorry, Tom, how are you?"

"Well, nothing that about twenty years wouldn't cure, but I won't complain. So, this is a surprise. I haven't heard from you in a while. Everything all right?"

"Oh, sure. Yeah, everything's fine. I was just in the mood for a beer and a burger. I thought maybe you might want to venture over to the Highland Taproom?"

"Oh, that does sound good," answered Tom. "I was just about to make another one of those blasted healthy frozen meals my sister leaves in my freezer and watch reruns of some damn TV show."

"Well, do you want me to pick you up? It's mostly on my way."

"No, I'm okay. They haven't taken away my license yet, you know. I'm only 77, and I can still see straight, so I figure I'm as good as half the drivers on the road."

"Probably better than that. Well, good. How about 6:30? Or is that too late?"

"Oh, I can handle it."

Jay drove in silence to the bar, thinking about Tom. Father Tom had been at the end of a long stint at the nearby St. Timothy's church when Jay got his first real placement as a priest, and Jay had found Tom to be an invaluable resource. Tom sought out Jay and took him under his wing, helping Jay when he ran into trouble with the congregation, the staff, or the parish leadership. Jay felt like he learned ten years' worth of the priesthood in that first year.

Jay found a parking spot on the street and walked up to the restaurant, where Father Tom was already standing outside, hands in the pockets of his tan spring coat. Jay realized that he hadn't seen Tom in a few years and noticed immediately that he was a little more hunched over and his hair was almost a bright white at this point. But the twinkle of good will was still in his eye as he looked up to Jay and reached out to shake his hand.

They got a seat in a booth at the back, where it was more of a pub than a restaurant, a pool table in the middle and beer signs all around.

"Too loud for you?" asked Jay, noticing the sound and the hearing aid in Tom's ear.

"Ah, not too bad." A waitress appeared and they ordered beer and burger baskets for both.

Tom eyed Jay for a moment. "So, how is St. Stephen's treating you these days?" He watched Jay closely.

"Oh, it's going fine," Jay answered. The waitress appeared with the drinks and Jay took a long draught from his tall glass. "Can't complain," he finished, looking down at his glass.

"Really?" replied Tom, smiling, but with a note of disbelief in his voice. "If I recall from conversations with your predecessor, St. Stephen's wasn't an easy assignment. They had a few long-time parish leaders who were kind of entrenched and hard to work with. And a couple staff members who weren't easy to work with, either." Jay looked up from his glass to see Tom watching him. Jay remembered why he always liked Tom's counsel. Tom was an acute observer, kind and thoughtful, but wasn't afraid to be direct. Jay smiled and gave a slight shrug.

"Well, that's...not inaccurate," said Jay.

"They're breaking your balls, aren't they?"

Jay laughed. "No, no...well, most of the congregation is great. There are just a couple people on the parish council that seem to have it in for me. Don't know why. And our bookkeeper pretty much ignores everything I say. And the music director hates me." He looked up at Tom. "But other than that, it's fine." He took a big swig of beer. Tom sat back and nodded, a knowing smile on his face.

"That can get tiring, always pushing against someone or something."

"Yeah," Jay nodded.

"You gotta be there for others, but if you don't have people around you that lift you up, it'll wear you down."

"Yeah." He sat quietly for a moment. "It's a tough job."

"It's a damn tough job," agreed Father Tom.

Jay continued quickly. "You are providing leadership, but the members of the parish know that they'll probably be there long after you're gone, and they have leadership roles and a vision of their own."

"You are right. Somehow, you have to assert yourself but do so in a way that brings others along. I guess that's the challenge of leadership, isn't it?"

"I guess so," answered Jay. They both took another swig of beer. Tom looked at Jay.

"I'm going to tell you something that you might already know. I don't mean it to be disrespectful, so I hope you aren't offended. But I don't think the leadership thing is your forte. That's not a knock on you. It doesn't mean you're a bad priest by any means. Priests have to be a lot of different things, and they can't be good at all of them. Some are better at management. Some have a vision. Some are likeable and compassionate. I think you are likeable and compassionate. I don't think you're a driver, however. You'd rather step out of the way and let someone else drive. But that's okay, as long as you are okay with the direction things are headed. The problem comes in when someone wants to take you in a direction you aren't happy with. Then stepping in gets a little harder." Jay frowned a little. The message stung a bit, but not too much, because Jay instinctively knew that it was true - it was just that no one had ever articulated it before, including himself. Jay didn't say anything, so Tom continued.

"You just need to surround yourself with people you trust

who can get things done. And again, if there is something you disagree with, you need to be smart about it. Head-butting usually doesn't work. You need to reach out to others one-on-one. Build your case, build support." Jay looked doubtful. "I know, it isn't easy."

The food arrived and they dug in. Jay ordered another beer. Eventually, they both pushed away their empty baskets, leaning back, patting protruding bellies. Jay sat in silence, staring into his beer. Tom watched him.

"Anything else going on, Jay?"

"Oh, no. Not really."

Tom didn't reply, just waited. Jay debated what to tell Tom. He didn't want to mention Zin, and he didn't know what to say about her, anyway. Finally, Jay continued.

"So, I've got a question for you."

"Shoot."

"Did you ever question your decision to enter the priesthood?"

"Oh, boy," said Tom, a mock grimace appearing on his face before replacing it with a smile.

"I don't mean to be dramatic, I'm just curious." Tom looked off to a corner of the ceiling for a long moment before replying.

"The priesthood is not an easy life, as you know. Especially these days. We're a pretty easy target for ridicule and, frankly, we deserve it. Can't swing a dead cat without hitting someone who got mixed up in some kind of scandal."

"That's for sure."

"This bullshit about only men wearing a collar is ridiculous, but you and I both know that'll never change." Jay nodded his head in agreement. Tom leaned forward and dropped his voice. "And between you and me, half the bishops in this country keep acting like a jackass. Couldn't see hypocrisy if it sat on their nose. Thank God they let some of us have a little free reign in the inner-city churches, or I'd probably have quit a long time ago." Jay's eyes grew as he listened to Father Tom. Jay wondered if he was hearing something that Father Tom may not have revealed to anyone before. He suspected the beer may have had something to do with it, but either way, he was eager to hear more, and remained quiet as Father Tom continued. "But to your question—I'm guessing most of us ask ourselves that question at one point in our career."

"You, too?"

"Of course."

"What was your main reason? I mean, was it the politics or the policy stuff you were just mentioning? I get it. It's just that, well, you, maybe as much as any priest I know, seemed to have it together. Every time I meet someone from St. Tim's, I still hear them talk about you. For Pete's sake, you got a plaque from the mayor for that community partnership. Felt like half the city showed up for your retirement."

"I had a good run at St. Tim's," he admitted. "Really felt like I had my groove there. But it wasn't always easy. You know the story. You change parishes, congregations, towns. It's hard. It's lonely." Jay sensed there was more to the story.

"And which was your hardest stint?" It was Tom's turn to look at his glass, now empty. He took his time before he answered.

"So, in my early-40s, I was assigned to a parish south of the cities. I was a city boy, you know. Grew up here in St. Paul on the West Side. Getting plunked down in a small town at the outskirts of the cities was hard for me. I didn't really know anyone." Tom glanced up at Jay and then he started again, slowly. "Anyway, a lot of things were going on. I suppose it was a bit of a mid-life crisis. I'd hear about high school buddies who were now doing well in business or whatever and I'd look at where I was in life and felt like I hadn't done jack—hadn't made anything of myself."

"And I was lonely. I didn't seem to connect well when I was down there, at least not the first few years. And I may have had a bit of a 'better than this' attitude. Bottom line—I really wasn't happy with the appointment. And it was about this time that an old high school friend reached out. A woman." He glanced up at Jay when he said it. "We were always friends in high school, but I wasn't the dating type. Was totally afraid of girls back then, to be honest. I was young for my grade and a late bloomer, so I felt like a little kid all the time. Anyway, she was going through a divorce and wanted advice. She lived quite a ways away, so we met in the middle, some small town west of the cities, at a cafe for lunch. We talked and talked. And I gotta be honest, it felt good. We both enjoyed it. So, we decided to meet again. And then it just became a thing we did. We'd meet in a different town every other week. It felt a little dangerous, like I was having an affair or something, kind of exciting. For her, too, at least I thought. We must have met eight or nine times over a few months. Just for lunch. But I won't lie—I really looked forward to it." Jay was listening quietly. Tom looked up with a sad smile. "And then one day, we meet for lunch, and she's acting all sheepish and distracted. I pressed her on it. She hemmed and hawwed a bit, but eventually it came out. It turns out she was getting back together with her husband and was embarrassed to tell me. I was kind of blindsided by it. I guess I was a little cold with her the rest of that meeting. We hugged when she left, and that was about the last I heard from her." Tom eyed his empty glass.

"Huh," said Jay. "I can see how that would make you think hard about the priesthood."

"Well, that wasn't the end of my problems. I sort of fell apart after that. Fell into a dark place. I didn't look forward to anything. I didn't want to do anything, didn't even want to get out of bed in the morning. I couldn't sleep, and then I tried drinking to help me sleep, then tried pills. I didn't want to talk about it and didn't really have anyone to talk to about it. And people noticed. The bishop got wind of the complaints and dragged me in to chew me out, which didn't exactly help. In fact, it made me resent the congregation for ratting me out. That's when I nearly quit. I was thinking about it non-stop for a few months. Just didn't know how to do it, and frankly, was a little freaked out at the idea. I mean, what would I have done? Mid-40s, no money, no skills. It's kind of scary to be that vulnerable." Tom paused and flagged down the waitress for a glass of water.

"So, what happened? Did you get help?"

"Not exactly. I kind of got lucky. I was at an event, an anniversary or something at a golf course, and I got talking to this doctor. He played racquetball. Said I should join him. I wanted to say no, but for some reason I didn't. We'd play, go get breakfast or lunch. Got into a routine. He introduced me to a small group of guys, my age or a little older. None of the guys went to my church, so I didn't have to be their priest. We'd talk, joke around, whatever. Sounds weird, but it was kind of the therapy I needed—something to do, someone to talk to, some exercise. It felt like a knot was slowly being untangled over the course of a year." He looked up and smiled at Jay. "Probably more than you wanted to know, but yes, I have questioned my being in the priesthood."

"Wow," said Jay. "I had no idea. I mean, about, your, ah, problems."

"Not too many people do. Or did at the time, even. No one talks about this stuff—certainly not 30, 40 years ago."

Jay sat, nodding, his mind racing. He looked up and noticed Tom watching him.

"So, back to the question. Having second thoughts about your current profession?" Jay shook his head.

"No, no. Nothing like that. Just...you know."

"What bothers you the most? Are you having a hard time towing the line? They don't take too kindly to undercutting the doctrine, do they?"

"No, they don't. And, yes, towing the line gets tough at times. But I don't know. You want to believe you are making a difference, and if you aren't, why are you doing it?

Tom leaned forward. "Jay, believe me. You are making a difference."

Jay twisted his lips with a look of doubt. "Like you said. It gets tough at times. Makes you wonder. The road not taken and all."

"Yeah, you only get one life. Sometimes you wish you could have it all, but that isn't an option." He looked at Jay earnestly. "Anyway, if you find yourself in that dark place. Make sure you reach out to someone. You can't do life alone."

Jay drove home afterwards, the radio off, deep in thought. He got back to the house, opened the cupboard for the bottle of Jim Beam, grabbed a couple ice cubes from a tray in the freezer, and poured himself a glass. He paced around the house, still trying to parse the information he learned tonight. When Jay met Tom, it seemed like the entire city knew who he was. Everyone would call upon Tom. He was recognized by the mayor for his work in the community. The congregation revered him. Jay always thought of his position in the world as being stable, but maybe everyone's station in life was much more precarious than he realized. People can skid off the path, and what if you can't get back on it? And what if you shouldn't be on it in the first place?

15

"Well, hi!"

Zin stopped in her tracks. She knew that voice, and hoped that it wasn't aimed at her, but she didn't want to be rude. Zin turned around to see if he was hailing Zin, or some other poor sap, but no such luck; there he was, walking briskly now to catch up with Zin.

"Hello Patrick," replied Zin, rather flatly.

"Well, hello. Say, nice weather we're having, huh?" He had stopped in front of Zin, now shuffling his feet.

"I'm not so sure," answered Zin. "A little cold for me. I could do with more sun."

"Yeah, I suppose," Patrick ran his hand through greasy black hair and adjusted his thick glasses. "What are you doing?"

"Oh, I'm just out for a walk. How about you?"

"I'm out for a walk, too. It's good for my health. I have a bad back, so I can't do much else. Have you ever hurt your back? It's a real problem. Sometimes I have a hard time sitting. But it's not been bad lately. Have you ever had back problems?"

"No, Patrick. Can't say I have."

"Oh. That's good." He paused for a second and Zin thought she could make her escape. Patrick brightened up suddenly.

"So, the Twins look good this year. Their pitching staff looks good. I like the looks of Ortega. He has a really strong arm. I think he can throw 98 miles per hour. That's fast. I think they have a strong bullpen. Do you like the Twins?" Zin had to smile a bit. Patrick and his stream-of-conscious runnings.

"I do like the Twins. Probably will watch them today. I was just getting back to watch them."

"Oh, that would be nice," answered Patrick. He rubbed the back of his neck and shuffled some more. "I'll probably listen to them on the radio. I don't get the channel they play on." Zin closed her eyes. She was surprised at what she was going to do.

Two hours later, Zin was sitting on her couch, watching the Minnesota Twins baseball game. Sitting next to her was Patrick. Zin leaned back on the couch, glass of wine in hand, half watching the game, half watching Patrick, who was focused on the game, sitting forward, hands crossed, occasionally sweeping some greasy hair out of his eyes, but never taking his eyes off the game.

Zin looked back down at the phone in her hands and decided to check email. At the top of the list was a message from a colleague at school about a fundraiser for needy students. Zin had volunteered at it for years, but as she thought about volunteering again, she decided she had enough problems of her own. She didn't need to be bothered with this right now. Maybe next year, she thought, and swiped to delete the message.

Out of the corner of her eye, Zin saw some movement out on the street in front of her house. She glanced back to her phone for the time: 2:55 p.m. Father Jay would be arriving any moment. She propped herself up to get a better view of the outside and saw someone large, wearing black pants and a grey coat, walk past her house. Zin thought that was curious but went back to watching her game. Five minutes later, she saw movement again, and this time someone was coming up the sidewalk. Then the doorbell rang, and Zin got up to answer the door.

"Hello Father," answered Zin, attempting to send Jay a signal with her eyes. "Come on in." Zin stepped aside to let Jay in.

"Thanks," he said, a big smile on his face, but when he entered the living room, he saw Patrick sitting forward on the couch, watching a baseball game intently, and Jay's expression soured.

"Father, this is Patrick. Patrick, Father O'Brian." Patrick glanced at the priest.

"Oh, hi, Father."

"Hi Patrick," answered Jay, sounding less enthusiastic.

"You two know each other?"

"Everyone knows Patrick," answered Jay.

"It's the top of the seventh," informed Patrick. "Two to one, the Twins are winning. Ortega held them to one run through six. Now Rogers is pitching." Patrick was rocking ever so slightly. Zin looked at Jay, her eyebrows up, lips pursed, head nodding, 'help me' written all over her expression.

"Yep. Patrick's been here for the WHOLE game," she said. Jay nodded in understanding. Zin pointed to a chair. "So, have a seat. Take off your coat." She walked toward the kitchen and called back. "I'm getting a little more wine. Want anything? Wine? Beer?" Jay looked at Patrick and frowned.

"Well, it's a baseball game. I feel like I should have a beer." Then added, "if it's not too much trouble."

"No trouble."

Jay tossed his coat on the back of a chair and slumped into it. Zin returned with a bottle of beer and handed it to him.

"On second thought, maybe I should go," he said.

"No, you should stay. I'm guessing Patrick won't be too long." They both watched Patrick for a bit—he seemed oblivious to their presence.

Zin shrugged her shoulders and stayed standing for a while, half watching, half making small talk with Jay, talking about not much more than baseball, Easter, and the weather. When the last out had been made, Patrick popped up off the couch.

"The Twins won. That was a good game. Ortega has a strong arm. I need to go now. Thanks for letting me watch the game." He suddenly looked desperate to leave, and Zin saw him to the door. Jay checked his watch. It was after four, and he had to get back and get ready for service. Zin plopped down in a chair and looked at Jay.

"Sorry, Father. I didn't think Patrick was going to stay long. I suppose we can't have our little talk now?"

"Unfortunately, I have to run," said Jay, standing up. He was quiet, and Zin sensed it.

"Ok. Well, we can reschedule again, if you would like."

"It's up to you," answered Jay, heading to the door.

"I'm fine with meeting again," answered Zin, sensing Jay's disappointment.

"Okay, we'll figure it out. Thanks again." Jay headed out into a gray afternoon, zipping his coat up. Zin stood in the doorway and watched as Jay walked to the corner and took a left turn, hands in his coat pocket, head down. Up the block, a car started and crawled past Zin's house, turning at the corner to head in the opposite direction from Jay.

Zin pulled into a parking lot at the Mall of America and weaved back and forth through parking aisles for ten minutes until she found a spot. A cold, gray day in early April, the Mall was packed. Zin hated the mall and its crowds, especially on nice days when she didn't understand why so many people would choose to be indoors. Today was kind of miserable, however, so she understood it. She had raced here after Jay had left, having forgotten that she was supposed to meet Henry at precisely 5:47 p.m. in anticipation of their 6:07 p.m. scheduled time together. What a nut! He still insisted on meeting. It seemed ridiculous, but it was the most interesting thing going on in her life, and for some reason, she still felt obligated to go, so she continued to play along. She had toyed with the idea of offering Henry a ride to the mall, seeing that this was a long way from downtown St. Paul where she assumed Henry was living, possibly in a homeless shelter, but then thought better of it. The mall was a good location to meet, because it was on public transit rail lines, was obviously a public place where she would feel safe, and there would be plenty of people for them to watch—that was a given.

Zin made her way through a department store and to a bench

near an elevator and a shoe store. She checked the time; she was early, so she sat by a railing, looking down into the massive central indoor park area which held walking paths through an indoor garden forest and an amusement park with rides. She watched the families with tired kids in strollers and excited eight-year-olds running through paths to the next ride. Fat couples, little old ladies, and confident looking teenagers, all shapes, sizes, colors. She sat for a couple minutes and tried to guess the stories of those walking by.

As she watched the scenes below, one person in particular caught her eye. A man was leaving the walking path and heading into a grove of indoor trees. He was blonde and was wearing a bright blue windbreaker over a yellow shirt and blue jeans. He was squatting, seeming to look at something through some sort of instrument. Then, she looked out across the park and could see two mall security guards making their way across the amusement park, looking like they had a purpose. She swore out loud. Henry!

Zin jumped up and ran over to a nearby stairway, zigzagging through and apologizing to shoppers who gave her hard stares as she pushed past. She reached the bottom and dashed into the amusement park area. As she approached the spot where Henry had left the trail, she could see passers-by staring at him and pointing. She called out in a fierce whisper.

"Henry! Henry!" She glanced nervously at the cops who were rounding the bend, scanning the area. Henry popped up.

"Oh, hello Zin," he said, looking pleased. "You should see how the watering system works for these trees."

"Not now!" she called. "Get out of there!" The cops were coming closer, and would soon see Henry, so she decided she had to take matters into her own hands. She headed briskly in their direction and marched right up to them.

"Officers," she said, standing right in front of them, a tall, thin black man whose uniform looked like it was too big for him, and a shorter, round white officer with sleepy eyes.

"Yes," said the white cop. The tall black cop kept trying to look past her.

"Did you know there were some kids hanging out by the south entrance that looked like they were going to fight?"

"Hmmm," said the black cop, not looking at her but still trying to look past. "We were just there. Didn't see any trouble."

"Well, my daughter just texted me. To tell me. About the fight. I was going to go get her. To make sure she was safe." The black cop looked at her now.

"You know kids under sixteen aren't supposed to be left unattended."

"Well, umm, that's because she is sixteen. So, she is with her friends," she stammered. "And there is a fight. Or might be one." The white cop finally spoke up.

"Okay lady. We just gotta check one thing out and we'll go right back there. There are other security guards around, you know. So, I think it's probably okay. Thanks for letting us know." They stepped around Zin, who looked back to see Henry standing on the path now. He had a confused look on his face but brightened up when he saw Zin and waved at her. The officers looked at Henry and then turned to look back at Zin, who turned away from all of them and hurried away down a side path.

It took a couple minutes for Zin to circle back around and find Henry while trying to avoid the cops.

"Why did you walk away from me?" asked Henry.

"Because I had just lied to the cops to save your butt. What were you doing digging in the mall forest?"

"I told you, I was looking at the watering system for the indoor plants. It is really quite ingenious." Zin just shook her head, as they walked back to the original meeting place.

"Henry, don't you know you can't do stuff like that?"

"No," answered Henry. "I do not see what harm I was doing."

"You weren't, but there are rules."

"I did not see any signs that said that we could not go in among the trees."

"What did you think that little chain was for?"

"Decorations? Besides, I would not do harm to the trees."

"It doesn't work that way." Zin shook her head and headed back to the bench where she had started, Henry trailing silently behind her. "How much time do we have?"

"Two minutes," answered Henry, without looking at anything in particular. Zin dug her phone out of her purse and checked it—6:05 p.m. She nodded. They sat in silence for the two minutes until Henry called out. "Starting now."

This was the most difficult of the minutes they had spent together. People were everywhere. Gaggles of teenagers chatting away. Older couples ambling past storefronts. Exacerbated moms with strollers and straggling children. Pairs of women or young men, couples holding hands, single men with a purpose or older single men, looking lost and lonely. Country folks in Wrangler jeans and plaid shirts. Urban youth with oversized hoodies and expensive shoes. Every size, skin tone, and age.

Zin focused on a lady who looked exhausted, making her way to a bench opposite them. She was plump if not heavy, wore a plain beige jacket and had a small bag from a card shop. She looked about 60. Something about her seemed to imply that she wasn't married. Zin wondered if she would be like this lady, spending her days alone.

"Okay. Time," said Henry. He looked at Zin. "Well, what did you see?"

"I saw a lot of humanity. Not sure what to make of it."

"Hmmpf," answered Henry. They sat in silence a bit more. Zin felt that rush of guilt again. She wondered, yet again, if her cup was always half empty.

"I'm hungry," said Zin, finally. "You wanna get a bite?"

"That does sound good," answered Henry, standing up. Zin looked at him, his mismatched clothes (although not as bad today) and remembered that she was likely going to have to buy lunch.

"All right, let's find something."

Zin and Henry sat in the corner of the busy food court at a tiny table. The place was a cacophony of sound, with hundreds of conversations happening at once and countless kids crying and yelling. Next to them, a family of six was crammed around a couple of small tables, ketchup packets, empty bags, and half-eaten lunch plates littered the table. Zin wasn't happy about eating here, but knowing that she'd have to buy Henry's lunch, she decided to go cheap.

"How's your burrito?" she half yelled across the table. Henry finished chewing and looked up.

"It is wonderful. I have never had anything like it." Zin looked at him with disbelief but decided not to say anything. Henry was a riddle, wrapped in a mystery. Or maybe in clothing from a lost and found box. They continued to eat in silence until they both pushed themselves away, stuffed full of carbs.

"So, how many of these sessions have we had?" asked Zin.

"Five," answered Henry without hesitating.

"Whaddya think? Is humanity worth it?" Henry's face darkened.

"I am not sure. I have made extensive notes about our observation periods. But I do not know what your assessment is. That is what is important." Zin was caught off guard. She didn't think he'd still be taking this so seriously.

"Well, I'm not sure either," she answered. "I'd...have to consult my notes." She took a sip from her straw and gave a noncommittal shrug. Henry looked around the food court. Zin picked up the conversation again.

"So, what've you been doing, besides meeting me at random times to watch people? You've been here for, what, a week now? And you've got another week to go?"

"Yes, I have one more week in St. Paul. I have been observing and interacting with people in different settings."

"Yeah? So, where have you been?"

"I have tried many different venues," he said. I tried to go to hotels, but they would not let me talk to people. I also tried office buildings, but I usually get asked to leave. I have tried to talk to people on the street, but that has not gone well."

"Nope. That's not going to go over well."

"Apparently not. I tried the government buildings, but the people at the help desks seem to get scared and call an armed police officer to take me outside after a while. I tried the library, but no one wants to talk there, either."

"Sounds like you can't find anyone to talk to."

"Well, you need to find the right places. There is a group of people who are waiting outside of the Dorothy Day shelter every afternoon. Most of those people will talk to me. I found the bus station and people sitting in the bus station will often talk to me. Sometimes I can go to a bar and find people who will talk to me, except I need to buy alcoholic drinks, and I do not usually want to do that." Zin nodded her head, remembering seeing him drink. "I stopped in that big church and a few people would talk to me. There was a man who said he was a priest who listened to me, but then tried to get me to go to the Dorothy Day Center. I told him I had already been there. He seemed to think I needed help, but I assured him I did not. He was quite adamant that I go get help." Zin suppressed a smile, imagining the scene, the good-intentioned priest trying to steer this clearly troubled man toward help.

"Well, you are getting first-hand experience with how people treat a stranger. But I'm not sure how this fits into your thesis."

"I am not certain, either. The human equation is very complex. People are not as they might appear at first."

"Yeah? How so?" Henry frowned and thought about it for a moment before answering.

"Most people seem polite and friendly at first. But if you ask them to do something that is outside of their usual experience, everyone seems to be afraid. There is little trust. People quickly identify outsiders and push them away. It is very tribal. It seems to be that only those who have lost their tribe will be willing to really take you in and get to know you." Zin pondered that for a moment. She opened her mouth to retort, but only emitted a thoughtful "huh."

They sat in silence a bit longer and then said their goodbyes, Henry waving off an offer of a ride back downtown. Zin wasn't just being kind, she really wanted to know where he was staying. Was it the Dorothy Day shelter? A halfway house? Under a bridge? She felt like following him, but somehow it seemed that would break their trust. Zin wandered through the maze of parking lots until she found her car, and then joined the herd of vehicles heading for an exit. She tried to imagine what it would be like to be a true outsider trying to get a foothold in a society that protected its own and was suspicious of others. A person like Henry, stuck on the fringes of society, could never find the keys to get back in on his own.

16

Jay's eyes wouldn't open. He tried, but they seemed stuck. It had been about two minutes since his alarm started going off, and he still felt like he only had one foot out of the dream world. He grabbed another pillow and stuffed it on top of his head, pushing on his temple and forehead to address the dense headache that was sitting there. And wow, was he thirsty.

Jay stayed in that position for another couple of minutes until, with one big move, he threw the pillow off his head, threw his legs over the side of the bed, and sat up. Jay ran his fingers through his wispy hair and then reached over and hit the stop button on his phone about ten times before finally hitting it the right way and bringing a blessed silence to the room. Jay stood up, scratched his belly, and headed to the bathroom, tripping over a week's worth of clothes lying on the floor of his bedroom. He relieved himself and then drank approximately three cups of water straight from the bathroom sink tap. He looked in the mirror. It was not a pleasant sight.

Jay found some Ibuprofen and popped them, and then got in the shower. It was Palm Sunday, and he had to get his act together. He got out, got dressed, and made his way downstairs to get some coffee in him, plus a little toast to settle his stomach. Jay stood at the counter, waiting for coffee to brew and bread to toast. He surveyed the scene. Papers were strewn about the kitchen table along with two-day-old dishes, unopened mail, and a mostly empty Jim Beam bottle, along with a couple cans of Coke. Last night's damage. It wasn't his plan to drink heavily. He had started the evening trying to be productive, reviewing his sermon and doing some laundry, but then he got thinking about Zin. He was confused as hell, and mad at himself. He was bothered by the way Zin had used up or ignored their planned meetings. He knew this was irrational, and she hadn't done anything malicious. He was mad at himself for the way he was feeling. Plus, he was confused about what Tom had told him. What was the true message in that story? Was it that he should find the life that is right for him? Or was it that he needs to work through the rough patches, as they will lead to brighter days? Somehow, the meeting with Tom had left him more unsure of what to do, rather than less.

Jay finally finished up his breakfast, got cleaned up, and wandered over to church. He unlocked the side door, then the front door, then the other side door, and finally the office. He still had a little alone time before the choir director would show up, the other members of the choir would trickle in, and some volunteers would arrive to organize the palms. It was a much-needed bit of quiet time, and he went into the office to hide and work out the last kinks of his sermon.

Jay sat in his office for a while until he could tell by the buzz of people coming and going that the service preparations were well underway. He wanted to clarify how the processional would happen today, as they started outside and would wind up processing to the altar, so he went and consulted the choir director and the lead of the worship team.

During the first and second reading, Jay scanned the seats looking for Zin. He didn't see her, which disappointed him, but at the same time was a relief. He didn't like knowing she was watching him, and he also knew he wanted to seem less priestly to her and standing at the altar in a robe and reading a sermon was not the way to do that.

After mass, Jay wandered downstairs to coffee hour, a relatively unusual event in that he almost always avoided coffee hour. As he got downstairs and looked around, he remembered why. First, Delores Crawford cornered Jay to talk about the Spring Festival.

"Have you heard anything about the donations yet? Maybe you could bring it up during next week's mass?" Jay assured her they were working on it, and he would try to bring it up, all the while, glancing above her head to the crowd milling about the folding chairs and plastic tables. Jay got halfway across the room, deflecting some brief chit-chat and good mornings before Mel Hunter stopped him.

"Not sure if you caught that email, but the trustees want to get someone in to look at the water damage coming in along the roofline in the northeast corner. Looks like there might be leaks around the flashing on the roof that we've had trouble with. We're just worried about staining the wood in the front entrance there." Jay agreed they should get someone in and told Mel to send him the email again in case he missed it (he hadn't, but he just thought the committee could handle this one on their own).

As he started again, he noticed the back half of the room hosted piles of cots, blankets, and boxes of various sizes. Looking around he saw Barb Adler, the long-time church secretary. Barb was a saint that Jay knew he couldn't live without. She would know what that pile was about.

"Good morning, Barb."

"Hello Father. How are you today?"

"Oh, I can't complain." Jay wanted to get in and out quickly, but Barb deserved better. "Did you ever get your washing machine fixed?"

"No. They came and looked at it and told me it wasn't under warranty, and then told me that the labor and the parts would be about $375, and it was $95 just for them to tell me that. But I figure the thing is fifteen years old and $375 could get me a long way to a new one. So, Bill says he'll just buy me a new one."

"Well, it sounds like you came out ahead—you get a new washer out of it?"

"I suppose. It just makes me so mad. It's a rip off."

"I hear you. I should have opened a repair shop instead of donning the cloth. Say, question for you. What's with the cots and boxes?" He nodded toward the back of the large room.

"Did you forget? Project Hope starts up here this week." Jay batted his forehead. He had completely forgotten about the temporary housing that would be occupying half his basement for a month.

"Oh, duh. Of course."

"They called Friday and said that the first families would probably show up around Tuesday or so."

"Is everything going okay?"

"Yup. As far as I know, we've gotten everything taken care of. Easter Sunday coffee hour will be held upstairs in the Narthex. But it will be fine."

Jay thanked Barb and plowed through the remaining congregants again toward the back of the room, sweeping the room as he went, looking for Zin. Instead, he caught Marvin Schneider's eye. Jay nodded and quickly walked toward the back door, but he could see Marvin coming up alongside him.

"Good morning, Father," Marvin called to Jay, who obliged by turning toward Marvin, a grim smile forced on his lips. "Looking for someone?" Marvin asked with a look in his eye that Jay didn't like.

"Nope. Just saying hi to folks. How are you?" Jay responded.

"Oh, I'm fine. It just looked like you were trying to find someone."

"Nope," answered Jay. They looked at each other. Marvin broke the awkward silence.

"Well, have a good day then." Jay nodded and Marvin wound his way back to his wife, a heavy woman with short grey hair and an intense expression who was busy gossiping with Sheila Price. Jay sighed and left the room, heading back to his house for a nap, feeling slightly dejected for not seeing Zin, and on top of that, he just realized that he didn't even get a doughnut.

17

Zin paced the train platform wearing sunglasses and a Minnesota Twins hat, looking anxiously down the track to see if the next train was coming. She checked the time again; Henry was five minutes late, which was unusual for him. After another minute, she saw someone crossing the street to get to the platform. Zin watched the person as he approached, a man with a riot of blonde hair, wearing a bright pink Twins t-shirt and a pair of black pants. A group of young men at the end of the platform watched Henry as he walked up the steps and guffawed as he went past them.

"I am ready to watch the Minnesota Twins baseball game," announced Henry as he walked up to Zin. Zin twisted her lips into a smile.

"I see that." Zin thought about telling Henry that the pink shirts were women's shirts but decided to just let it go. Besides, who cares? It was kind of liberating hanging out with a self-proclaimed visitor. Rules and norms seemed so arbitrary when viewed from an outside lens, even if that lens was imaginary. The Green Line train pulled up to the station a minute later and people shuffled on board. On the train, Henry sat near the aisle and watched every person that boarded at each stop. When a few people came on board wearing Twins uniforms, Henry felt compelled to talk to them.

"Are you going to the Minnesota Twins baseball game this afternoon?" asked Henry.

"Yup," came the response.

"We are, too. I think it will be great entertainment." They looked down at Henry, momentarily confused by his appearance. Zin chimed in.

"He's from out of town. First baseball game." They nodded now, happier to have a classification for the odd little man. After asking a third group of people the same question, Zin had to stop him.

"Henry, you can pretty much assume that anyone boarding this train wearing Minnesota Twins clothing is going to the game."

"Yes, I was going to make that same assumption myself." They rode in silence the rest of the way until they approached the stadium, where they all poured out and joined the throngs of fans heading towards the game.

Zin led Henry to the mall in front of the stadium, where larger-than-life statues of former players were scattered about. Henry stood in front of one.

"Was he that large? No wonder he was an exceptional athlete."

"No, he wasn't that big."

"Oh. Is this a sort of worship? An idol for the masses?"

"Yeah, sort of." Zin pulled Henry to the ticket booth, where Zin bought the cheapest tickets she could get, an upper balcony seat along the third base line. She handed a ticket to Henry.

"My treat," she said.

"Thank you," Henry replied. They made their way to their seats and Henry proceeded to grill Zin for the next three hours on the rules of the game. The weather was nice, and the Twins were winning, so Zin didn't care. At least she had a companion and someone who wanted to be there.

The game ended all too soon, and the throngs all shuffled out in good spirits because the home team had hung on to win. As they left the mall and reached the corner of First Avenue, they observed a haggard-looking man sitting on an old upside-down five-gallon paint can, holding a square of cardboard that read:

Looking for work. Family to feed. Anything Helps.

The man had a hat on the ground and in it were a couple crumbled bills and a handful of coins. The crowds were mostly ignoring the man. Zin tried to walk along past, but Henry was focused on the man and kept staring at him, even after they had passed him.

"Why is no one helping this man?" asked Henry, visibly distraught.

"I don't know. It's complicated," answered Zin, not wanting to get into it with Henry. Henry wasn't so easily placated, however.

"It does not seem complicated. He needs help."

"I think people worry about giving money to someone like that. They may feel that he might use it to buy alcohol instead of food. They may not believe he has a family. Who knows?"

"But what if he is telling the truth?"

"Then that is pretty sad."

"So, we should help him." Henry had stopped, causing a bit of a ripple in the flow of bodies around him.

"What should we do?" sighed Zin with resignation.

"Give him some money."

"Sure," said Zin, digging in her purse. She handed Henry a five. "How about you give him the money?"

"This is not much money," said Henry.

"What? Well then you go give him some of your own money!"

"I do not have any to give."

"Then you shouldn't be telling people how to spend their money."

"All right," he said, looking down at the bill. "I will be right back." He pushed his way toward the man, a salmon swimming upstream, until he reached the panhandler. Zin watched the man talking to Henry. He smiled and shook his hand. Then Henry surprised her by standing on top of the bucket. Zin's heart sank as she watched Henry call out to the crowd.

"Hello everyone. This man is in need of assistance. He just needs some money for food for his family. If each of you could give one dollar, he would be happy." Zin could see across the street a couple of police officers were walking toward the stadium. When they saw Henry, they looked at each other and started moving in a straight line toward them. Luckily, the traffic on First Avenue was busy, and they had to pause and wait. Zin pushed her way back toward Henry, but then she noticed something unusual; the flow of people had slowed down. Zin could see what was happening; people were pausing to throw money into the hat as they went by. Zin finally reached them, and they were both beaming.

"This is Marcus," said Henry. "Marcus, this is my friend, Zin." Marcus extended his hand and shook with Zin.

"Hey, thanks a bunch," he said to Zin, pumping her fist hard.

"Oh, you're welcome, but I didn't do anything."

"Marcus was a landscape worker who hurt his back two years ago and cannot find work."

"Yeah, been scraping by, but this helps."

"Say, it was nice to meet you, but a couple of cops are coming over to pay us a visit," said Zin, nodding up the street, where the cops were doing a quick step across the last lane of traffic. Marcus bent into action.

"Okay, that's my signal. Anyway, thanks a bunch." He flipped the paint can over, threw everything into it, and waded away through the crowd. Zin grabbed Henry's hand and pulled him back towards the train.

On board the train, Zin suddenly remembered the reason they were together.

"Henry, what about our minute?" she asked. She was surprised at how much it bothered her that they had missed it.

"It was at 4:17 p.m."

"I know, but I don't..."

"It was right after I stood up on the can," Henry said.

"You know, you're not supposed to alter the experiment. You are just supposed to observe."

"Let us just say that I introduced a variable in a controlled environment," said Henry, smiling.

18

Zin glared at the phone sitting on her nightstand. When she was living with Rick, she was always the early riser and the phone was right there, at arm's length. Now, she sprawled over the bed, mornings came too soon, and the phone was an annoying five feet away. She let it buzz for another minute before crawling over and tapping it quiet. At least it would be a short week, with the school closed on Friday, a sort of unofficial Easter break. Unfortunately, she had conferences tomorrow night, which meant a night of preparing mini reports for her students.

Zin made her way to school and managed to get through first hour without any crises. In fact, the day was going well for a Monday. For some reason, kids had done their assignments over the weekend, and no one was looking for trouble. It just goes to show you that you never know what to expect as a teacher.

Zin sat at her desk grading assignments while her fourth hour students wrestled with the quiz on Western European countries. She had finished half of the stack of papers before she came across Adrian's assignment. She frowned. It had started out well, but the second half of the assignment looked slipshod, as if he had tried to do it in five minutes. That kid was perplexing; he seemed sharp, but then would just fall off a cliff.

The classroom was a little warm, and a post-lunch mini coma

had started to settle in. Zin's head drifted downward slowly and then snapped back up. She checked to make sure no one had seen it, but they all looked intent on their quiz. Within another minute, however, her head was drooping again. The announcement on the intercom caused her to jump in her seat.

"Attention. We are in lock down. An intruder is in the building. I repeat, we are in lock down. An intruder is in the building. This is not a drill." Zin looked around with wild eyes. Every student looked up at her at once. For a moment, the room was deathly quiet, and Zin could feel her heart pounding her chest. Then an immediate commotion broke out.

Zin ran for the door and locked it, turning off the lights. "Emily, Deshaun. Windows!" A skinny boy with a mop of dreadlocks and a tall girl with a fuzzy sweater were already at the windows, throwing locks. Zin ran over to help lower the shades. The rest of the room pushed desks into a pile and then sat behind it on the floor, as far from the door as they could be. Emily, Deshaun, and Zin then jogged over behind the desks to join them. Zin crouched looking at the door. All was quiet. Half the kids were on their phones, texting friends, trying to find any information. Zin looked back at the kids. Some looked serious, others looked scared. Zin wanted to offer comfort, but honestly, she didn't want to lie to them, either. She didn't know what was happening.

Zin scanned the room for a weapon. She had played this mental game a couple times before, but now she couldn't remember what would make for a weapon. Nothing in the room looked like it would help much against an intruder. A tall file cabinet stood behind the door and Zin thought about pushing it in front of the door, but knew it would make a lot of noise, so she decided to sit still.

A twenty second eternity ticked by before the class was jolted by a knock on the door. Zin held her breath. No one made a sound. Again, a knock, but this time, a voice from the other side.

"Zin? Zin?" The door handle twisted a couple times, the person outside trying to open the door. Zin's head spun in confusion. Something about that voice sounded familiar, although muffled by distance and a door. She looked at the kids, who were all staring at her. She stood up slowly. Another knock at the door.

"Zin? Is this your room?" Zin's mind was racing. She got up and crept along the wall to the door. When she got near it, she hissed.

"Henry? Is that you?"

"Yes," he answered. "Can you let me in?" Zin took a deep breath and unlocked the door, opening it a few inches and looking out. Henry was standing outside and gave a little wave. With a motion faster than she thought she was capable of, she swung the door open with her left hand, grabbed Henry with her right, and yanked him in, closing the door behind him and locking it. Henry looked around the room with confusion.

"What are you doing in the dark?"

"What the hell are you doing here?" Zin hissed.

"I came to see you. It is our time for observation. It is in about three minutes." Zin looked at Henry with a dawning realization. Henry was wearing a black hoodie pulled up over his messy hair, his hands were in his pockets, and he seemed to be holding something. He wore black, baggy pants and his black canvas hi-tops. *Oh. Shit.*

"Henry, did you check in at the office when you came in?"

"No. I knew where your room was." Zin shook her head and walked over to her desk, where she picked up the phone. She punched a couple numbers and waited for several rings before someone answered it.

"Cindy, it's Zin. Who reported an intruder?" Zin listened in. "What did he look like?" Zin nodded her head. "U-huh. U-huh. Yeah. Listen, I think there was a mistake. I think the man is in my room. Yeah. U-huh. Send them to my room." She looked at Henry.

"I think we have a problem, Henry. You should have checked in at the front desk."

"He's the intruder?" called Liam, a heavy-set kid with wavey, brown hair who was now up on his knees."

"We don't know," said Zin to the class. "There might be a

mistake here." She heard a low whistle.

"Oh, boy. You are in b-i-i-i-g trouble," called a skinny kid with a sing-song voice. Several kids nodded their heads.

"Yeah, this ain't gonna be good," said Jayden, a tall black girl with braids, to the group of girls around her. To Zin's horror, the kids were looking at her with wide eyes and then tapping wildly on their phones. A couple were taking pictures. The pitchforks and torches were going to start showing up at the school entrance in about fifteen minutes.

Zin turned to Henry and grabbed him with urgency, leaning in close and whispering, "Listen and listen good. In about a minute, police are going to come here. Whatever you do, don't tell them you are from a different country or whatever you think you are. Just tell them you are homeless and thought you were supposed to meet me today."

"But that would be a lie."

"Henry, if you tell them some weird story, like you're from another country, they're going to ask for identification, and if I'm guessing correctly, you don't have any. And if that happens, they'll lock you up for an eternity in a detention center. And if you tell them something even more crazy, they'll lock you up in a loony bin and throw away the key. So do me a favor and tell them you're homeless and I was helping you. Okay?"

Henry frowned but nodded his head. Zin went over to the door and unlocked it. Just then, she heard a couple sets of footsteps pounding down the hall. They slowed as they approached the room and then all was quiet. Then a fist pounded on the door and a voice barked from the other side of the door.

"This is the police. We are coming in. Step away from the door." Henry and Zin took a couple steps back. The door flew open, and four police officers jumped into the room wearing bullet-proof vests, weapons drawn. Two led the way—a burly, middle-aged officer with a crew cut, the other a tall, thinner man with a mustache. They practically ran into and around the room, weapons drawn, with the first two pointing their weapons at Henry. The burly officer shouted at Henry.

"You. Put your hands where I can see them. NOW!" Henry looked confused. Zin tried to speak up.

"Officers. This is just a mistake. He's a friend of mine."

"Hands in the air, slowly. NOW!" Henry obeyed. "Now step forward and face the wall." Henry walked forward and both officers raced to him, the other officers standing nearby, checking the room out and watching Henry. The burly officer kept his gun trained on Henry while the other forced him against the wall and patted him down. "Do not move," he commanded. The officer felt in Henry's pockets and pulled out two packets of Little Debbie Treats.

"Hey! Those are my Little Debbie Treats!" protested Henry.

"Shut your face!" The thin officer continued to pat down Henry until he was satisfied. Zin paced behind them. When the tall officer was done, he looked at the other officer and nodded. The burly officer lowered his weapon and then walked over to Henry and pushed him into Zin's chair. By now, a couple more officers and the school security guard had filed into the room. One of the officers was speaking into a radio attached to his uniform. The burly officer sat on Zin's desk and looked down at Henry, the officer's partner standing beside him, arms crossed.

"So, would you mind telling me what the hell is going on here?"

Henry looked at Zin, who jumped in.

"Henry was just looking for me. He thought we were supposed to get together. He didn't know he had to check in." The officer looked at Zin.

"Ma'am, I'm talking to this guy here," pointing at Henry. He looked back at Henry. "What's your name, mister?"

"Henry."

"Henry. Got a last name?" Henry looked away for a second at the corner of Zin's desk before returning his gaze back to the officer.

"Ford. Henry Ford."

A flash of anger crossed the officer's face. "You some kind of wiseass or something?" Henry looked confused.

Zin chimed in from the side. "No, that's his name," she said, trying to neutralize her expression. The officer looked at her and frowned hard, shaking his head.

"All right, *Henry Ford*, telling me what the hell you are doing here."

"Ummm. I was here to visit Zin. I thought we were supposed to get together at this time."

"And why was that?"

"Because we get together every day to observe humanity." A couple of the officers standing behind them exchanged glances.

"Observe humanity. Huh. Not sure what the hell that means. So, you just waltz right into school in the middle of the day, dressed like some punk serial killer, and don't tell anyone. How come you're not at work?"

"I am…" he paused and looked at Zin. "I do not have a job."

"He's been trying to get on his feet again," inserted Zin. "He's been going through a tough stretch. I've been helping him a bit," offered Zin, her voice trailing off. The first two officers looked at each other, their mouths a grim line, their heads shaking side-to-side. The first officer returned his glare at Henry again and then stood up. He went back to the other officers and the security guard behind him, and they conferred for a bit. Zin could hear other police officers in the hall. The first officer broke from the group and approached Zin, looking down at a notepad where he had been taking some notes.

"Ma'am. Can I get your name?"

"Zin. Zin McGuire." The officer scribbled on the notepad and looked up at her.

"So, here's what's going to happen, Zin. We need to complete a sweep of the school, but I'm guessing we've found the problem. Mr. Henry Ford here is going to have to come down to the station with us for questioning. We'll probably need you down there as well to answer a few questions." Zin nodded. The officer's tone softened a bit and dropped in volume. "So, really. What's going on here? Is this guy all right? I mean, is he a nutcase or something?" Zin looked at Henry, then back at the officer.

"Officer, he's a good guy. He's just a little...socially clueless. I think he might be autistic or something. Anyway, he just needs a little help. He wouldn't harm a fly."

"Hmmpf," grunted the officer. "That's what a lot of people say before a serial killer goes off. He was really coming to see you?"

"Yeah. We try to get together every day. Just to...check in. I guess he thought it was a good time."

"He's damn lucky he found you before we found him," answered the cop. "It could have been ugly. Can you get someone to take care of your class and come down to the precinct station down on University ASAP? I don't think I need to escort you there, but I do need you to show up and make a statement soon. Okay?" Zin nodded. "All right." He turned back to the group of officers. "Let's get this guy out of the building quickly." His partner grabbed Henry by the arm and hauled him up. They escorted him out the door, Henry looking back over his shoulder at Zin with a worried look on his face. Zin was happy to see that they didn't put him in handcuffs. When the officers and the security guard had cleared out, Principal Harris appeared in the doorway. A tall, black woman in her mid-forties with hair in a long ponytail halfway down her back, she had her arms crossed with an irritated look on her face. Zin approached, her stomach dropping away as she remembered the torches and pitchforks.

"Zin. They are telling me that some man was visiting you? That was the scare?" Zin nodded.

"Yeah. It's this homeless guy I've been helping. He's harmless but clueless. He was just coming to visit." The principal sighed and looked up at the ceiling.

"This is going to be really bad. We've got press everywhere. Every parent in the district is either on the phone or on their way here."

"I know," was all Zin could manage to say. She felt like she should have apologized, but when it came down to it, she didn't want to. They stood in silence for a moment.

"Well, I guess we were lucky," Principal Harris said. "These situations can turn out to be much worse than this." Zin nodded.

"They want me to come down to the police station. I'm going to need someone to cover my class."

"I'll tell Julie," she answered. She turned and walked out of the classroom. Zin exhaled, her body seeming to deflate. Her head was spinning, and she walked over to her desk and sat down. Zin looked up to see her students, now all standing at the back of the room. They were alone now, and all the kids were staring at her. She was shaken and emotionally drained and just wanted to be alone for a bit, but the kids were there, needing attention. Zin took a deep breath and tried to get back into teacher mode.

"Wow. Okay guys. I'm sorry about this. I know that was traumatic."

"They gonna jail that guy?" It was Liam again.

"I don't know. I hope not. He wasn't here to cause any trouble, he's just a little clueless at times."

"I'll say," chimed Jayden.

"He looked like a loner school shooter type," said Erica, a small, thin girl also dressed in all black, with a black hoodie and black lipstick.

"You should know," said Dylan. A couple kids snickered.

"Hey, we don't need that," said Zin. She stood up. "All right, let's get this place back together. The kids started pushing chairs into place. Zin opened the shades on the windows and straightened her desk. There was only about five minutes left in the class.

"I don't think there's much sense in doing anything else today. Why don't you hand me your quizzes? I don't know if we'll finish them or not tomorrow, but I'm not going to worry about that now." She walked around the room and collected the papers.

"Let's talk," she said, sitting on the edge of her desk. "What were you guys thinking when I let Henry into the room?"

"I thought you were crazy," said Sammy.

"Yeah, I thought he was going to come into the room and start shooting us up," said another girl. A few heads nodded.

"Wow. I'm sure that seemed frightening to you," said Zin. "I knew who it was, so I wasn't as worried, but I can see how that might have seemed like a bad idea." Zin thought about it. She still didn't know much about Henry. He was certainly odd, and definitely not mentally stable. Maybe that was naive of her. What if Henry wasn't so harmless? She was constantly putting herself into situations with Henry that she would never suggest to another woman. Still, whenever she was with him, any notion of him being harmful dissolved like a silly dream.

Zin wrapped up the class and grabbed her backpack and lunch bag, getting ready to leave. She pulled her coat off a hook and put it on. Slipping her hand into her pocket, she realized she didn't have her keys. She felt her pockets and looked in her purse but couldn't find them. Turning back to her desk, she spotted them on the corner, and went back to grab them. As she did, something caught her eye that gave her pause; the key fob was turned up with the *Ford* logo clearly visible to anyone sitting on the opposite side of the desk.

A substitute relieved Zin for her last class, so she headed down to the precinct station where she reported in and was then escorted to a windowless room with a small table and a few chairs. While she waited, Zin debated whether she should tell them that Henry needed help. Given his story, he probably did need help. She sat for what seemed to be a long time before an officer appeared, a middle-aged woman with blond hair pulled back in a tight ponytail, muscular arms, and a serious expression. To her surprise, it wasn't one of the officers she remembered from the school. The officer asked about Henry and how she knew him, and Zin realized that she might be caught in a trap— they would already have asked Henry the same thing, and if her story was much different than his, things might get complicated fast. Henry didn't come off as the best liar, so his story would probably be pretty straight up. Zin decided to stick close to the truth.

"I met Henry about a week ago," she said. "I had an accident and he helped me out. Then we got talking. I thought he could use a meal, so I bought him dinner. And then we decided to meet every day. So, we just meet and talk for a little bit every day." The officer made notes.

"What do you know about Henry?"

"Not a lot, I guess."

"Does he have family?"

"Not that I know of."

"A job?"

"I don't think so."

"Do you know where he lives?" Zin just shook her head.

"From what you know, could he be a threat to himself or anyone else?"

"No. Not Henry. He is gentle. But really clueless at times." The officer continued making notes before looking up.

"Well, here's what he told us. He said you threw something at him when he was visiting the cathedral. Then you went with him and had some drinks. Then you discussed the problems with humanity and decided you would get together to judge humanity every day for ten days to see if humans were really worth the trouble. And now you get together every day to watch people. For one minute." She looked up at Zin. "And this afternoon was supposed to be another minute." Zin looked at her blankly. Yeah, that sounded a bit crazy.

"I didn't throw something at him. I dropped it. Accidentally." The officer just stared at her. Zin continued.

"We had dinner and a couple drinks. We were joking about all of the trouble in the world."

"Henry said you meet every day at prescribed times."

"I guess so. It's a different time and place every day."

"So, you knew he was coming to school today?"

"No. I definitely did not."

"He said he provided you with a listing of all the times you would meet." Zin thought about the paper in her coat pocket.

"He scribbled some dates and times on a piece of paper and handed it to me the first night we met. I didn't really pay it much attention."

"So, he just surprises you?"

"Sometimes, I guess. If I forget to ask him when we will meet, he will just show up." The officer wrote a few more notes and looked up.

"Does that worry you? That he shows up without you expecting him? Does it feel like he's stalking you or something that makes you uncomfortable?" Zin hesitated, but then shook her head.

"Umm, no. Not really. I mean, it caught me off guard once or twice."

"Like today?"

"Uhhh, yeah. Like today. But it is more of just a miscommunication. I don't feel like he's hunting me down or anything. We meet for a few minutes, then he goes." Zin knew this still wasn't sounding good. "I've wanted to do this. I just need to get better at setting parameters."

The officer looked at Zin with a hard stare. Zin tried to look earnest.

"You need to be smart about this, okay? You might think you understand someone like this, but he may have challenges that you aren't aware of, and some weird behavior might appear out of the blue."

"I understand. Thank you for your advice." The officer gave her one more hard look before pushing back her chair.

"Okay, I think that just about does it."

"What's going to happen to Henry?"

"We've been talking to the school. I don't think we are going to charge him with anything."

"So, he is free to go?"

"We are having him meet with a social worker from the county first. He probably needs some services, like mental health counseling or housing assistance."

"Can I meet with him? When he's done."

"Yeah. How about I take your number and call you when he is wrapping up. You can come by then. I can tell him you want to see him when you are done."

Zin thanked the officer and walked out to her car. She drove home to crash on her couch, feeling exhausted. She wanted to nap, but there was so much to process. Was Henry a threat? Was she really so naive? And what would happen now? Would she get disciplined by the school board? She closed her eyes, dreading the next few days, wondering if her job was in jeopardy. Maybe she needed to call this off with Henry.

Zin got the call a couple hours later and drove back to the precinct station. She found Henry sitting in a waiting area, holding a manila folder full of papers. She stood above him.

"How are you doing, Henry?" she asked, her mouth a grim line.

"I am fine. They said you wanted to see me, and I should wait for you."

"Yeah, I wanted to know if you were okay."

"I am."

"What's with the papers?"

"There was a nice lady from the Ramsey County social services department that was trying to get me to see a doctor and find me a place to stay."

"Did she set you up with anything?"

"I told her I did not need any such services." Zin was quiet for a moment. She had calmed down by now but was still upset.

"Henry, you can't be causing trouble like this. You scared a lot of people today. And I don't know what is going to happen. My job might be on the line for this, you know."

Henry hung his head. "I am sorry I caused so much trouble." Zin stood, hands on hips, frowning. Her voice took a gentler turn.

"Are you sure you're okay? That was a pretty traumatic event today." Henry nodded.

"I found it very interesting."

"Did they treat you okay here? Did they rough you up at all or give you a hard time?"

"They treated me decently. They were a little upset. I think they were frustrated with me, but not really angry, from what I could tell. The big officer without much hair scolded me, but he was not mean. He seemed to believe that every person should know to check into the office when visiting a school. I admit, I did not bother reading all of the signs on the door."

"Yeah, the schools are pretty uptight about that these days." Zin patted Henry on the knee. "So now what? Do you want me to take you home?"

"Actually, we are right next to the Green Line train," answered Henry, standing up. "I think I will just head back." He started walking out the door, but Zin called out to him.

"Henry?" He stopped with the door half open and looked back at Zin.

"I have something of yours." She held out her hand. In it were two Little Debbie Treats. Henry smiled and walked back to her and took the treats. "Thank you, Zin." He paused for a second. "And thank you for your concern, Zin." Zin nodded and smiled. Somehow, that seemed like progress.

19

Jay lined his club up with the ball and took a couple of easy practice swings. He took a half step forward and lined his club up again, sensing the quiet that had descended on the spot behind him. He wasn't supposed to think this much when golfing, but now he was self-conscious, and when he did swing, he shanked the ball. He stood up and watched it squibble away to the side, maybe 60 yards. Jay waited for what he knew was coming.

"You're pulling up too soon. Keep your head down all the way through the swing."

Jay looked straight ahead, nostrils flaring. He didn't want to listen to a lesson; he just wanted to hit some balls and relieve some stress. It was Tuesday, after all, and he had already endured his dose of Mabel Jorgenson that morning. He took a deep breath and decided not to acknowledge the critique. Lon was a decent guy, and he was good enough to drag Jay out to golf or get a drink once in a blue moon, but dammit if the guy wasn't just a little too serious about his golf. Jay could picture Lon standing behind him, arms crossed, a serious look on his face, ready to critique his next swing. Jay put another ball down on the grass in front of him and eyed up a target 150 yards out. He grabbed a mid-range iron and went through the same routine, this time topping the ball, causing it to bounce for about 50 yards. Jay sighed.

"You did it again."

"Looks like it," said Jay, walking back to his clubs. He grabbed a towel to wipe his club, the only thing he could think to do to avoid more lessons and having to tee up again. Jay shivered and did some active stretching to warm himself up. It was much too early to be golfing in Minnesota—there were still patches of snow in places—but the driving range had opened up and when Lon had called, he thought it was just what he needed. Now, he wasn't so sure. He wasn't in the mood to listen to Lon. He decided to change the topic.

"So, how're the kids doing?" Jay asked.

"Good, good. Tim's a sophomore at the U. Seems to realize he needs to study a bit. Megan is a senior at Central. Got a graduation party to get ready for pretty soon. Thankfully, Sheila makes a little money so we can fix the place up for the party. Heaven knows we men of the cloth don't get paid anything."

"And how's Sheila been?"

"She's good. She's running a lot, probably will run Grandma's marathon in June." Lon's wife, a physical therapist for athletes, was as athletic as Lon, possibly more so. The two of them pretty much made Jay feel like, well, the big lump that he was. Lon must have gotten the signal, as he didn't seem to press Jay on his form. Instead, he lined up and got ready for his own swing, carefully selecting his club and then eyeing the target at the far end of the driving range. Lon swung, driving the ball long and straight, bounding out near the 200-yard mark. He took off his baseball cap and ran his fingers through his crew cut. "She's a big help at the church, too. He looked off in the distance. "Not sure what I'd do without her. Not sure how you priests do it, not getting married." He looked back at Jay. "I'll hand it to you—you guys deserve a thousand bonus points in Heaven for that sacrifice. I sure couldn't do it." Jay frowned, but Lon lit up. "Hey, you'll never guess who Sheila got as a client last week? Brandon Richardson."

"The wide receiver?"

"Yeah. Apparently, he's had a calf problem all year. Needs to work it out before summer. Sheila says he's ripped. Pure muscle."

"That's cool." He thought about Sheila and Lon, and not for the first time, felt a stab of injustice. Why can a Lutheran Pastor get married when he couldn't? And even though she might be ten years older than Jay, he had to admit she was a very attractive woman. Jay walked back to his spot and set another ball down, waited to hear the swoosh and ping of Lon's stroke, and then swung himself, this time getting under it and getting some distance, although still pulling.

"So, how're things at St. Stephens?" Another swoosh and ping. Jay lined up another.

"Ah. Okay, I guess. Can't complain."

"Sounds like maybe you could?" Jay stood up and turned to Lon, who was leaning on a club.

"Ahh, you know. Church politics and personalities. Can get under your skin at times."

Lon nodded. "Yeah, I know what you mean. Don't take it too personally."

"Ummm, how can I not take it personally? I mean, if your parishioners don't like you, that's, well, personal."

"You don't think they like you?"

"I dunno. At least a chunk of them don't. They miss their previous priest." Lon nodded his head and made a wry smile.

"They probably complained about him all the time he was there, and now that he's gone, they're nostalgic for a time they never had. Don't worry about it. I've had a few of those. I pretty much ignore it. I know I'm damn good at what I do—they can jump in a lake if they don't like it. I'm not going anywhere." Lon reached in his basket for another ball and set it down in front of him, lining up his club. Jay looked at him and shook his head. He knew Lon was confident—probably cocksure, but his advice seemed a little shady. He didn't think ignoring his parishioners was likely the best route.

"I read once that the doctors that don't get sued for malpractice aren't the best doctors, but the ones that give their patients the best personal attention," said Jay.

Lon snorted in disgust. "Doctors? Lawsuits? That analogy doesn't have anything to do with this. We're more like a politician, and a politician is never going to make all his constituents happy, it just isn't possible. Just keep smiling and stick to your guns. Besides, what're they going to do? They're Catholic. They have to attend church, and they can't leave the church, or their souls will burn in hell for eternity." He looked at Jay and laughed. "Jay, you've got the easiest gig ever!" Lon patted Jay on the shoulder, then squared up again and focused on the ball. "Hell, we've practically got to offer yoga studios and climbing walls to get families to come to our church. You could probably have mass in the basement of the 7-Eleven and still pack-em in." Jay turned around and grabbed a ball, still bewildered by Lon's comments. Lon was a good golf buddy, but he made a mental note not to ask him for professional advice again.

Jay thought about golfing with Lon again, and suddenly had an idea—maybe Zin likes to golf? He could ask her. A golf outing would be harmless, wouldn't it? Maybe find a few people from church who liked to golf—make it into a church social thing. He let the idea run its course for all of three seconds before realizing it was a ridiculous idea. He set a ball down, took a deep breath, and took a swing. He pulled it, of course, and behind him, he heard a soft chuckle.

By 8:00 p.m. that evening, Jay was wiped out. He rubbed his temples and closed his eyes. Hell, he figured, was being stuck in a two-hour meeting while enduring a pounding headache. He placed himself in ring two or three of Dante's Inferno, probably reserved for gluttons or lust-filled souls. Or was this his personal Purgatory? Jay tried to remember the difference between Limbo and Purgatory. Limbo was kind of a waiting place for those who didn't do wrong, necessarily, but were just born at the wrong time, like people who died before Jesus or babies who didn't get baptized. Purgatory was more about doing hard time so you could go to Heaven one day. This must be Purgatory, he decided.

Jay became aware of the quiet. He stopped doodling on his agenda (which he realized was a drawing of nine cascading rings) and looked up. The rest of the committee members were staring at him from their seats around the plastic folding table.

Sylvia Gomez tried again. "Father?" Jay shook his head.

"Oh, sorry. Could you repeat that?"

"I asked if you felt like it would be appropriate to use some of the recent Hoffman donation money to fund the capital campaign study?"

"Oh. Hoffman money. Yeah. I think so. It wasn't earmarked for anything specific, and we want to do the study before embarking on the plan. I think we should."

"We'll have to have a motion approved by the church council," reminded Steve Dawson.

"Of course," replied Jay. The committee moved on and Jay did his best to keep his eyes open. Jay sat listening to the capital campaign plans, looking at finance reports, reviewing the spreadsheets on projects they envisioned. One of the documents that was passed around was last year's line-item budget. Jay looked at the maintenance costs for this year and the previous one and shook his head, the costs were significant. Boiler repairs, plumbing issues, electrical work, water damage—it seemed like the church was constantly falling apart. It's why we needed a capital campaign, he thought. But man, these projects are expensive.

20

Zin finished entering a few grade reports into her laptop and closed it. She grabbed the laptop, a pen, a water bottle, and a stack of papers off her desk and headed to the gym. It was parent-teacher conference night, a night she pretty much dreaded. It was a long day, having taught all day and then dealing with parents for hours. Most parents were pretty good; they wanted a general idea of what was going on and wanted to look for some way they could help their child, if needed. But once in a while there were the others. The talkers, who kept going and going, needing to know everything, or just couldn't take the hint when five sets of parents had queued up behind her. Or the helicopter parent who had 'helped' with every assignment and wanted to argue points on the recent essay. Or the occasional hothead—they usually didn't bother showing up, but when they did, they were unimpressed with your curriculum and materials and were angry with your treatment of their child.

Tonight, however, was different. It was the worst of timing—right after the school lock down. At least twenty-nine students had first-hand knowledge of Zin's involvement. She knew she'd have to answer questions but deflect as much as possible. She wouldn't get into details, at least that was the plan.

Zin sat down at the table with her name on a placard and

waited, grading papers. Parents, with the occasional student by their side, trickled in after 3:30 and Zin got her usual share, keeping her halfway busy until 5:00. After that, she pretty much was talking to someone non-stop. Zin liked to keep it short and sweet, and that kept her line moving. Half of the parents had heard that the intruder had been found in her classroom, and Zin had to repeat her prepared remarks. *Yes, the intruder had come to visit her. He was a man who needed some help—he didn't understand about checking into the building.* But that message didn't sit well with many parents. *Is he getting help?* (Zin answered in the affirmative, which she decided was slightly true. Maybe). *How do we know he isn't dangerous?* (Zin answered that he was just coming to visit a friend. He had no violent tendencies, no violent past, and was just in the wrong place. He is a good person). That part got more personal than Zin wanted; she wanted to distance herself from this stranger who had done this foolish act, and tying herself to him made her culpable in a way, but she didn't know how to suppress the fire of retribution without her personal testimony. *Does he know not to come back?* (Yes, he understands now). *I heard he was a drug dealer.* (No, nothing of the sort. He had a cupcake in his pocket) which was Zin's favorite response of the night.

Zin got up for a fifteen-minute break and grabbed a drink from the vending machine. She stood in a quiet corner of a hallway, relishing the peace. She leaned back against the cool block wall and closed her eyes. She was thinking about the kids who needed a parent to show up tonight. Usually, those who should show up didn't. She was wondering about Adrian—a kid who seemed smart and with it, but sometimes would just tank assignments, and whose attendance had gotten worse and worse since the beginning of the year. She'd like to talk to his parents tonight.

"You okay Zin?" It was Principal Harris, in athletic pants and a warm-up top, looking like she was ready for a volleyball match. Zin realized that she very well could be. Here was a woman who had given birth to two kids and was older than Zin, but somehow had a body twenty years younger.

"Yeah, just taking a little break."

"It's a long night. It's so tiring to have to deal with the parents all night long."

"Yeah, you know it."

"Are they asking about the incident yesterday?"

"Half of them are. I'm trying to assure them that there was never a risk from this guy."

"That's good. They all want to know how he got as far as he did. I don't have a great answer for that yet. But at least we responded appropriately across the board." Zin nodded.

"Well, I better get back to the gym," said Zin, resenting that she was ending her break a little early to escape the principal. "See you later."

Zin headed back to the gym and as soon as she sat at her table, a couple parents queued up to talk to her. Zin looked at the clock—only an hour to go. The after-work parents kept up a steady stream and time was moving quickly. After a bit, Emily's mom sat down, an annoying woman with blonde hair pulled back in a tight ponytail and skin that looked like it had never seen the sun. She gave a perfunctory smile as she introduced herself. Zin found Emily's grades on the computer and started talking about her recent assignments. Emily's mom nodded and didn't ask any questions, which, if Zin remembered, was unusual, as she had grilled Zin at the last conference with questions regarding curriculum, how fast it took to get assignments graded, and what extra credit opportunities were available for her little angel. It didn't take Zin long to realize why she had held off on the questions to that point.

"Well then, do you have any other questions about Emily's work?" Zin was trying to wrap it up and stay on the subject of Emily. Neither worked.

"Nope. I'm good there. I did have one more question about your class, however."

"Sure."

"Emily said that the school lockdown yesterday was because a friend of yours had come into the school and was trying to find you." Emily's mom took on the 'reasonable but concerned parent' look. Zin took a deep breath and kept her face blank. She was starting to reel off her usual statement when she glanced behind Emily's mom and noticed the next person in line. It was Henry. Zin froze in a state of panic. She didn't know what to do. So far, it didn't seem like anyone had noticed Henry. He was dressed almost normally, in a pair of blue jeans and an ugly green sweater, but it wasn't garish, and he didn't stand out. And thank goodness, there weren't any of her students in the line with their parents at that moment, or they might have recognized him. Emily's mom was starting to turn her head to look behind her when Zin rushed back into the conversation.

"Oh, that! Yes. Big mistake. Just wrong place at the wrong time. Very big misunderstanding."

"So, he was a friend of yours?" She had a way of asking questions with her head slightly tilted. Zin fought the urge to tilt her own head while responding.

"Yes. Well, an acquaintance."

"Emily said that he was a mentally ill man." Still tilting, still concerned.

"Mentally ill? No. No, just a man I was helping. Tutoring. He, ah, was, ah, working on his GED and he thought we were supposed to meet during school and had come to my class, like we had planned. After school, of course. Nothing strange about him, just a normal guy. You see. Wrong place, wrong time. Big mistake." Zin grinned, as if she had just told a funny story. Emily's mom's head was nodding now, in the 'I don't really believe you' nod.

"Hmmpf." She nodded again. "So, he's not dangerous."

"No, no, no," Zin shook her head and pursed her lips in an exaggerated 'don't be silly'.

"Is he still coming to school to meet with you?"

Zin shook her head slowly and let out a high, brief "Nope." It came out like a chirp. Emily's mom looked at her quizzically. She turned to take a quick glance behind her, and Zin let out a little gasp. Emily's mom turned back to Zin and started to get up.

"Okay. Well, it looks like there is a line behind me." She

stood up and again emitted the perfunctory smile. She stuck out her hand and Zin stood up to shake it. "Thank you for the time." Zin smiled big and kept the smile as she waved Henry forward. Henry approached and she reached out to shake his hand. Henry looked at her with confusion and reached out to shake her hand. Zin sat down and pointed at the chair opposite her.

"Have a seat." Still smiling. Henry didn't sit.

"Why? It is almost our time to meet."

Zin hissed through her smile and nodded to the chair. "Henry, sit down!" Henry complied. Zin brought her laptop to the middle of the table and leaned in as if showing Henry a grade report. Henry leaned in, curious.

"What are you doing here?"

"It is our time, of course." Zin gritted her teeth.

"Henry, you can't come back to the school! Don't you know how much trouble you will be in? If they catch you here, you will go to jail." Zin was finding it hard to keep her calm teacher demeanor while wanting to yell at Henry and ring his neck. Henry sat back. Principal Harris was walking around the gym and Zin gave her a smile and a nod. "Henry, sit up and pretend to look at this paper with me." Henry obliged.

"Why do I have to look at a paper?"

"Because you need to pretend you are a parent."

"Our minute is starting now." He started looking around.

"Henry," Zin demanded. "You need to look at me. Right now." Henry turned back to her. "Here is what is going to happen. You have to pretend to be a parent. That means when you are sitting here with me, you are looking at me or at a paper I give you. Then, when we are done, you will stand up, shake my hand, and walk straight out of the building. Don't stop for anyone. Don't talk to anyone. If anyone looks at you, just give them a little smile and nod. Do you understand?" Henry nodded. Zin dug in her folder and pulled out a paper and handed it to Henry. "Take this paper with you, so it looks like you are a parent."

"Our minute is up." said Henry, not looking anywhere in particular.

"Then it is time for you to go." Zin reached out her hand and gestured with her head to get him to stand. Henry stood, sticking out his hand in confusion. Zin felt a piece of paper pressed into her palm as they shook hands. Then Henry turned and walked stiffly, straight out of the gym, a little too quickly. Zin watched him go a bit and glanced down at the paper. On it was scribbled:

7:36 at the big church

Zin looked up and smiled big for the next parent, who sat down with a concerned look on his face.

"I heard you had quite a big day yesterday," said the man, with an "I'm reasonable, but concerned" expression. Zin sighed and forced a smile. Only twenty minutes to go.

21

Jay headed to his office early the next morning and immediately looked for Miranda. She wasn't around, but Barb was already there, working on the church calendar.

"Barb, have you seen Miranda today?"

"She said she had an appointment this morning and would be in around eleven."

"Okay, thanks." Jay rolled his eyes—Miranda had an "appointment" of some sort every week. She was part-time, so he couldn't get too uptight about her hours. Plus, she seemed to work a number of evenings, helping Marvin Schneider with audits and budget reports, so maybe she was just a night owl. Jay had been thinking about the maintenance costs since last night's committee meeting, and they were really bothering him. Looking at those line items, they could hire a full-time maintenance person just to deal with everything, and still come out ahead.

Miranda rolled in just before noon and Jay pounced on her as she walked into her office.

"Good morning," he said, but then glanced at the clock. Technically, it was still morning.

"Hello, Father. How are you?"
"Fine, fine. Say, could I ask a favor of you?"

"Sure."

"Can you spit out all of the church expenses from our main church checking account for this year and last?" Miranda eyed him suspiciously.

"Uhh, sure. I guess. Is there something you need help with? I can find the information and get back to you."

"No, no. I'd just like to review everything. Get a handle on what we do with all our money."

"We prepare budget summaries for the finance committee meetings. Do you want me to get you that?"

"No, I've got that. I was just wanting to look at the details."

"That's just a lot of minutiae. I'm sure you don't have time for all of that."

"You know what? Never mind about that. I think I'm good." Miranda seemed to not want to go there, and Jay decided not to press it.

"You sure? If you need something, just put it in an email and I'll get you the info."

"Sure. I might take you up on it." Jay went back to his office to make a phone call before noon. He dialed the number, but it didn't pick up. He debated what to do, but when the beep sounded, he found himself talking.

"Uh, hey Zin. Umm, this is Jay. Father Jay, I mean, from church. Umm, yeah. I was wondering if Saturday afternoon would work. For our meeting. I was thinking of maybe 3 o'clock or something. But if you can't, I totally understand, no worries, not a big deal. Well, then, I guess I'll talk to you later. Maybe. Okay. Have a nice day."

Jay hung up and dropped his forehead to his desk. That was just...pathetic. He shook it off and got up, grabbed his coat, and left the church, headed to a lunch meeting.

When Jay got back a couple hours later, Barb was packing up, and Miranda was nowhere to be found.

"Barb, any idea where Miranda is?"

Barbara looked up from her computer. "Running errands. I think she said she might be back." She gave Jay a look that he would classify as 'you know what I think about her, so I'm keeping my mouth shut'. Jay nodded in understanding.

"Well, I hate to bother you, but I needed something. I don't think I have access to the accounting software. Do you have a log-in for that? I needed to look something up."

"Yeah, I should still have that." She opened a drawer, pulled out a little notebook and thumbed through it. Then walked over to Miranda's office and sat down at the computer, tapping in some information from her notebook. The computer unlocked and Barb pointed at the screen.

"That's the software right there. I haven't had to work in this for a few years, but I could give you a tour if you need it."

"No, no, that isn't necessary. Thanks a bunch."

"You're welcome. I'll leave you to it." Jay watched her leave and waited to hear the door close. Then he sat down and opened up the software. He poked around until he was looking at expenses. Fortunately, it allowed him to filter the data by category, which he did. There were quite a few maintenance expenses over the last couple of years—and probably twice what they were spending on maintenance the couple of years prior to that. This bothered Jay. There were a handful of vendors they used, some of which were the same as in the past. He wondered if a specific vendor was gouging them, but it looked like increases were happening across the board—electrician, plumbers, heating, flooring, miscellaneous repairs. Aside from noticing a little naming inconsistency with the vendors, he couldn't see anything other than work going on.

Jay sent a report to the printer and then shut down the software. These old churches were built when more people went to church and the church was flush. Now, they were burdens on congregations, who might be able to do more with less. But it was their building to keep for the next generation—it was just the price of doing business. He grabbed the papers from the printer and stuffed them into his bag. He could go over this tonight and see if there was anything that they could do to save some money. And besides, pouring over these reports would be a good cure for his insomnia.

***

Marvin Schneider frowned at the computer in front of him; he had a report to generate by the end of the week and he realized he had just found a mistake that would cost him an hour of re-work. He saved the spreadsheet under a new name and had opened up the original version when his office phone rang. He looked at the number and picked it up, speaking quietly so as to not be heard by his cube neighbors.

"Hello? Can I help you?" he answered, stiffly.

"Hey, it's me."

"Yes, I know."

Miranda could hear his impatience through the phone. "Sorry, I know you can't talk. But can I tell you something?"

Marvin closed his eyes. "Sure. What is it?"

"So, I was working on the endowment fund reports and realized that I didn't know what to do with the Hoffman money, so I was going down the hall to ask Father Jay, but his door was open a bit and I could hear him. I think he was making plans again to meet with Zin McGuire! I think they were going to get together on Saturday at like three o'clock."

"Really? That *is* interesting. Did you hear anything else? Any details?"

"No, not really. I only caught the end of it. But I thought you would find it interesting. Anyway, I think he's got a thing for her. He's all nice and such on the phone."

"I'll bet he is."

"So, waddya think?"

"I think we should put that on our calendar," said Marvin.

"Okay. Will I see you before then?"

Marvin glanced back at his computer. "I don't think so."

"Awwww. You sure?"

"Is there anything else I can help you with, *Sir*?"

"Yeah, there's one more thing." Miranda paused, and Marvin could sense she was nervous about something. "It's probably nothing, but I thought you should know."

"Know what?"

"Well, Father Jay comes into my office this morning. He says he wants a report on all expenses. Like details and stuff."

"All expenses? "Did he say why? Was he looking for certain years or something?"

"The last couple of years, I think he said. He said he wanted to look at the details. I didn't know what he meant."

"Did you give him the reports?"

"No, I offered to find information for him. And then I told him we did summaries of expenses that are in all budget reports, and I could give him those. After a while he said 'never mind' and let me go. But then I came back to the office this afternoon and I saw that Barb had logged into the computer. She hasn't done that in years. I tried to act nice—I told her I saw that she had logged in and asked her if there was anything I could help her with. She said Jay just wanted to get some numbers from the accounting software, so she helped him log in."

"Yeah, I don't like that. That doesn't sound good."

"Do you want me to do anything?"

"No, but if anything else happens or if he asks you to do something like that again, let me know right away."

"Sure."

"Is that all I can do for you?" he said, a little louder. "Thank you for your time."

"Oh, you're no fun," laughed Miranda.

"Yes, sir. Have a good day," replied Marvin, still louder than necessary.

"Whatever! Bye!"

Marvin hung up the phone and sat back in his chair, crossing his arms. It felt a little premature, but it seemed his hand was being forced. Marvin thought about it another minute, then leaned into his computer. He searched for the website of the archdiocese, then grabbed a piece of paper and wrote down a name and a number. He pushed back his office chair, stood up, and then walked over to a corner conference room. It was dark, so he popped in, closed the door behind him and turned on the lights. He sat down in front of the office phone and punched in the number on his paper. It picked up after a couple rings.

"Hello, this is Jim."

"Deacon Ketterling?

"Yep, that's me."

"This is Marvin Schneider from St. Stephen's. You may not remember me, but we talked a couple times about Father Murphy a few years ago."

"Marvin Schneider. Yes. You were upset with some changes he was proposing. Wanted my office to intervene." Marvin almost groaned. The deacon hadn't been particularly helpful at that time.

"Yes, well, we worked that out in the end." Marvin continued. "Do you have a moment? Some information has come to our attention that I think is critical that we discuss."

"Regarding?"

"It's about Father O'Brian."

22

Zin arrived at the cathedral parking lot at little past seven, just as most cars were leaving from the evening mass. Zin parked her little Ford, grabbed her coat from the front seat, and started to walk to the front steps of the church. She assumed Henry had meant p.m., and she assumed this church—what other big church would he be thinking of? She walked up the steps and scanned the area but didn't see him. Zin sat down on the top step and surveyed the downtown buildings arrayed below her and the state capital building to her left. The sun was getting low, and the western sky was a soft rose blanket, but there was a light breeze and no warmth from that setting sun. Zin shivered, pulling her coat tightly around her.

"Are you okay?" Zin turned around to find Henry who had appeared out of nowhere in classic form, wearing what appeared to be red and blue zebra-striped Zubaz pants, a green Minnesota Wild hockey jersey, and a grey puffy jacket. Zin shook her head yet again.

"How do you do it?"

"Do what?"

"Your clothes? Where do you get them?"

"I have my sources," answered Henry. "Why, do you not like them?"

"No, no. They're great. Just...unique, that's all." She turned back to enjoy the view and Henry joined her, sitting on the top step.

"You did not answer my question."

"Am I okay? Sure," Zin shrugged.

"The last time you were here, you were not okay."

"No, I wasn't." Zin thought about it quietly. "But I wasn't going to jump, if that's what you were thinking. I was upset, but I wasn't suicidal. I was being stupid, I guess."

"I did not think you were planning on jumping, by the way."

Zin looked at him. She smiled and nodded her head but didn't say anything.

"You were upset about your husband."

"Yeah, he tends to do that to me. There is a direct correlation these days between the number of times his name is mentioned and how upset I am."

"I will not mention his name, then."

"Good idea." After a moment, she continued. "But I was upset about a lot that day. He was at the heart of it, but I didn't even talk to him that day. It was...it was just a bad day."

They sat in silence for a minute, watching lights starting to appear across the city as the sun slipped behind the urban forest canopy in the distance.

"Do you talk to your husband often?"

That didn't take long. She answered, almost to herself. "I can't believe he's still my husband. Sometimes I forget. To answer your question, once in a while. Once a week or so I get a message from him, or I have to do something related to the divorce. That puts me in a pretty foul mood for the rest of the day."

"Was he always a terrible person?"

"No, he wasn't terrible. He isn't terrible. I think he stopped caring a long time ago, and that indifference allowed him to do some lousy things—not because he necessarily wanted to hurt me, but more because he thought it didn't matter and stopped worrying about the consequences. How our marriage went on that long in that state is still amazing to me. I guess you just get used to some things and then it becomes the new normal."

Henry pondered that a bit. "So, you decided it was time to leave him?" Zin frowned. She didn't want to have to go over this territory right now.

"He kind of forced my hand. He cheated on me, and I caught him."

"Hmmm." Henry frowned. He watched the traffic trickle by. "I have been here about two weeks, and I can say that I do not understand most people."

"You and me both." She turned to Henry, "So, have you seen enough to make up your mind about humanity? You still think humankind was worth it? Or maybe you never did."

"I have not made up my mind, and I have not formulated an opinion on whether or not humanity was a net benefit. However, I am waiting for more data points to come in." Henry paused and then called out, "Our minute starts now." Zin stood up and Henry followed suit, turning toward downtown to watch the world go by. A handful of cars were crawling along Summit Avenue, a couple bicycles mixed in, folks who were working late and leaving downtown. There were a few people out for an evening walk, most seemingly tuned out with earbuds in their ears or looking down at a phone. Zin hugged herself a bit to warm up. After a bit, Henry called out, "Time."

"Well, that was pretty uneventful," said Zin.

"Yes, I agree. We did not see much human interaction."

"I don't know where you're going to get your data points. Half of the time we don't see anything happening."

"There is usually something I can observe. But tomorrow we need to meet where we will see people."

"Okay, let's meet at Como Lake one more time. Can you meet at 4:30? Same place as before?"

"Yes, I can do that."

"Okay. I'm getting a little chilled. Gotta get home and find that fantastic meal that's waiting for me in the freezer." Henry looked at her closely.

"That was sarcasm, was it not?"

"Now you're getting it, Henry. So, do you need me to give you a ride?"

"No, I am fine."

"All right, mystery man. I will see you tomorrow." She headed down the stairs and to the church parking lot. After crossing the street, she glanced back to make sure Henry wasn't following her, but he was out of sight already. Zin wandered back to her car, deep in thought. The church at this hour wasn't a good place to watch people. He had chosen the location so they could talk about her situation. Maybe he wasn't as clueless as he seemed to be.

Zin headed home to an empty house, which made her a little sad. She poured herself a glass of wine, turned on the TV, and found the series she had started to watch. She glanced at her phone and noticed a couple voice messages. The first was her mother, asking what time Zin could be over for Easter dinner. The second was Rick, saying that he was going to come over and get some stuff tomorrow. Zin deleted that voicemail with a flourish of her thumb. She checked her email and saw that there was one from Carol, the woman running the social justice committee at church.

Hello. Our stint as hosts for Project Hope has started, but we are getting a little desperate, as we don't have anyone to staff the overnight position Saturday night. We still need two volunteers. I know it is Easter, which might make it very hard for you, but please consider helping out if you can. Call me at the number below if you think you can take this shift.
Carol

Zin sipped her wine and thought about this. She tried to find a good reason why she couldn't help, but try as she might, no good answer emerged. She sat, looking at the email for a few minutes until she finally called her parents, doing it quickly so she couldn't talk herself out of it.

"Hello?"

"Hi Mom."

"Oh, hi, Zin. I was just thinking about you. I was wondering what time you would be able to come out for Easter dinner?"

"I think any time works."

"Okay, let's plan on one o'clock."

"Sure, that's fine."

"So how are you doing? I heard there was a lockdown at your school. It was on the news. But they said it was someone who was there by mistake or something."

"Yeah, it was nothing. Just a mistake."

"I bet that's scary. What do you do when that happens? Lock your doors and hide?"

"Pretty much. Lock the doors. Lock the windows and pull the shades. Go sit in a corner. It's a little scary."

"That makes me sick, thinking about it. I'm so glad it was nothing. There are so many crazy weirdos out there. You never know. There's always the story about those loners that no one suspected to be violent, and then they do something awful. But someone should have noticed something."

Zin closed her eyes and planted her palm on her face. "Yup. Crazy stuff," she answered, changing the subject as fast as she could. "So, how are you guys?" Zin listened to the latest news, which included gossip about a cousin of Zin's who was expecting a baby and the man in question was no longer part of the scene. When Zin heard a lull in the conversation, she jumped in.

"Say, is Dad around? I was going to ask him something."

"Oh?" Judy's surprise wasn't masked well. "Okay. Ummm, let me see. I think he was reading the paper in the living room. Let me get him." Zin listened as her mom walked through their house. She immediately had pangs of regret. This was not a good idea. What was she thinking? She did not need this right now. She had enough problems of her own.

Her dad picked up the "Zin? Everything okay?" he started, a worried voice permeating the line. *I obviously don't talk to dad often enough.*

"Uhhh, yeah. Umm, I just had a question for you. About my car. Ummm, how do you know when to buy new tires?" It was all that she could think of, but it did the trick. Her dad told her about tread depth, something about a penny and Lincoln's head, and something called a tread wear indicator. He seemed happy to be needed, and she thanked him and got herself off the phone. It made sense. This was not the time for her to be doing these kinds of things. This was time for her to take care of number one. But as she told herself this, she couldn't help wondering about Henry, what he might say about this, and where he might be sleeping tonight.

23

Thursday afternoon, Zin parked at the Como Lake parking lot, grabbed her water bottle, and walked to the pavilion to look for Henry. It was a nice day. She was now starting a long weekend, and she felt the need for a walk. She tied her running shoes a little tighter and stretched lightly before looking around for Henry. He wasn't the athletic type, but she could probably make him power walk with her on this, their last session together. All day she had been thinking about the fact that this was her last scheduled meeting with Henry. He was an enigma to be sure, and despite knowing and talking to him for ten straight days, she was still confused. She had originally pegged him as someone with Asperger's Syndrome, a soul that didn't need the social interaction that others might crave—at least in the way she was familiar with, and one who missed the usual social queues. But that wasn't quite right. He became more interested in her after a bit, and was obviously interested in others, apparently even talking to strangers. And their relationship was, from what she could tell, completely platonic. She had expected that he would hit her up for money by now, and although she had bought him dinner a couple times, it didn't feel like he was working toward asking for money. So, what would Henry do today? Would he cut off their relationship cold? Deep down, she feared that he would. Rejected by a homeless person! She didn't know if her ego could handle that.

Zin walked up into the open pavilion to get a view of the lake below. Lots of people were milling about, but she couldn't see Henry, which was surprising as he was usually attired in something attention grabbing. She scanned back and forth for a bit until she noticed a person whom she had dismissed before. There, at the end of one of the docks, standing perfectly still, was a man in a light blue suit and a crazy blonde head of hair. Zin smiled and headed down to the docks.

"Nice suit," she said, as she approached Henry. Henry whipped around with a huge grin on his face.

"It is," he said, like a five-year-old girl with a new party dress. Zin inspected Henry; his suit was lightweight, pale, and pretty blue, he had a red Iron Man t-shirt under the suit coat, and he was wearing black canvas hi-top sneakers. The suit looked like it had been around the block once or twice, but Zin had to admit—it was a good look. Zin peered down at her stretchy pants and polyester workout shirt.

"I feel a little underdressed," she said.

"Oh, it is fine," answered Henry, seriously. "No one will notice you."

Not if I'm standing next to you, thought Zin. "I feel like walking today. So, you might need to power walk with me."

"I can do that." They headed out around the lake, the late afternoon sun warming them quickly.

"I'd ask you where you got the suit, but I suspect you wouldn't tell me, anyway."

"I have to keep some secrets," answered Henry, not being coy at all, but serious as usual. Zin brought up the subject that was at the top of mind.

"So, this is session number ten."

"Yes."

"So, what happens now?"

"Well, according to our plan, after we do our tenth observation, we will document our scores and see what we think of mankind."

"Yup. And then what happens?"

"I still need to finish my research. This is information for my study."

"Okay, but I guess I was wondering more about you. What happens next for you? Will I see you again?"

"As I said before, I will be leaving this city on Sunday and will move to do more observations in another city. So, no. I do not think we will see each other again. But you never can know." Zin frowned. She had hoped that he would drop his story, or he'd say something that left a glaring hole in it, but he had kept the same story, and it looked like he was sticking to it.

"That's too bad. Well, hopefully I'll get a good mention in your study."

"You will not be mentioned by name."

"Of course. Not sure why privacy matters here, but I'll go with it." They walked along briskly. After a minute or two of silence, Henry asked Zin a question in a quiet voice.

"Zin, are you embarrassed by me?"

Zin was caught off guard and didn't respond immediately, before asserting herself. "No, no. Of course not."

"Well, there are times when I feel as if you are." Zin shook her head.

"No, Henry. You're just...unique, that's all. And sometimes I'm not expecting it."

"Hmmpf." Henry was silent for a bit before calling out, "our time begins in one minute," without looking at a timepiece. Zin climbed a little hill off the path and plunked down on a bench with a nice view of the walking trail. Henry followed her to the bench, sitting stiffly and attentively in his blue suit.

"It is time," announced Henry. Zin sat back on the bench, legs and arms crossed, taking it all in. Down below, a tall, lean, woman jogger in a running jacket and blonde ponytail huffed down the trail and past them, pushing a stroller with a toddler bundled thickly in its hold. An older couple in heavy coats, him in a wool flat cap and her with a scarf, meandered along the trail in the opposite direction of the jogger. Two heavy-set women in sweatpants, sweatshirts, and bright white running shoes came along behind the older couple, chatting happily as they power walked, swinging their arms. After a bit, a thin, bearded young man came along, talking on his phone, a little boy on a 12-inch bike with training wheels churning madly along in front of him. Finally, a middle-aged woman in glasses and running pants jogged along slowly, carrying a white trash bag. She rounded the corner and then veered off the trail, picked up a Styrofoam cup, threw it in her bag, and then returned to the trail, jogging at a pace that wasn't faster than Zin's brisk walk.

"That is the end of our minute," said Henry. They both sat in silence, watching the world below. Zin, at least, was a little sad that it was over. She sat forward and turned to Henry.

"How about a last meal together? There's a little cafe just a couple blocks from here. My treat."

"But now is the time to do our assessment."

"We can walk and talk. Or eat and talk."

Henry considered it skeptically. "Okay. I think that would work." He stood up and Zin led him across the street. "Do you have your notes?" Zin gave him an apologetic shrug and just tapped her head.

"It's all right here." Zin led them around a corner and up the street.

"All right," said Henry, all business. "How did you rate our first minute?"

Zin sighed. He wanted to get to business. No small talk, apparently. She thought about it for a moment and then remembered it. "Oh, that day. Yeah. You showed up at my school unannounced and surprised me. Definitely not good."

"So that was negative?"

"Yup. Definitely."

"Okay. Day two. Do you remember that one? We met at the church?"

"No, you surprised me again outside the church," she corrected. "At night. When I was alone."

"You knew that I was coming."

"Whatever."

"What is your rating of that minute?" Zin looked up and

scratched her chin.

"Hmmm, I don't remember seeing much of anything." She thought some more. "Nope. I couldn't say good or bad."

"So, neutral then?"

"I guess so."

"Okay. Day three. It was a Thursday, and we went for a walk at Como Lake."

"Damn, you have a good memory."

"Thank you."

"Let's see. I think I remember fighting with Rick beforehand, but that wasn't during our minute. Just saw a few joggers if I remember. Not much going on. Probably neutral again."

"Hmmm," said Henry. "Are you sure you did not take any notes?"

"No." Zin pointed to a cafe at the corner of the next block and then made a beeline toward it.

"Okay. Day four."

"Well, that would be the Friday night we went down to the boulevard and watched traffic."

"That is correct."

"I remember that being negative. That homeless person in the median asking for money and no one stopping." She shot a glance at Henry to see if he reacted to the mention of a homeless man. He didn't appear fazed.

"All right. Another negative." They had arrived at the little cafe, with a couple small tables with umbrellas on the sidewalk and an artsy sign above the door. Zin was suddenly very conscious about the fact that they looked like the odd couple. Henry was oblivious, as usual. The cafe was mostly empty, and they grabbed a seat by the window.

"Okay. Day five."

"Can we get our orders in first, so we aren't interrupted?" Henry frowned.

"Yes." He studied the menu but quickly set it down, looking around for a waitress. Zin watched him. It didn't appear that he had looked at the menu. Zin eyed what she wanted on the menu and then set it down. The waitress was slow to come, and Zin picked up her phone, scrolling through social media, frowning, and not looking up.

"You seem to be upset by something you are looking at," said Henry. Zin put her phone down and looked up, embarrassed to have gotten so absorbed.

"Oh, it's nothing," she said. "Just someone posting nonsense. Just makes me mad that there are so many idiots out there that go unchecked."

Henry thought about it. "Do you think the person who posted this is representative of most people? Or does it just get a lot of attention?"

Zin wasn't sure what to say, but the waitress came over to the table at that moment and took their orders. Zin got a Caesar chicken wrap and a side salad, and Henry copied her order. As soon as she left, Henry was back to keeping score.

"Okay. Day five. We went to the Mall of America." Zin squeezed her eyes shut, trying to pin down a memory that was flitting by, just out of reach, but it proved too elusive.

"Sorry, I can't remember much about that day. Can you jog my memory a bit? Was there anything that happened?" Henry looked at her with a mild scowl of disapproval.

"We met in the amusement park area…"

"You mean I saved your ass from the mall cops," interrupted Zin. Henry just looked at her as if she had spoken gibberish.

"And after that, we went upstairs and sat on the bench in the east wing. There were hundreds of people visible during our minute."

"Oh, yeah, yeah, yeah. It's coming back to me. Oh yeah, there was this sad older lady who looked all by herself. That got me down." Henry raised his eyebrows.

"So, your assessment?"

"I don't know. I guess it was a little negative. Maybe neutral."

"You must choose a rating: good, bad, or neutral."

"Gee! Okay, neutral."

"Fine." Henry was all business. "Day six."

"The Twins Game. That was a fun day, wasn't it?" answered Zin, brightly.

"Yes, I enjoyed it immensely. I especially liked Cracker Jacks. With the little prize in the box."

"And then you go and jump on a bucket and make a scene in the middle of all those people leaving the game. I couldn't believe you! But it looked like it worked. That guy was certainly happy."

"Yes, Marcus is a good person."

"Wow, you remember his name."

"You did not?"

"No, and I don't imagine anyone else would have either, so I'm not going to feel guilty about it."

"And your rating for that day?"

"Well, it was positive, although I must point out that you manipulated the situation—we weren't exactly watching as objective observers."

"I will note your qualified response." Zin chuckled to herself. He probably would. Of course, what was she thinking? He's not going to be writing a report tonight, he's probably going to be sleeping under a bridge. Henry plowed on.

"Day seven. That was Monday when I met you in your classroom."

"Ha! Met me? You mean, when you sneaked into school, caused a major disturbance that brought the school into a lockdown mode and brought half the Saint Paul police force into my room, and caused me to deal with dozens of irate parents, a couple calls from school board members, and interviews with police and my boss? That day?" Henry's eyes looked away for a second and then back.

"Umm, yes. That day."

"Yeah. Not so positive."

"You mean…"

"Negative!" Zin looked up to see the waitress had arrived with their food. They took a few bites, Henry appearing pensive. She watched him until he looked up from his food.

"Okay. Day eight. We met at the school again."

"Yeah, you never told me what the hell you were thinking, coming back into the school when half of the people in school were looking for you. That was..." she stopped herself, "not a good idea."

"I am sorry to have upset you so much. I thought our meetings were important."

"They were, but for Pete's sake, couldn't you have, I don't know, been a little more flexible with your schedule?"

"That would have ruined the randomness of the experiment," Henry replied, hands in lap, looking like a boy that had just been scolded for spilling his milk. Zin just shook her head.

"Who is Pete?"

"Huh?"

"You said, *for Pete's sake*?"

"That's just an expression, Henry. It means exasperation, or frustration at the situation."

"Oh. Henry ventured back to the topic at hand. "And your rating of that time?"

"I was furious. But I guess, mankind was...whatever. Neutral, I guess."

"Okay. Day nine."

"What day was that?"

"Yesterday."

"Oh, yeah. Seems like longer ago. That's right, we went to the cathedral where we first met. I don't remember seeing much of anything during our minute." She looked over at Henry. He gave her a non-committal shrug. "Okay, call it neutral."

"And that brings us to today."

"Well, just a bunch of joggers and walkers. Not much going on. I guess I'd have to say neutral." Henry put down his fork and sat back in his chair, glaring at Zin. "What?" asked Zin.

"Neutral? Really?"

"Yes," she answered. "Why is that so strange?" Henry sat back from the table and folded his arms.

"What about the jogger with the garbage bag?"

"Her? She's down there all the time. I see her around a lot."

"So, this is a woman who uses her free time to pick up garbage in her community and you do not see that as a positive?"

Henry's voice was rising.

"Sure, yeah, you're probably right. Not sure it matters. What was my score? Is mankind worth it?"

"If it was up to you, no, mankind would not be worth it. You had six of the times marked as neutral, three as negative, and only one was positive." Zin gave a little shrug. Henry shook his head.

"You obviously do not care." Henry's face flushed, his mouth a grim line.

"I said I was wrong about the last one. You're right, that one should have been positive."

"That is all?"

"What do you mean? You were there. You saw what I saw. What would you have rated those days?"

Henry's nostrils flared. "Seven positive, one negative, two neutral."

"What? How could that be? What about the school lockdown?"

"Your school was in danger. People were scared. And the entire school and police force worked together to make sure that all of the children were safe. And when they found me, they asked me tough questions, but they did not harm me. They did not treat me poorly. You did not lose your job for your association with me. I thought everyone acted admirably." Zin sat, arms crossed.

"What was so great about the Mall of America?"

"There were hundreds of people, every size, shape, color, religion, and culture, from different communities, cities, even countries, all intermingling peacefully in one common place. I think that is a wonderful thing."

"Hmmpf," snorted Zin, eyes rolling up at the ceiling. She eyed Henry who obviously had pent up frustration. "What?"

"This makes me very upset," he replied, the disappointment etched with anger. "I could have felt much better about my assessment. Instead, I do not know what to think."

"Whatever. You're right. I'm changing my score."

"Zin, it does not work that way. This was not only about

what we saw. It was also about how it was perceived, by you and by me. And I cannot ignore what I perceived."

Zin set her jaw and stared at Henry. "Christ, Henry. You know what? Get over it. I'm sick and tired of this stupid game. You've dragged me all over the place, followed me, scared me, nearly got me fired—I don't give a rat's ass what the damn score is! It doesn't take a stupid science experiment to figure out that mankind's pretty messed up—just turn on the news some night. So can we be done with this?"

Henry's gaze dropped to the table in front of him, and he sat quietly for a long moment. Then he stood up and held out his hand toward Zin who shook it, confused. "It is time I left. Thank you for helping me with my assessment this past week. It was quite…enlightening." He headed toward the door.

Zin watched Henry leave. She was not in the mood to apologize for anything, but she couldn't just let him walk off like that, so she got up and ran out onto the sidewalk. "Henry, wait!" she called, jogging to catch up to him.

Henry stopped and turned back toward her. He looked at her with cold eyes before softening a bit. "I am sorry if I was short with you today."

"No, it's me. I'm stupid. Come back inside. Let's finish the meal."

"No, I think it is time for me to move on." They stood, considering each other for a long moment.

"Are you going to be okay?"

"Yes," he replied. "Thank you for asking. And thank you for helping me the last ten days. I wish you much luck. Goodbye." He turned and started walking away down the sidewalk. Zin watched him go. She was about to call out to him when she heard a familiar voice from behind.

"Zin?" Zin turned around to find Camille Sutton, a woman she used to work with years ago. She was walking her beagle and watching Henry leave.

"Camille! Good to see you."

"You, too. I just saw you and had to say hi. She looked back at Henry. "I wasn't interrupting anything, was I?" Zin glanced back at Henry, waving it off.

"No, no. Just...just a homeless man, looking for a dime," she said. The two exchanged updates before Camille turned away. Zin glanced back to the restaurant window and caught the waitress's eye and decided she had better get back before they make an issue of it. She scanned the street, trying to find Henry one last time, but he was gone.

"Goodbye Henry," she said softly. Zin stood and stared at the empty sidewalk, shivering as the last bit of color left the sky, the guilt sitting squarely in her gut, wondering if she had become the callous, bitter woman she always prayed she'd never be.

24

Zin wound her way home, but couldn't stop fretting all evening, wondering what would happen to Henry, feeling bad about how they left things. She went to bed but tossed and turned, cycling through worry after worry, question after question. In the dead of the night, every worry was amplified. The divorce would leave her broke and never to find another partner. Her recklessness with Henry would cost her her job. And somehow worst of all, she felt guilty for letting Henry down. She resolved that she would go find him in the morning to make amends, after which she finally was relieved of her ghosts and was able to sleep.

When morning came, she felt dull and had a fatigue headache, but at least she had a quiet day to recover. The monsters that frightened her in the middle of the night didn't seem quite so bad. She told herself that she was being ridiculous for feeling so guilty about Henry—she had befriended him, after all, which was more than she thought most people would do— and set herself at the dining room table to get some grading done. But by mid-morning, she found her mind wandering again, and by noon she was too distracted to get anything done. Her rational brain kept arguing that it was silly, that he would be all right, and that it was improbable that she would find him, anyway, but eventually it gave in because the emotional side of her brain wouldn't let the matter rest.

Zin drove to downtown St. Paul and started walking around. St. Paul isn't a big city, and she figured she could hit the most likely spots. She started at the homeless shelter for men, where a couple dozen single men had started to congregate a couple hours before the doors were to open for the evening meal. She walked past the group, trying to scope them out without looking at them. Henry didn't appear to be in the group, but she expected they'd recognize him if she asked, so at the end of the block she circled back and mustered the courage to go talk to some of them. A lean, middle-aged black man with a short grey beard was sitting on a short block wall, talking to a couple other men, his backpack by his side. He was somewhat close and seemed approachable, so she chose to start with him. She was trying to decide how to approach the man when one of the men in the group noticed Zin and nodded towards her. The other two men immediately stopped talking and stared at Zin, who was now approaching gingerly. Zin no longer knew who to address, so she started to address them all, looking at each one in turn as she spoke, finishing with the man on the wall.

"Ummm, hi. Say, I was wondering if you could help me? I'm looking for someone?" The man on the wall looked at her a little suspiciously.

"Yeah? Who're you lookin' for?"

"Well, his name is Henry."

"Henry what?"

"Well, I don't know," she answered. But I thought he might be...I thought he might hang out here. From something he said," she added quickly.

"I don't know any Henry." He looked at his buddies. "You guys know any Henry?" They both shook their heads in silence, still unsure about this woman. "What's he look like?"

"Well, he's, uh, well, he's white," she said, "about five ten. Messy blonde hair. Teeth a little crooked. He dresses a little funny sometimes. If you ever heard him talk, he'd sound kinda funny too—not funny, just...very formal." Her voice trailed off. It sounded preposterous when she described it, and the men seemed to pick up on that, the thinnest of smiles starting to appear on each of their faces. They exchanged glances and the older man on the wall answered for them.

"Nope. I'm pretty sure I'd remember a guy like that."

"Okay. Well, thanks anyway," answered Zin, feeling a little relieved. She had been anxious to engage a group of single, homeless men and now felt a little silly that she had been so nervous. She turned and started to walk away.

"Good luck," the man called out to her. "Hope you find him."

Zin went into government buildings and roamed through the skyway connecting the buildings above the street. She trudged down to the train depot and asked around there, and down along the river to see if anyone was hanging out under bridges. She asked security guards and shopkeepers, but the answer was always the same—they didn't recognize the guy.

Zin wandered around until she noticed it was late and she was getting hungry. She was also chilled by this point, so she stopped at a little cafe, sat at a table next to the window, and had a sandwich as she watched people pass on the street. By now, the emotional side of her brain was appeased. She had tried, but it wasn't meant to be. She still felt guilty, and only time would let that heal. It was so strange that this man had come into her life for a very short period of time, was now gone, and she'd never see him again, but he seemed to have left her a lesson she'd never forget. She wondered if she would ever tell anyone of this time with Henry. It sounded absurd and foolish.

Zin left the restaurant and headed back to her car. The sun was starting to set but the storm clouds had assembled to the west covering most of the sky, and the sun was fighting to hold a thin, deep pink line at the horizon, a seemingly futile effort against the pending darkness. She could hear the bells of St. Paul's Cathedral starting to clang, calling people to the Good Friday mass. For some reason, the bells seemed to ring out a death toll for the sunset, and it made Zin feel a little lonely and sad.

Zin headed home and plopped down on the couch, thinking she'd watch a movie. But after scrolling through hundreds of options, nothing seemed to match her mood. She found an old TV series she'd seen a dozen times already and started playing from the beginning again. She picked up her phone and started scrolling through posts, all of which made her more depressed. Finally, she checked her email. She saw another letter from her social justice committee at church.

Hi Folks,

I just wanted to give you an update. We had a last-minute cancellation for a Saturday night host for Project Hope. We now need two overnight hosts. I know it is last minute and not a great night, but if you or someone you know could help us out in this pinch, we would all be very grateful. Let me know right away if you can help.

Thanks again,

Carol

Zin put the phone down next to her on the couch and gave it a hard stare, as if it had conspired with Carol to send this email. She turned this over in her head again. Hadn't she already decided this wasn't the right time for her? She got up to grab a glass of water, and when she came back, the phone was still lying there, looking up at her.

"This is your fault," she said as she picked up the phone and dialed her parents' number.

"Zin?" answered her mom, sounding surprised. "How are you doing? Is everything okay?"

"Oh, I'm fine, fine," she said, pointing her remote at the TV and hitting the mute button. "Just hanging out. How are you? What were you up to today?"

"Oh, not much. I had a hair appointment this morning, and then I made your father take the afternoon off and go pick out paint with me."

"Paint? What are you painting now?"

"We're redoing the dining room. I hate that lame mustard

color in there." She paused a bit. "So, what can I do for you tonight?"

"Actually, I was hoping to talk to Dad again."

"Twice in one week? This is a record. I'll go grab him." She heard her mom call to her dad, and then heard him pick up.

"Well, hello Zin. Did you end up getting new tires?"

"No. Not yet. But if I have any more questions about them, I'll call you. I, uhh, just wanted to ask you something."

"Okay. Well then, what's up?"

"Are you free Saturday night?"

"Umm, I'd have to check with your mom. You know, she runs the calendar around here. But I think so. Why? What are you thinking about?"

"So, there's this thing our church is doing. A temporary homeless shelter in the basement of the church. They need volunteers to staff it overnight and no one has volunteered for Saturday night. I was thinking of volunteering, and I wanted to know if you would do it with me?" Zin was met by a moment of silence. "Dad?"

"Oh, umm, yeah. So. Can you tell me a little more about this?" Zin cringed at the delay tactics.

"Well, the county relies on other organizations to provide temporary homeless shelters, so there is this program where churches take turns hosting some of the families. So, there would be cots and little room partitions in the church basement. We'd put out snacks for bedtime, help get things wound down, and then put out breakfast in the morning."

"Hmmpf. So, we'd turn out the lights, go home, and be back bright and early the next day?"

"Not quite. We'd have our own cots and stay overnight in case anyone needed anything."

"Oh." More silence. Clearly, this was a road too far. Zin gave him the out.

"Yeah, I know. Very last minute. You probably already have plans. And sleeping on the cot is going to wreak havoc on your back. Say, don't worry about it. I'm sure they'll find another volunteer. It's no big deal, really."

"Yeah, I don't know what I'd be doing. Maybe something else might be better? If you want to do something like that in the future, we could plan it." He was trying.

"Sure. Listen, I've gotta run. But I'll see you on Easter. Okay?"

"Yes. See you then."

"Bye, Dad."

"Bye, Zin." Zin put down the phone. She wasn't sure if she was relieved or disappointed. She thought it would be a good experience for him, for both of them, really. Henry had made her remember that they lived in a bubble of prosperity that prevented them from seeing the world of many people who lived around them. Her dad was always complaining about people on "the dole". She had thought it might be good for him to meet someone who needed help.

Zin started composing a response to Carol's email when her phone buzzed. She checked and saw that it was her parent's number.

"Hello?"

"Hi, Zin." Her dad's sheepish voice responded, the usually gruff, low rumble of his baritone softened. "Just me again. I was thinking. About that shelter thing. I talked to your mom, and we don't have anything going on Saturday night. I was thinking I could do that thing with you. If that's all right." Zin stuttered with a little shock.

"Ummm, yeah. Of course. That would be great. I'm sure it won't be hard—just show up and they'll tell us what to do. I think the families pretty much take care of themselves."

"I'm sure it will be fine. What time do I need to be there? It's at your church, right?" The business dad had returned, more confident, needing details. Zin filled him in. Do they need to bring anything? No. Pack anything special? No. Can he bring treats? Sure (that surprised her). What time were they done in the morning? Probably by 8:30 or 9. Are there other volunteers overnight? No. Satisfied, he made arrangements to meet Zin at her house and they hung up. Zin sat back and took it in. She was more than a bit surprised. It may have been her mom pushing, but Dad was showing up, so she'd give him the credit. She hadn't had more than an hour of alone time with her dad in many years. There was likely a reason for that. This volunteer opportunity could be very good for them, but it could also go south fast. He was trying. Maybe she could play nice.

25

Jay was pacing again. It was 2:30 p.m. on a Saturday, and he was holding his second vodka and tonic in a little red plastic cup (nothing else was clean). It was not something he would normally be having on an early Saturday afternoon, but he needed a drink to calm his nerves. He took a deep breath and closed his eyes; he was exhausted from another night of tossing and turning, and the insomnia from the week was taking its toll. Jay took another swallow and tried to ignore the implications of what he was thinking. He was just meeting a congregant. Stop making it into more than it was.

Jay noticed that, although it wasn't hot, he had already perspired through his t-shirt armpits, so he trekked upstairs to his bathroom, pulled his shirt and t-shirt off, grabbed a towel, patted himself dry, and then threw on some deodorant before heading back to his bedroom to pull out clean shirts. Then back to the bathroom one more time, where he opened the medicine cabinet, pulled out a little bottle of cologne, and spritzed it into the air in front of him.

Back in the kitchen, Jay grabbed the red cup and took one last swig, then marched to the front closet, grabbed a grey hoodie (he thought it would look younger and more fun than his tan spring coat), took a deep breath, and headed out the front door.

When he got to Zin's block, Jay slowed again. He stood at the corner and surveyed Zin's house before steeling himself and proceeding. He rapped on the door and waited, his heartbeat noticeable in his ears. A few seconds later, Zin appeared in the door, dressed in casual black leggings and a colorful blouse.

"Hey, Father. Good to see you, she said. She waved him in. "Make yourself at home."

"Please, call me Jay."

"I'll try," she said, leading him to her kitchen where she turned to her cupboard and pulled out two wine glasses. "I'll probably feel guilty every time I do, however. I'm gonna have a glass of wine. Can I get you anything?"

"A glass of wine sounds good," answered Jay, noticing that the table wasn't quite the mess it was last time. He took a seat.

"Red okay?"

"Sure." Zin poured a couple glasses and sat one down in front of Jay, then sat near him at the end of the table, legs crossed.

"I feel like this is exactly where we finished off last time I was here," said Jay.

"Pretty much. Except I was crying more that day. I'm sorry about that, by the way."

"You don't have to apologize for anything. I know you must be going through some tough times. You seem to be holding up pretty well."

"I have my good days and not so good days," she answered, looking at her glass. "Maybe that's true for everyone."

"I think it is," answered Jay. Both of them looked down at their glasses and the quiet got uncomfortable.

"So, you wanted to meet?"

"Ummm, yeah. I mean, I like to reach out to members who have kind of fallen off the radar. Just to connect. I'm not trying to do any kind of arm-twisting or guilt trip. But you never know what's going on in people's lives, and it's good to hear. Most of the time I can't reach people, but sometimes I do, and it is interesting. I mean, I like to know what's going on with them, and what is happening that has caused them to stop attending church. Sometimes it's just something like a move. Sometimes, people aren't happy with our church or the Catholic church, and they have complaints, maybe legitimate, and it is good to understand where they are coming from. Sometimes, people just have something big going on in their lives." He looked at Zin. "Like you." Then added. "Sorry, that was dumb—way too much information. Let me start over. I just wanted to check in." He gave a sheepish grin and Zin looked at him for a few seconds, trying to assess the situation.

"Well, thanks for checking in. As for falling off the radar— to be honest, I go hot and cold on church in general. This was happening before the Rick thing, but after that, I just wanted to hide from pretty much everyone. I still am hiding. I hate bringing up the whole separation thing, so doing stuff like going to church means people who know me are going to talk about me, or ask me about it, and I'm not ready to deal with that right now."

Jay nodded. "I understand. You are embarrassed, and you don't want anyone to know, or you are ashamed to be in that spot, so you just hide away." Jay looked down at his glass and swirled. Zin looked at him curiously.

"Yeah. That's basically right." She paused, but Jay didn't say anything. "You sound like this comes from experience?" Zin asked, raising her eyebrows in an invitation to divulge more. Jay looked at her with a wistful smile.

"Oh, I guess so," he said. Zin watched him but didn't say anything. Jay glanced up at Zin.

"What?"

"Well, you look like you were going to say something about being embarrassed and hiding."

"Ummm."

"Sorry. Didn't mean to push it. Never mind."

"No, it's okay. It's a long story."

"I'm not going anywhere," Zin sat back in her chair with a smile that said that she was intrigued. Jay looked away for a few seconds before turning back to Zin.

"So, I wasn't always going to be a priest," he said.

"No? Let me guess. You wanted to be a musician." Jay smiled and shook his head.

"Nope. Never could carry a tune. No, I was planning on being an accountant."

"Really?" Zin leaned forward, examining Jay, as if seeing something she hadn't noticed before. She tilted her head. "Hmmm, maybe? I dunno. I'm not sure I see it."

"I was always good with numbers, and it made sense to me. Or so I told myself. Anyway, that's what I studied in college."

"So, why aren't you an accountant?"

"Well, I had, what shall we say? A self-inflicted wound."

Zin looked at him. "Wound?"

"When you are wrapping up your schooling, you need to take certain tests. I was an okay student in college, but not a star or anything. And I was nervous about these tests. And...so I cheated," he said, looking up at Zin. "And I got caught."

Zin cringed. "Ouch."

"Yeah," Jay took a sip from his glass. "Looking back, I can't remember why I did it. It seems so long ago. I could try and explain it, but I don't think I can put myself in those shoes anymore. I have no idea why I did it. It doesn't even seem like it was me—maybe just something I remember from a movie or something. The more I think about that, the more I realize that people do change. You really become a different person over time."

"So, what happened?"

"I got expelled. Got kicked out, if I remember correctly, at least from the program. I don't think I actually have a degree— I don't think I technically finished. Honestly, once it happened, I just walked away from everything. I didn't tell anyone. I stopped opening letters from the school. I couldn't explain it to anyone, so I didn't tell anyone, even my friends."

"Your parents?"

"Nope. It was spring of my senior year, and I told my parents I was going on a road trip instead of going through commencement ceremonies, and I didn't want a graduation party. After that, I just pretended I was having a hard time getting a job, which was true, so I went to work at a sporting goods store for a couple of years. I got a cheap little apartment by myself and did my own thing. But that was lonely, and, I don't know, I guess it felt like I was wasting my time, wasting my talent."

"And how does one go from selling basketballs to being a priest?"

"I'm not sure how it happened. I think I had gone through every kind of possible career option in my head, and not much made sense, or else I just wasn't confident enough to go there, as if I would be called out in front of others as a liar and a cheat. I think I was always trying to find a way to earn back my respectability and somehow make up for that lost education. I always hated how I had wasted my education and disappointed people, and I felt so guilty carrying this secret around." Jay paused and took a drink before continuing.

"Somewhere along the line, the idea of the priesthood came along. I remember meeting someone who was in the seminary once and he was a decent guy and I think the idea kind of took root. It seemed a way to vindicate myself and gain the respect of my parents, who never said anything, but seemed disappointed that I gave up on everything after college. And I didn't need to lie about my past—it's not like a job where you have to lie on a resume about your degree. In fact, the faculty at the seminary were the first people I told about my cheating incident, and it felt good to finally tell someone. I don't know; it kind of felt right, like it was a penance and I wanted to pay." Jay took a sip of his drink and looked sheepishly at Zin. "So, there you have it. Probably all the wrong reasons to become a priest." Jay studied his shoes.

"I don't think so. You obviously wanted your life to matter. And you've found a way to make it so. I don't think that's the wrong reason at all."

Jay shook his head. "I don't know. I look at some people in the priesthood and they know what they are doing, and they know why they are there. And people respect them. I'm not like that."

"People respect you. A bunch."

"Not half the church leadership. Not some of my staff." Jay sat up. "You know, what, sorry. I shouldn't have said that. I'm sounding pitiful and ungrateful. I apologize."

"Aww, don't apologize. There are definitely a few curmudgeons in the mix at church. But I attended church a bit before, well, before I fell off. And I know that people like you. You have a great rapport with a lot of people. And the kids like you." Jay frowned and sat back, becoming more assertive.

"Listen, I appreciate the pep talk, but I didn't come here for a therapy session. I came to talk to you. And to listen." He made an abrupt change to a more cheerful tone. "So, what's happening with you? When I stopped by last time, you described Rick as your soon to be ex-husband."

"No, I said my soon to be asshole ex-husband."

"It sounds like we need to talk about forgiveness," Jay gave her a sly grin.

"Whatever." Zin rolled her eyes.

"Anyway, has anything changed with you two? Are you still of the mind that you need to be divorced?"

"Yup."

"And is he of the same opinion?"

"I really don't care," Zin answered, looking at Jay firmly.

"I know I'm not here to preach, although that is a bit ironic, and I don't have a lot of the background in this matter. I just want to point out that talking is important, even if it brings out the reality that you aren't able to save your marriage. At least you will both be heard and won't have any regrets."

"Listen, Father."

"Jay."

"Listen, Father Jay. I know you are trying to help. But you probably would think differently if you had the details."

"Maybe I would. Do you want to tell me any, or do you want to pass on that subject?" Zin took a drink and looked out the window, then back to Jay.

"Okay. So, here's the deal. Rick always traveled. He was a salesman for Michelson Tech. Technically, director of business something or other. Anyway, there were always excuses for being gone, either out of town or just entertaining in town. I would often see texts pop up on his phone from CJ, his assistant. I assumed it was just the details of events, etc., and didn't pay them much attention, although sometimes things just seemed...funny. I couldn't put a finger on it. Or maybe I chose not to look into it very hard because I didn't want to find out. Anyway, a couple of months ago, he was getting ready to catch a flight and his phone was sitting on the dresser in plain sight when I saw a text from CJ pop up—it said: *Loews—1204*. So, he's standing in the closet, getting dressed, and I sit down on the bed and grab a magazine and just start a conversation. Where are you headed? Cleveland, he says. I'm going to visit so-and-so manufacturing. How many nights? I ask. Just one. Be back tomorrow after work. I left it at that, so it didn't sound like I was snooping. He comes out of the closet. I don't even look up, just page through my magazine. He comes over to the bed, gives me a peck on the cheek, says he's gotta run. And I can smell his cologne, and he's looking kinda sharp, wearing nice pants and a sports coat. And I'm pretty sure if he was flying out this late to Cleveland, he wouldn't have any reason to dress up—he wouldn't get there 'til nine, ten o'clock."

"That sounds suspicious to me."

"Yeah. I think he was getting to the point where he didn't care if I found out—getting careless, maybe subconsciously or on purpose. So, I decide to see what flights are going to Cleveland that evening. I found a total of three, two which were leaving within the hour that he never could have caught, and the other was on some cheapo airline which I'm pretty sure he'd never stoop to use. And I look for Loew's hotel locations, and there isn't any in Cleveland, but there is in Minneapolis. So, I grab my coat and drive downtown to find the hotel. Of course, he's a good twenty minutes ahead of me, so I figure I should stake things out. I park and then go sit in the lobby of the Loews hotel, hiding behind a magazine off to the side. I don't know whether he's here or not, or if he'll come later or not, or what the deal is. I was tempted to go up to room 1204, but I figure if he's up to no good, it is too early to bust him."

"I just sit there for a while and am about to go up to the room when who walks into the lobby? Rick and CJ. They're meeting some business people. So, I play my best James Bond and follow them to a restaurant, and then to a basketball game. I can't go to the game, but curiosity is killing this cat, so even though I was scared to death, I go talk the front desk person into giving me a room key. I am his wife, after all. I went up to the room, and guess what I found?"

"Two suitcases?"

"Yup. Looked like an old married couple—toiletry bags in the bathroom, clothes hung up in the closet. Only difference was her lingerie was sexier than mine."

"So, there was no flight to Cleveland."

"Nope. Just going to a game on the company dime and shacking up with his assistant."

"Oh boy. I'm sorry Zin."

"Not your fault." They sat in silence for a moment.

"So how did you approach Rick?"

"I didn't, really. I wrote "Goodbye" on some hotel stationery and left it under the covers in the middle of the bed." She paused and looked at the ceiling. "Oh, and I left a lot of ice with the note. I'm guessing they had a fun little surprise when they hit the sack."

Jay covered his eyes with his hand and chuckled. "Yeah, that would tend to put a damper on the evening." He shook his head. "I'm sorry. I shouldn't be laughing."

Zin ignored him. "He called me right away, too. He had this story that CJ wasn't staying in his room; she had just brought a change of clothes from work so she could go to the game without driving home first. I hung up on him."

"So, he denies it?"

"He denied it at first. Then he made it sound like it was just a one-time thing, no big deal. And for a couple days, I tried to downplay it. Not deny it, but pretend it was a mistake, one that a lot of people make. But then, I got thinking about all the travel and special projects, and I knew it wasn't good. I tried to do some digging. I see him connected to her on Facebook, so I look at her account and go back through her pictures and start finding a lot of pictures from the same places and times that Rick had been to when he traveled. And this goes back a long time. I press him on it, and then he changes his tune and says it was for a 'few months'—which is a load of b.s. I'm guessing it was years. And he claims it meant nothing. Said it was like getting a massage."

"Well. I guess I understand that you aren't wanting to talk to him right now. I'd understand if this was something you couldn't come back from."

"You know, he pissed me off. Made me feel like dirt. Still makes me angry to think of it." She paused, tilted her head, and stared out the window for several seconds before looking back at Jay. She seemed to be fighting back tears. "But I think I've realized something that I hadn't admitted before. It doesn't bother me that I'm losing him. I'm depressed about everything else, but not that. I don't see him in my life anymore. I don't know what happens next for me, which is scary, but I know it isn't going to be with him."

"Interesting. Does he want to stay married?"

"He claimed he did. I think he just wanted the best of both worlds. And didn't want me to take half of his money. When he found out I wasn't interested, then he got nasty. So, no. We're ending this."

"And you told him to move out?"

"Yeah. He didn't like that. But I needed him to be somewhere else."

Jay nodded his head. He took another sip of his wine and realized it was empty. He started to reach for the bottle, but Zin beat him to it, pouring him the rest of the bottle.

"Thanks," he said.

"Yeah, so that's my world right now."

Jay took a drink from his glass, and they looked at each other for a bit. "So, do you have anyone to talk to about this? It's important that you do."

"Well, I tried to see a shrink—that didn't work out well. I have a friend from work that I've been close to that I've started to open up to. At some point, I'll have to tell some or all of this to others. But maybe not quite yet...And I have my priest." She smiled at Jay who gave a soft chuckle.

"That's what I'm here for," he said.

"And you're cheaper than my shrink was."

"Hmmm, not if you tithe," he said, with a mischievous smile.

"I don't make enough right now for that to matter." There was a moment of quiet as they both sipped their wine. Jay sensed he should wrap it up.

"Well, I want you to know that if you ever need to talk—about anything—please, just give me a call. Any time. I mean it."

"Thanks, Father. I mean Jay. I might take you up on that some time."

Jay leaned in toward her. "You know..." He paused, looking.

"What?"

"Oh, nothing," Jay said, shaking his head and sitting back. The wine was clouding his judgement, but he knew this was not the time nor the place for what he was about to say.

"You can't leave me hanging like that!" Zin complained, but at that moment, they heard a loud, familiar voice coming from the porch.

"Well, Hello!"

26

Marvin paced outside of his Volvo in the church parking lot, looking at his watch. No one had shown up yet, although it was only a couple minutes after their planned meeting time. But still, timing could be everything, and he didn't want to screw this up. *Miranda should know better*, he thought. That woman was such a pain. It was an annoying coincidence that he had to deal with her on these church matters, as well as fooling around with her. Things would be much easier if those aspects of his life weren't intertwined, but in the end, that's how it all started, anyway, so no sense wishing that away now.

As if on cue, Miranda's big SUV turned into the parking lot, rumbling over next to him. She rolled down her window and leaned out.

"Hey, sexy."

Marvin winced. There was no one around, but she was so careless. This was going to be their undoing one day; he knew it. A little tan Buick pulled in after her and Barb Adler pulled herself out, walking over to the group with a frown on her face, wearing a blue fleece vest over a white turtleneck sweater. She acknowledged Miranda, who by now was standing next to Marvin.

"Miranda," she nodded. She turned to Marvin, a tight

grimace on her face. "So, Marvin. What's this about?" Marvin noticed two more cars were entering the parking lot.

"Just a minute. Let's get everyone here and then I'll let you know."

"Who's everyone?" asked Barb.

"William Leland and Deacon Ketterling from the archdiocese Parish Services department." Barb looked at Marvin with suspicion but didn't say anything. The other two men parked and walked up to the group. Marvin introduced the deacon to everyone. He had arranged to have two members of the parish council (himself and chair William Leland) and two staff (Miranda and Barb, the church administrator).

"So, what's going on?" asked William. Marvin glanced at Miranda and then faced the group.

"Miranda and I have become aware of a potentially disastrous situation that we want to deal with quickly and discreetly." A few eyebrows went up in the group. "We know how sensitive clergy abuse issues are these days, and we want to address it before it becomes a problem for the church."

Barb looked taken aback. "Clergy abuse? Father O'Brian?" She looked at Deacon Ketterling who stood quietly, arms crossed, listening to Marvin.

"I'm afraid so. Here is the situation. Miranda started observing that Father O'Brian was making arrangements to meet with a parishioner, a single woman, multiple times. At her house. I heard them arrange to meet once, myself."

"So?" Asked William.

"So, these arrangements didn't always sound...innocent," answered Marvin, figuring the embellishment was needed. He looked at Miranda who nodded in agreement. "And on one occasion, we observed them hugging." At this, William and Barbs expressions changed. Barb chimed in.

"So, you think he's having an affair with someone from the parish?"

"Yes."

"Who?"

"Zin McGuire."

Barb frowned. "You know, she's in the middle of a divorce. He's probably just giving them marriage counseling."

"Well, if he is, it's only with her, and the counseling includes hugs." Barb and William looked at each other. "And it goes without saying that having an affair with someone you are counseling is grounds for serious discipline in the church."

William followed up. "So, what are we doing here?"

"Zin and Father O'Brian are having another 'counseling' session, right now," replied Marvin, using air quotes. "We thought we should try to find out more of what's going on and get a few additional people to observe this."

"You've got to be kidding," replied Barb.

"No. How else are we going to get to the bottom of this quickly?" No one said anything. "Miranda and I can take you there. It's just a minute away. Miranda, can we pile into your vehicle? It's the biggest."

"Sure." She headed over to the big SUV and the group followed her except Barb, who stayed put, hands on her hips, until nearly everyone was in the car. She finally shook her head and muttered something as she climbed in the back. Deacon Ketterling was offered the front seat and settled into the leather seats, admiring the high-tech dashboard.

"Nice vehicle."

"Thanks. Yeah, it's my favorite toy. I got it a couple months ago." The deacon seemed to be processing something.

"What does your husband do for a living?"

"Oh, I'm not married. Never found the right man." Marvin saw Miranda trying to catch his eye in the rear-view mirror, but he ignored her. The deacon looked confused for a moment—likely unable to align the expensive vehicle with the part-time church bookkeeper's salary. Marvin crossed his fingers that the Deacon would let it go, and given that he didn't say any more about it, it seemed that he did. They drove the short distance to Zin's street, pulling over on the opposite side of the street, half a block away.

"Let's park here," said Marvin. He wanted to remain stealthy and this crew in the giant vehicle was not going to go unnoticed.

They got out of the car tentatively, Marvin waiting for them on the sidewalk.

"Okay, here's the situation. We think Father Jay is in the house right now. It's the green house, second from the end," he pointed. He started walking in that direction, the others following in a line.

"This is nuts," said Barb, trailing behind. Marvin ignored her. When they got to the corner of Zin's lot, he stopped and addressed them in a quiet voice.

"All right. So, the idea is to catch them maybe in...you know...a situation of some sort that would...make it clear what's going on, so to speak. So let's try to be quiet."

"We're spying on them? Really?" said Barb, shaking her head. "This is ridiculous. I'm heading back to church." Barb stomped away down the sidewalk.

"It's fine," he said. "I know she is close to Father Jay, and I'm sure this is hard for her," he said, trying to sound sympathetic. He slinked up to the side of the house, peeking in a window while the others hung back, looking confused.

Marvin returned to the group. "It was just a window to the staircase. Couldn't see anything." He studied the house, thinking. "Let's go up to the house," he said, still in a hushed voice. The others looked at each other and shrugged. Marvin opened the porch door slowly and tip-toed softly onto the porch, the others following suit. "Don't let the door slam," he whispered to Miranda at the end of the line. They all huddled behind Marvin, who was spying through the top window of the front door, standing on his toes to see. He watched for a few moments.

"I see them. They're sitting at the dining room table. Looks like they are drinking wine," he said with a tinge of excitement, his eyes gleaming as he turned back to the group. He looked at the big window that was facing into the porch and hunched over, motioning the others to follow. He then got on his knees and all four followed suit, crawling over to the big window which was wide enough for all of them to look into. Marvin peeked up just enough to see over the back of a chair that was placed in front of the window. Half of four heads slowly appeared above the window ledge. Inside, they could see Jay take a sip from a wine glass and Zin pouring the rest of the bottle into his glass. A few moments later, Jay leaned in toward Zin in a rather intimate way. All four held their breath, but Jay leaned back, looking away. None of them noticed the little man with glasses and dark, greasy hair, walking up the front steps. They all turned in unison as the porch door opened.

"Well, hello!" Patrick walked up behind them, beaming. Marvin and Deacon Ketterling jumped up immediately. Miranda tried to hop up but tipped back, toppling into William Leland, who fell backwards into a small table, knocking it over and crashing on top of it.

"Are you here to watch the game?" Patrick asked the group. "I'm a big Twins fan. They are starting out well this year, aren't they? I really like Ortega. He's starting today. He's from the Dominican Republic. Did you know that there are lots of big-league ball players from the Dominican Republic? They must play a lot of baseball there."

"Get up!" hissed Marvin to Miranda but didn't move to offer a hand. Miranda was shaking her wrist in pain and sitting on the floor, William was getting up and righting the table. Marvin looked around wildly for an escape route, but there was no way the four of them could move quickly enough and the funny man was blocking their exit. Out of the corner of his eye, he noticed that Zin and Jay had left the table and were approaching the front door. The door opened and Marvin decided on the spot what he had to do.

27

Jay tried to make sense of the scene. There on the porch were members of his church, his bookkeeper sitting on the floor, looking flustered and angry, a deacon from the archdiocese that he recognized but couldn't name, and most bizarre of all, Patrick, looking aghast. Patrick perked up when he saw Zin and Jay at the door.

"Hi, Father Jay! Hi Zin!"

"Uhhh, hi, Patrick," replied Jay. Turning back to the others, he noticed that three looked sheepish or embarrassed, but Marvin Schneider looked cross. "Miranda? William? Marvin?" He looked at the Deacon. "Deacon..." Jay remembered the face, but not the name.

"Deacon Ketterling," the man replied, nodding. "Jim Ketterling."

"Right," answered Jay. Zin looked up at Jay, then back at the group.

"Ummm. What's going on?" asked Zin. Marvin took charge.

"We came to see you." He looked at Jay. "To see both of you."

"Really?" asked Zin, still seeming baffled. She looked at the group, but no one said anything. "Well," she shrugged. "Come on in." She held the door and waved them in. Jay stepped aside to let the four from church file into the house, followed by Patrick. When they got inside, the group stood around the living room awkwardly, only Patrick plopped down comfortably in the middle of the couch.

"Have a seat," Zin pointed. Miranda started to move, but Marvin gave her a hard look.

"I think we'll just stand," said Marvin from across the room, arms crossed. Zin looked at Jay before turning back to Marvin.

"Okay then. To what do I owe this pleasure?"

Marvin assumed the role of interrogator. "We can't help but notice that you and Father Jay were enjoying each other's company today." Jay rolled his eyes and Zin's expression turned hard.

"Yeah. Father Jay was meeting with me about not being at church."

"I see," said Marvin. He looked at Jay. "I didn't know you took such an interest in lost sheep, Father." he said. Jay didn't reply. A number of things suddenly clicked for Jay, and he realized there might be some danger in this odd little situation. Marvin glanced at the dining room. "And it looks like you were enjoying a little wine with your meeting?" Marvin's head tilted, a hint of a smile appearing on his lips." Zin glanced back at the dining room table where an empty bottle stood next to two empty wine glasses.

"Yeah. I offered him a glass of wine. Thought it might be the nice thing to do."

"I'm sure it was," replied Marvin. "This isn't the first time you too have met for a glass of wine."

"Now wait," said Jay, shifting his feet. "Zin and I met to discuss how she felt about the church. And to talk about her divorce," he added, cringing ever so slightly, then glancing around the room. A couple eyebrows went up.

"Oh, yes. Ms. McGuire's divorce." Marvin looked at Zin with mock sympathy. "I'm very sorry to hear about that. I'm sure it is a difficult time. I'm glad that Father Jay has been able to provide you with...support."

"What's your point?" Zin asked, folding her arms across her

chest.

"So, you met once before this as well?"

"Yes. Jay and I met to talk about...stuff," she said.

"Oh? And when was that?"

"Last Saturday. And Patrick was here," she said, pointing at Patrick. "We watched the game together." Marvin eyed Patrick.

"Patrick?"

"Yes, Patrick," replied Zin.

"And you watched a baseball game. The three of you?"

"Yes."

"I see," Marvin, making it clear he didn't believe a word. "Well then. Other than that, you didn't meet another time?"

"Nope."

"Not even a week ago Thursday?" Zin looked confused. "Jay didn't visit you a week ago, Thursday. And you didn't hug him on the porch?"

"Huh?"

"Miranda and I happened to observe you that evening. And Jay was here, then, as well. And we observed you hugging him on the porch when he left." Marvin looked at Miranda, who nodded her head, a serious expression on her face.

Zin's expression hardened. "Happened to observe us? What the hell does that mean?"

"We happened to be driving by and saw you two."

"You two happened to be driving by?"

"Yes." William LeLand frowned and looked at Marvin now, but Marvin turned to Deacon Ketterling and kept going. "The point is, it appears that Father Jay has been taking advantage of someone who he should be counseling. I'm not sure that Ms. McGuire is making good choices right now—I can imagine that this is a stressful time for her, but..." Zin stepped forward and grabbed the back of a chair, her voice jumping a notch in pitch and volume.

"What are you talking about? Not making good choices. Are you talking about my divorce?"

"Oh, no. I have no idea why you are getting a divorce. None of my business. But besides this...situation...with Father Jay, you've also been seen in the company of other questionable men."

"Huh? Now what the hell are you talking about?"

"I'm talking about you taking a bag from what appeared to be a drug dealer and giving him money. Right in the church parking lot. A week ago, Friday. Isn't that right, Miranda?"

Miranda nodded again. "Yeah, he was a pretty shady looking guy. She took a bag from him a week ago Friday and put it in her trunk, then gave the man some money."

"Oh my God," groaned Zin. "That was Henry. He's harmless."

"Sure." Marvin turned back to the deacon. "Anyway, we're not here to talk about Ms. McGuire's, umm, relationships, other than as it pertains to Father Jay. So far, we've heard about three rendezvous that Father Jay has had with Zin, and those are only the ones we've observed. Which means that's probably just the tip of the iceberg."

"That's ridiculous. This is crazy, you know that!" Zin was now leaning in, her voice jumping again.

"On the contrary, I think it is the only thing that makes sense here."

"You can't come into my house and make up shit like that! Who do you think you are? Sitting on my porch, spying on me with your girlfriend, dragging half the church into my house! This is some sort of witch hunt!"

Marvin stepped forward. "She is NOT my girlfriend," he asserted. The room got quiet and William Leland's eyes grew wide. Marvin continued in a quieter voice, "I'm happily married. And I'm only trying to save the church from being ruined by a scandal between a priest and the floozy he's supposed to be counseling."

"Floozy? You little..." Zin was in Marvin's face now, hands down at her side, fists clenched. "I should wipe that stupid smirk right off your face! First, I'm not having an affair with Henry, who is a sweet little homeless man that just needs a hand, nor am I having an affair with Father Jay, who happens to be a great guy. In fact, I don't even..." she stopped herself abruptly, an air of expectation descended into the room, but she seemed to find her footing and continued. "And second, you have no right spying on me or coming into my home! You need to get OUT!" Zin stared at Marvin, her body starting to shake, her hand pointing at the front door.

The room fell quiet. Everyone in the room peered around carefully as if to verify that they weren't the only witness to the scene before them. Jay realized his mouth was agape, his eyes as big as saucers. He wanted to go put his hands on Zin's shoulders and pull her away, but then stopped himself. Zin seemed to be handling it, and he didn't want to make things worse by looking to comfort Zin in their presence. Jay saw that Marvin's nostrils were flaring, but Deacon Ketterling looked angry. Apparently, he had had enough. He stepped forward.

"Ms. McGuire. I think we owe you an apology. This looks like it was a big misunderstanding. Please forgive us. We'll get out of your hair now." He looked up at Jay and nodded, and then headed out the door. William Leland followed suit, mumbling an apology as he followed quickly out the door, head down, looking like he was trying to become invisible. Miranda shuffled out, glancing up at Jay, a fearful look on her face. Jay gave her a half grin and nodded cordially. Marvin looked at Jay and Zin, gave a small snort, and marched out.

Patrick looked up at Zin and Jay and then stood up, running his hand through his hair, not making eye contact. He shifted on his feet.

"Well, I guess I should get going home. The Twins are on TV tonight. Channel five. I should go watch the Twins." He started heading out.

"Patrick, we'll watch again another time, okay?" called Zin.

"Okay," replied Patrick, already on the porch, racing away.

Jay was still standing behind Zin when Patrick made his exit. Zin turned around the room with a stricken look at her face, as if she had just been mugged. It seemed to take a moment to register that Jay was the only one left.

"Wow," she said, and took a few deep breaths. "I'm not sure

what happened there, but it looks like Marvin was gunning to get rid of you. I mean, was he really spying on us?"

"I guess so," said Jay. "That guy's a little more devilish than I would have thought." They both turned to the front door, as if the group might re-appear. Jay spun toward Zin. "But you were something else! I guess I better not get on your bad side, or I'll go home in pieces!"

"Would you have forgiven me if I would have pelted him? Right in the cheek? I was about to, I really was. Floozy! I can't believe he said that!"

"I'd have let you off with a light sentence. Ten Hail Marys."

Jay watched Zin march back to the dining room table, sit down, and pick up the wine bottle, tipping it upside down over her glass. "Well, I sure could use a drink, but I think I'm out." She was still breathing hard, staring off into space, her jaw set, her fists clenching and unclenching. Jay came to sit down at the table with her. She glanced up at the clock. "And I've got to work at Project Hope tonight. I might need to sneak a bottle into the church."

"Don't go stealing my communion wine," Jay winked. Given the look on her face, he wouldn't put anything past her tonight.

Zin frowned and shook her head. "Word of this scandal will probably reach church before I get there."

"Yeah. This is one for the ages. There's no way this doesn't spread far and fast."

They both sat in silence for about a minute, both gazing out the big window onto the porch, lost in thought. Zin turned to Jay. "So, before we got so rudely interrupted, you were going to tell me something."

Jay gave a small, sad smile. Thankfully, he hadn't said anything foolish, and given the time and what had just transpired, he had an easy out. "No, not really. But it is time I got out of here before people start talking some more." He stood up. "Thank you again for sticking up for me and for listening to my story. I don't think I was much of a counselor to you—maybe the opposite is true. But I enjoyed our conversation."

"I did, too," said Zin, standing up and coming over to Jay. He looked down at Zin.

"You had quite a brawl with Marvin. Are you okay? If you aren't, please say so. It is important that you let me know."

Zin made a thoughtful face but nodded. "Yeah. I think I'm okay. It kind of felt good to yell at that loser. Plus, I'm hanging out with my dad tonight, which on some level seems comforting. So, yeah. I'm okay." Jay nodded and headed to the door. Zin followed and spoke up before he walked out the door.

"And Father? I mean Jay? Please be kind to yourself. You are a good priest, and you do make a difference." Jay stood awkwardly in the doorway for a second, then just smiled and nodded.

"See you around," he said, and headed out the door.

Jay strolled down the sidewalk feeling a sense of relief. It seemed to him that he had both dodged a bullet and suddenly gained clarity into what had been a murky situation. He'd been in a funk and not thinking clearly, but in just a matter of moments it all seemed to have been wiped away. And given that Marvin had just admitted to hanging out with Miranda frequently, and knowing what he knew about them, Jay suspected that he would come out looking much better than they would after people heard about this situation.

Jay's expression turned to surprise as he rounded the corner. There, coming toward him, was his church secretary.

"Barb? What're you doing here?" he called from a distance but closed that distance fast.

"Is the Marvin party over yet?"

"Yes, it is. How did you know about that? Did you hear something already?" Jay knew word would spread like wildfire, but this would have been ridiculous.

"No, Marvin roped me, William Leland, Miranda, and the deacon, what's his name, into coming to confront you about some crazy story regarding you and Zin McGuire. He thought you were having an affair or something. I didn't believe it for a second, but I tagged along at first. But when we got to Zin's house and I saw that they were planning on spying on you, I told them I wanted nothing to do with them. So, I left."

"They were spying, weren't they? Well, they came to the house to make some accusations, but Marvin pretty much just offended Zin to the point where I thought she was going to punch him. But you'll never guess who came by and crashed the party?"

"Patrick."

"Yeah!" said Jay, confused. "How did you guess? How do you know Patrick?"

"Patrick? Everyone knows Patrick," said Barb. "And who do you think sent him to the house in the first place?"

"What?"

"Yeah. I saw him walking down the street and told him to go knock on Zin's door. Figured he might gum up the works. I was trying to make up some excuse about why he needed to knock on the door of the green house, when he says 'Zin's house? Does she want to watch the game?' I just said 'yeah', and he was off. It was almost too easy."

Jay laughed out loud. "Oh, Barb. What would I do without you?"

Barb took his arm and turned to walk back toward church with him. "Probably not much," she said, seriously.

Probably not, thought Jay. *Probably not.*

28

Zin's doorbell rang at 5:15 p.m., and she scurried to the front to see her dad standing on the porch, a black duffel bag slung over his shoulder. Zin let him in.

"Hi, Dad." He squeezed her shoulder as he stepped into the house. Zin eyed him up—usually a sharp dresser, today he was in a comfortable pair of jeans and a college sweatshirt.

"Are you ready for this?" she asked.

"I guess so," he said. Zin noticed that he seemed a little nervous. She wasn't sure if it was just the prospect of spending time with her, or the prospect of immersing himself in the life from which he was usually far removed. Maybe both, she thought.

"Have a seat," she pointed to a dining room chair. "I just need to grab a few things." She noticed the empty bottle and two wine glasses and George noticed them, too, but didn't say anything. Zin ran upstairs and came back down with a bag and a pillow.

"Gotta have my pillow." She stood in front of her dad. "I appreciate you doing this with me. I know it's a pain."

"Naw, I'm glad you asked. Shall we?" They got up and walked out to the driveway, throwing their bags into the backseat of his BMW SUV and heading out.

"How was your day?" asked George. Zin shook her head a little.

"Oh, a little crazy for some reason. But it's all good, now." They pulled into the church parking lot and got out. Zin stood outside St. Stephen's church and, not for the first time, felt a pang of regret for having volunteered to help. It was a Saturday night, after all, and tomorrow would be Easter. She could have had a quiet evening to herself, but instead would be stuck in a church basement with a bunch of strangers, sleeping on a cot. And she hadn't been stuck in a house with her dad since the summer after her sophomore year in college, and that was a giant house where she could escape to her room, unlike tonight's situation where she and her dad would be stuck sleeping in a classroom. But she also knew that this meant she wouldn't have to sound so pathetic when her sister grilled her tomorrow about her life, or when her work colleagues asked about her Easter weekend.

Zin and George walked around to the side of the church. Pulling on the glass doors, she found them locked, so she pushed a button on the intercom and waited for a few seconds until she heard the buzz that indicated the lock was released. Zin stepped into the foyer with George behind, turned left down a hall, and found the stairs to the basement, where she heard a few other people talking and some kids shouting. She walked down the stairs and followed a hallway covered with grey, speckled tiles to a large open space where people were milling about. A few families sat at a couple of round tables on one end of the room near a counter that led to a kitchen, a handful of children were running and chasing each other at the other end of the space, and a group of adults were standing in the center of the room, chatting. Cots with makeshift dividers formed four small rooms along the sides of the space, a man in a t-shirt stood ironing clothes behind one of them, a teen-aged boy was lying in another, headphones covering his ears.

Zin headed toward the group in the middle of the room, which included a couple she recognized from church and a person she didn't recognize—a short, round, African American woman with shoulder-length straight hair and big, round glasses.

"Zin, good to see you." Carol Gunnerson waved as Zin approached.

"Hey, the night shift is here," joked a man at her side.

"Not so fast," Zin said and smiled. George stood a half step behind her.

"Zin, this is Cheryl Williams. She is the Director of Project Hope."

"Thanks for helping out tonight," said Cheryl, extending her hand and shaking Zin's. Cheryl's smile was somehow the biggest smile Zin ever remembered seeing on someone. "Tonight's a bit tough to staff, with the holiday and all. We appreciate you coming." Zin introduced her father to the group. She glanced around the room, a mild look of worry on her face.

"How's it been? Do we have a full house?"

"Always," answered Cheryl. "It used to be that we'd have some vacancies the first half of the month until people would start being evicted from homes or apartments. But for the last few years we've had to use a waiting list."

"How long do they have to wait on the waiting list?" asked Zin.

"Probably two to six weeks, less for smaller families. A couple years ago we started running two church basements at the same time. There's always demand."

George nodded toward the man ironing his clothes. "Looks like someone's getting ready for Easter." The others turned to look at the man, Mike and Carol exchanging a brief glance.

"Actually, he's just getting ready to go to work," informed Cheryl.

"Oh," replied George.

"Yeah. He works night shifts at a hotel." She noticed the confusion on George's face. "People are usually surprised when they find out that a large percentage of our adults are working. Or they want to be working but can't find childcare. Life doesn't always play fair with folks."

"I had no idea," answered Zin. Cheryl's smile faded.

"A lot of families live close to the edge, paycheck to paycheck. It doesn't take too much to tip that over: a job loss, an illness. You could probably have talked to each of these families two years ago and they would never believe they would be homeless one day. But it happens." The others nodded. They glanced around the room for a moment. Carol broke their silence.

"The kids are a little excited because of Easter," she observed. "You might be in for a late night!"

Cheryl's eyes lit up. "Speaking of which, I just stopped in to deliver the Easter goodies," answered Cheryl. "I'd better sneak them in."

"I brought a little something, too," said George. "Why don't I go out and help you with the goods." The two of them strode past a couple children pushing a plastic wagon and disappeared down the hall.

"How about I give you the tour?" asked Carol. They walked across the open room. "Lights are supposed to be out by 9:30, but if things are taking a while, you could delay it a bit. Still, there are young kids and some of these families are just plain tired at the end of the day." She pointed to the window opening to the kitchen. "Mike is in the kitchen, starting to assemble some snacks for the evening. That room over there is where you and your dad will sleep," she said, pointing to a door on the side of the room. Carol gave her the list of attendees and a little background on each. They talked about the schedule for the evening and morning, which was going to include an Easter egg hunt and Easter baskets for the children. Carol took Zin to the small room where she and George would sleep, and Zin dropped off their bags. Then they went to the small kitchen where Cheryl and George were waiting with Mike. Carol gave Zin and George final instructions and then said their goodbyes, leaving Zin and George to finish preparing the snacks.

"We just put them on the counter and let them help themselves," Zin told her dad.

"So, you know what you're doing here?"

"Nope. Not at all. But I think we'll manage." Zin set the

platters of banana bread slices and grape bunches on the counter and then walked around the room, letting the others know the snacks were ready. Zin returned to a spot behind the counter, trying to project friendliness. She watched the group assemble, which included what appeared to be a mix of single mothers, young couples, and children ranging from a baby to a young teen. Wanting to make a sign for the Easter egg hunt, Zin dug around and then headed upstairs to the craft room to find some paper and markers.

Zin returned after about ten minutes to find the kitchen cleaned up and George sitting, chatting with the man who had been ironing his shirt earlier. Zin left them alone and sneaked out to a separate activity room where Cheryl had left a bunch of plastic eggs and candy. She stuffed eggs for a bit until George showed up in the doorway.

"There you are," he said, sitting down next to her. "I thought you had sneaked out."

"Oh, I just didn't want to hover. Besides, I need to get the eggs hidden. Who were you chatting with?"

"That's Tomas. He works at the Days Inn on University. I was telling him about the days when I worked at a hotel."

"You worked at a hotel? I didn't know that?"

"Yeah. For a summer after my junior year in college. Worked the eleven to 7 a.m. shift—then I'd run around all day. I thought it was the greatest idea at the beginning of the summer, but by the end, I couldn't take it."

"Hmmm," said Zin, going back to her eggs. "I had no idea."

"That was a long time ago," said George, almost to himself. He got up and walked over to a cardboard box and pulled out little paper bags. He started stuffing them with items from the box.

"What do you have there?"

"Oh, just a little something extra for the families. How many people are here, do you think?"

"We have 16," said Zin, getting up to inspect a bag. Her dad had bought chocolate eggs, jellybeans, and gift cards for everyone. "Dad, that's so sweet," she said. She looked at her dad as if seeing him for the first time in a while. Maybe she hadn't allowed herself to look closely for a long time.

Zin and George went and hid the plastic eggs and bags in another room. When they came back, George headed to their sleeping room and Zin waded into the large room, scanning the room covertly; she didn't want to invade, and families were hunkering down and getting ready for the night. Before long, she and George were saying goodnight to everyone and turning out the lights.

Zin and George changed in the bathrooms and returned to the classroom where they were to sleep. Zin sat on her cot and her dad sat on his about ten feet away.

"Kinda wish I would have sneaked a bottle of wine into this fancy hotel," she said.

"Yeah. That would be good right about now. Or a shot of bourbon." They sat in silence for a few moments, looking around the room at crayon drawings taped to the wall, pictures of Bible scenes taped to the cupboards, books on a low shelf.

"I'm glad you came today," said Zin, looking at her dad. "I hope I didn't push you into something you didn't want to do."

"No, I'm glad to be here. We don't get to do anything together anymore."

"Well, I've got a little more time on my hands these days, so I'm available if you ever want to do anything." George smiled, looking down at his feet. He ventured a question.

"Are you and Rick through? For good?"

"Yep. I'm moving on. Not looking back." Her dad just nodded and looked up at a poster on the wall.

"He wasn't treating you right. I should've said something years ago. Didn't want to meddle, but I should've said something."

Zin was surprised. "Really? I thought you liked him?"

"Oh, I liked him well enough at first. He was always interesting to talk to, good to play a round of golf with. Seemed like you two got along well. Seemed like he'd take care of you. But later, I don't know, maybe after his career started doing better, he just seemed...indifferent. Not like it should be. I mean, you have to respect each other if you're married, and it seemed like that respect kind of eroded after a while." He looked at Zin. "That's why I was always pushing you about your career."

"I have a career, Dad," she answered, sitting up straighter on her cot.

"I know, I know," said her dad in a tired voice. "And I understand that now. But I was worried you'd be on your own and not able to pay the bills." He paused. "Are you okay now? I mean, financially? Because it would be plain silly to make yourself be miserable when you've got enough to deal with. Your mom and I wouldn't like to see that."

"I'm fine, Dad, but thanks for asking. My attorney says that although Rick's being an ass, he doesn't have a leg to stand on. George nodded but frowned. "Hmm. Well, all right." He looked at his watch. "Well, Sunshine, I think I'd better hit the hay. We have to rouse this roost early in the morning."

"Sounds good," said Zin, getting up to find the light switch. She fumbled her way back to the cot. "Good night, Dad."

"Good night, Zin."

Zin lay on her back, looking up at the water-stained, tiled ceiling, her mind running laps around her day. She was struck by seeing her father's softer side today. She had been butting heads with him for so long, had she missed something? Or had he just softened with age? He was tough on her when she was young, but was it justified? Was she just a stubborn girl who didn't want to be told what to do, and he, an alpha male who thought his role was to be in charge, a man who had learned lessons from experience and was frustrated that she ignored his advice? She had pretty much gone opposite directions every time he suggested something to her, going out of her way to reject his input. She had never entertained the idea that his suggestions were at least partly born of worry and concern. And to make matters worse, he was a man who didn't like to be wrong, and with Zin, he often was.

Zin cringed with guilt, but decided that this was water under the bridge, and she shouldn't beat herself up over this. Her thoughts wound back to the afternoon, and the bizarre incident at her house. What did that Marvin guy have against her? It didn't make sense. The more she thought about it, however, the more it seemed that the purpose of the crazy raid was to get Father Jay in trouble. He was a sweet guy; he didn't need these idiots to cause him trouble.

Zin heard her dad's deep breathing kick in and she glanced at him, envious of his ability to sleep soundly. She tossed and turned, wondering if Rick was still with C.J., thinking about the kids in her class that needed help, and finally, thinking about Henry. In looking back, their ten day experiment didn't seem random or by chance, but something more deliberate. But why? She had let him down, that much was clear, and she wanted another chance to talk to him and get some answers.

It was near midnight before Zin finally fell asleep, and when she did, she dreamt vividly. In her dreams, she wandered around a mansion only to realize it belonged to her ex-husband. She heard him calling her name and she kept searching, room-to-room, never finding him until she got to a large bedroom on the third floor. He was on a balcony, beckoning her to come out with him, but when she did, the balcony disappeared and she was falling, calling his name. Then she was following Henry, watching as he strolled down sidewalks, examined flowers, trees, insects, people, everything with his spoon device, and she followed him until they turned a corner and she found herself in a zoo. Then she was in a cage; Henry examining her from the outside amidst a group of others who were all laughing at her.

Zin woke with a start and glanced around at the whiteboard, the chairs, and the cupboards and remembered where she was. She sat up and rubbed her neck, rolling her head around, noticing that her dad's cot was empty. Zin checked the time—just ten minutes before her alarm would have gone off. She grabbed some clothes and a toiletry bag and waddled sleepily down the hall to the bathroom where she changed and freshened up. She returned her pajamas to the classroom and was digging in her purse when she came across a folded piece of paper. She pulled it out and held it up to the weak light. It was a check from her dad, written out to her. She cursed under her breath and held the check tightly in her hand, staring at it. *Dammit Dad! Why do you have to butt in?* She marched to the kitchen, the check in her clenched fist, planning what she would say to him. When she got to the kitchen door, she could see her dad on the other side of the room. He was already cutting bananas in half and had started the coffee pot. He was hunched over and, maybe for the first time, she saw that he looked old to her, not the man who commanded rooms, but an older man with some of the inherent frailties of old age. Zin's shoulders slumped and she sighed. She came up behind him.

"Good morning, Dad." He turned around, a big smile on his face.

"Well, good morning. How did you sleep?"

"Umm, okay, I guess. Had some weird dreams, though."

"Well, I slept like a baby."

"That's good," she said. She wanted to bring up the check, but thought she'd give it a moment. She joined George and they started working quietly, preparing breakfast. They turned on some lights as the signal for families to get going, and then set the food, plates, milk, glasses, and plasticware out on the counter. Zin called out gently—"food is ready". The families started wandering up, still sleepy, some little ones already excited about the prospect of Easter. Zin and George set out the breakfast and after a couple families had come forward, Zin made herself a plate of food and took her breakfast to a corner table to sit with her dad.

"So, Dad," she said, after they had started on their breakfast. "I found your check."

Her dad raised his eyebrows and looked at her warily. "I was just thinking it would help out," he answered, and then added, "It could be temporary if you want."

Zin gave him a mock scolding look, but her tone was kind. "I appreciate it. I really do. But I'm okay." She slid the check across the table to him. "If you feel like helping out, I'd rather you give this to a needy charity. That would make me happy." George nodded and took the check, stuffing into his pants pocket.

"All right," was all he said. They ate quietly for a bit, picking some safe topics for small talk. They were chatting idly when Zin glanced towards the kitchen counter and caught her breath. There, filling his plate, was a familiar figure with an unruly flop of hair.

29

Now that she saw him here, a wave of understanding passed over Zin along with a sense of resolution, as if something had just fallen into place. Zin thought about hiding and avoiding him to save him the embarrassment, but she thought better of it—he probably had already seen her and avoiding him seemed cold. He turned from the counter and scanned the room for a table, and as he did, they made eye contact. Zin gave a slight nod and a smile, and he nodded in acknowledgement, heading to another table to sit. Zin decided she would seek him out later when they could have a private moment to talk.

Zin and George ate quickly and, after clearing away the dishes, called the families into the other room for the egg hunt. Parents lined the walls as the kids stood in the center of the room, hungrily eyeing the eggs, many of which were lying in plain sight. Zin explained the rules and got the hunt started, and then turned to her dad.

"You're in charge," she said. He looked surprised, but she patted him on the shoulder and then took a bag with some candy and slipped out of the room, heading back to the common area. She found him alone, sitting on his cot, lying on his back, white earbuds sticking out of his ears, his hands behind his head. When she appeared over the divider wall, he didn't look surprised, but possibly a little worried. She waited for him to pull his earbuds out of his ears before addressing him.

"Hi Adrian. Happy Easter." She handed him a bag and he smiled.

"Happy Easter Miss McGuire," he answered without smiling, giving his attention to the bag. Zin walked around the divider.

"Did you sleep well?"

"Umm, okay I guess," he answered, not looking at her, opening a carton of malted milk eggs and pouring them into his hands. "There's a guy who's been here for a couple nights now who snores and sometimes I can't tune him out."

"Can I ask how long you've been here?" asked Zin, leaning an arm on the divider.

"Almost two weeks, I think," he said. "My mom's friend was letting us stay with her for a couple weeks before that, but there just wasn't room." He kept focusing on the chocolate, popping a couple in his mouth at a time.

"Well, I know you must have had a rough month. I'm sorry about that."

"Yeah, it's kind of a pain." He paused and Zin gave him a few moments to see if he would open up a little more, which he did. "We knew it was going to happen, but it still sucks. I coulda stayed with Brandon's family, but then my mom would've been alone."

"Your dad isn't in the picture, I take it?"

"He died a couple years ago, that's what got this whole thing rolling."

"I'm sorry," said Zin, her face pained. Adrian munched on an egg for a moment before the silence led him into continuing.

"He had a good job and all," he said, defensively, "but he got sick and couldn't work. And then there were all these bills. My mom only worked part time and now she works a second job, but I guess it wasn't enough…" A defiant expression flashed across his face for a moment as if to say *don't pity me*, but just as quickly it melted, and he went digging for candy.

"I'm sorry about your dad," said Zin after a few moments.

Then added, "you know, this can happen to anyone."

"Sure," he said, frowning and uncomfortable. Zin wasn't sure what else to say—it was obvious that this was hard for him.

"Well, I better go back and help my dad," she said.

"Your dad? Oh, I thought that was your husband."

Zin laughed. "You must think I'm pretty old! No, that's my dad. My husband's an asshole, he'd never do anything like this."

Adrian's eyes shot wide open, and Zin realized that she might have gone too far—it was normally a very bad decision to broach any kind of personal subject with a student—but she also knew how vulnerable Adrian was now and wanted to share in that vulnerability. She knew this secret about him, a secret that he would do anything to keep from being exposed, and she felt like it was a kindness to share her own secret with him.

"Well, I should be clear. My husband left me recently, so let's just call him my ex."

"Oh," he said. "Umm, I'm sorry."

Zin chuckled, releasing Adrian's smile. "Don't be. It's for the best. Anyway, things happen in life that you can't control, and as you know, it is miserable when they do. So be kind to yourself and don't blame yourself." He nodded, looking back to his basket. Zin decided that was as much as she could expect to extract from a teenager.

"Well, I'm going to go see how the kids are doing. Happy Easter Adrian."

"You too," he said. Zin started to leave but he called her back. "Miss McGuire?" he said, a worried expression having broken through the mask of indifference. "You won't tell anyone about this, will you?"

"No, of course not," she said. The crack in the tough teenage shell made her almost go over and give him a hug, but she decided that might be too much for him. "This is your private matter, and I wouldn't talk about it with anyone. But Adrian, what if you and I sat down with the school counselor next week to go through this? It's okay to need help at times or get a break. It's just for a bit – we know you are a good student – but maybe she has some ideas for dealing with this. The counselors see all kinds of kids and have lots of resources or options for you. You're not the only kid who has things like this happening to them."

Adrian looked back to his candy bag for a few moments. "Uh, sure."

"Sounds good. We'll talk about it next week." Zin walked off to find the others, feeling like a giant weight had been lifted off her shoulders.

30

Jay walked out his front door early and was glad to see the weather was agreeable, unlike some Easters in Minnesota when winter refuses to give up and families don parkas instead of Easter bonnets. This would likely mean a full house at his church service, which always felt rewarding. Preparing for a service was a lot of work, and to have to hold it in front of sparsely filled pews was always a bit of a let-down. Jay unlocked the back door and was surprised to hear the light patter of a little child running on the tile floors. It took him a second to remember that Project Hope was occupying the lower level of the church, and the families would probably be in the middle of breakfast. Jay walked downstairs to the large reception room to find a scene he expected: families sitting quietly at tables, food out on the counter, a few kids chasing each other, a little more excited than usual, and to his surprise he saw Zin in the far corner, her back to Jay. Jay stood in the doorway, contemplating going over and saying hi, but decided to let the families be in peace. He turned around and headed upstairs to run through his sermon again.

Upstairs, he found a few families sitting around a table, moms and kids stuffing candies into plastic eggs, little paper bags and markers scattered on the table. Jay walked up to the table to survey the work.

"Well, good morning. Happy Easter." The crew looked up and greeted him. "Getting ready for the Easter egg hunt?" he asked.

"Yep," answered one of the moms, nodding to a series of paper bags on the floor, half full of eggs, half empty. "We're getting close. At least we're not hiding them in the snow this year." Jay stole a candy.

"I know," he said, "Looks like a nice day. See you later." Jay turned to head to the office, where a couple of volunteers were gathering some technical equipment and cords, but he was first drawn in by sounds from the altar. He wandered into the sanctuary, stood in a corner, and observed the activity. The choir was warming up. A few supporting musicians were setting up chairs and breaking out instruments.

Jay stood, half listening to the sounds of the church activities all around him. As he stood there, he became acutely aware of something that seemed obvious, but for some reason had been difficult for him to see for some time; he was grateful for the people around him. These were good people, doing good things. They didn't deserve his cynicism.

Jay slipped out and headed to his office with a sense of urgency. He had some last-minute corrections he needed to make to his sermon.

***

Jay stood at the pulpit to give his sermon, looking out at a full church, tapestries hanging along the walls, Easter lilies adorning the sanctuary, long time members sitting next to first time visitors. In the back row, something caught his eye—it was Zin, and next to her was a gray-haired main. A surprise twinge of nerves struck Jay, but he took a deep breath and started in.

Good morning. I hope the parents in the room got to sleep in this morning. I trust the Easter bunny was good to everyone? Well, as you know it's Easter. It's a joyous time. We've got lilies and trumpets on the altar. There are kids running around clenching Easter baskets and getting chocolate stains on their clothes. And just so we don't forget—Christ is

230

risen. It's easy to find joy and wonder on a day like today.

But to fully appreciate the joy that Easter brings, you have to understand the distance between Easter morning and the days leading up to it. Imagine what was running through the mind of Christ that week. He sees this coming. He doesn't know how, he doesn't know when, but he knows it isn't going to be easy—revolutions rarely are—and Christ was a revolutionary, preaching love, compassion, and piety over hate, selfishness, and greed, expecting the leaders of the community and church to follow a different path, a scary message for those who were clinging to the existing structures of power. No, Jesus wouldn't have been blind to the rumblings of the disgruntled power centers, and he would have had a sense of impending trouble, of something terrible coming his way, and as the week wore on, the picture would have gotten clearer and the dread even stronger.

And he would have asked himself—am I doing the right thing? Is it worth it? Is humankind worth it? He was born a man, and although he may have had a vision of what he needed to do, may have had an understanding deep down that this is what needed to be done, it would have been a monumental challenge to not try and avoid this fate. He would have looked around and asked himself why he was doing this, especially when he saw so much pain around him. All his life, he saw a powerful empire that was conquering his homeland and the corresponding suffering that the occupiers brought his people. He would have seen the priests and Pharisees despoiling the temples and living lives of false piety. At the end, he would have seen the Sanhedrin, the chief priests and elders, put him to trial. He would have seen crowds of people reject him, relegating him, instead of a known criminal, to death. He would have seen the barbarity of the guards and crowds who took him to Golgotha, stripped him, mocked him, and crucified him. He would have seen his friends abandon him at his darkest hour. He would have seen a friend and disciple betray him with a kiss.

It would have been impossible for Jesus to not wonder why he was doing this. There was so much cruelty in the world, so many times when he watched the darker side of people come out, whether it was the overt acts of the greedy and powerful, or the mindless or cowardly acts of the masses who wouldn't step forward to stem the tide of indecency. Why should he do anything to help these people? Why should he have to die?

But fortunately for us, Jesus also saw the good that permeated his life, and he didn't forget it. He remembered the friends and family he grew up *with, how they helped him, provided for him, cared for him. Loved him. He would have remembered his neighbors and communities that he lived in. He would have remembered little old ladies giving what little they could at the temple. He would have remembered throngs of people coming to see him during his travels, cheering for him, reaching for him, giving him food, shelter, the few pennies they may have had. Believing in him. He would have remembered his faithful disciples giving up their lives to follow him, having faith in him, despite the fact that they didn't know where that journey would take them. He would have remembered his mother and closest friends staying with him until the very end. And all of that gave him the strength he needed, the faith that humanity was, indeed, worth it.*

The question Jesus basically asked was—is humanity worth it? We don't usually ask that question. Instead, we ask a different form of that question: is mankind naturally good at heart, or are we inherently cruel? We're not asked to save humanity, but we do wonder—what is our true nature, and what does that mean for how I see the world, and how I interact with it? It is hard not to be cynical at times. We see war, terrorism and genocide around the world. We see violence that flames up in the form of rape, assault, murder, and we deal with a constant murmur of robberies and petty crimes. As a society, we take the easy road, choosing comfort over inconvenience, whether it be fighting poverty, protecting the environment, or ensuring equality, and then come up with weak justifications or we simply dismiss the problems as not necessarily that bad, all to clear our conscience. We vote for people who are void of character and morals, people who we wouldn't befriend and wouldn't want as role models for our children, because we are afraid to challenge our peers or unwilling to listen to reason. Yes, there are times when it is hard not to conclude that mankind is inherently selfish, self-serving, and ultimately, cruel.

I have to admit, there are times when that is my outlook on the world. When I shake my head and wonder if we aren't but a people with a savage core. It's a test of my faith that I fail too often. But what we need to remember is that for every one of these acts of darkness, there are hundreds, no, thousands of acts of kindness and compassion. These acts of kindness come in many, many forms. They can take the form of explicit acts of unselfishness: helping someone, volunteering, giving money. They can be clearly visible and newsworthy, but they are more often invisible, maybe even to the recipient of the act. It can be as simple as treating strangers with kindness and respect, or as complex as a lifetime dedication to a cause. And everyone you know does this, all the time, without giving it a second thought.

When I get down, when I start wondering about the good in the world, all it takes is a morning like today to reset my world: people helping prepare the worship, people volunteering in the choir, people helping get ready for Easter celebrations. The people helping out with Project Hope downstairs. All of you who came here today. You are the people who lift me up.

That's the message of Easter that no one talks about—humanity was, and is, worth saving. We all play a part. And we need to remember that every day.

Amen.

***

Zin listened intently to Father Jay's sermon. Her thoughts turned to Henry and her ten-day experiment with him. She had been indifferent about the world around her, but Henry had obviously taken it seriously, and the thought brought about a blush of shame. It was silly, of course. He was a disturbed man, and they were discussing a crazy hypothetical situation, but she couldn't help but feel a little guilty about her attitude in all of it, as if she had let everyone down.

Father Jay had finished up and was introducing Cheryl Williams, who told the congregation about Project Hope and what it did in the community. Then Cheryl made a plea.

"This year, we find ourselves in a precarious financial position. The building where our offices are housed is being sold, and we need to find a new home very soon. In addition, one of our main sponsors is unable to continue providing the support they have in the past. We run on a shoestring budget. Any gift would be much appreciated."

Father Jay thanked her and stepped forward. "As you know, each year we take an Easter offering for a special cause. This year, we are happy to be hosting Project Hope during the month of April, and our special offering will go to Project Hope. Please give generously."

George leaned over and asked Zin if she had a pen. Zin dug

around the bottom of her purse and found one, handing it to her dad. But she also found a small metal ball. She pulled it out and inspected it, Henry's so-called homing device. Her thoughts turned to the night she met Henry, that enigma, that goofy guy who claimed to be a visitor studying humanity. It was quite a line, one that only sounded remotely plausible after a lot of wine, and not really then either. In retrospect, she was crazy for letting herself get involved in that guy, and lucky he didn't turn out to be dangerous. This is the exact kind of situation everyone is cautioned against. But that was her cynical self again, wasn't it? He was a nice guy, after all, who didn't seem to have a mean bone in his body.

Zin thought about their first couple of get-togethers, but as she thought about them, a nagging problem kept bubbling to the surface of her consciousness...*how did he find me?* Yes, she had told him she was a teacher, but there are dozens of schools in the city. He must have called the district center to ask where she taught, but she was surprised that they would have told him. But there was no way he would have known to come to the church that next night. Zin hadn't told anyone she was going, and she hadn't planned on going until that morning. It made no sense. Zin sat racking her brain, but no possible explanation came to mind, and the more she thought about it—his dress, his behavior, his story, his speech – the more a pit starting to form in her stomach. Either he was anything but harmless, or he was telling the truth, and she didn't believe the former could be possible—at least she didn't want to believe it.

A test of humanity? It was ridiculous, really. Two people sitting down, watching a few other random people at a few random times. Who would do that? What could that tell about humanity? But she had found it interesting, maybe even enlightening. And as lonely as she had been, it was surprisingly cathartic. Talking out loud in a frank and open manner about something that you are observing, without fear of being judged or offending someone, is a great way to shine light on what you really are thinking. A phrase from the sermon came to Zin—'*It's a test of my faith that I fail too often*', and Zin's brain froze, her heart suddenly audible in her ears.

Zin leaned over to her dad and, with a sense of urgency, told him that she had to go and he shouldn't get up. He looked a little confused, but before he could object, she popped up and ran out the back of the church, jogging the rest of the way home. She had to find Henry. She needed to see him one more time. Because Zin knew now that Henry hadn't been testing humankind these past ten days.

Henry had been testing her.

***

Jay stood at the exit of the church, greeting the parishioners as they left. The crowd was big, and people wanted to chat, so the line took longer than usual. It was nearly empty before Jay saw a familiar face enter the aisle, making her way towards him. There was Mabel, walker in her hands, a frumpy blue hat sitting atop the straight, pure white mop of hair. Jay waited for her, the last one out.

"Good morning, Mabel," Jay called out to her. Mabel pulled up next to him, took both of Jay's hands, and looked up at him.

"You did a good job this morning," she said, almost sternly, and then promptly went back to her walker and pushed on past.

Jay watched Mabel plod out the door and chuckled to himself. *Now THAT is high praise.*

Jay headed to the church lawn to see how the Easter egg hunt was faring. He watched the kids scurrying about the church yard, scooping up plastic eggs, some sitting down immediately to stuff their faces with candy. Jay then made his way downstairs to mingle a little and see if he could steal a donut. He was chatting with Barb when James Taubert tapped him on the shoulder.

"Excuse me Father. Do you have a second?" Jay turned around and noticed that James seemed a little excited.

"Sure. What's up?"

"Well, Paul and I were counting the offering this morning, and, well, maybe you should come upstairs." Jay gave Barb a look that suggested he had no idea what was coming, and then followed James upstairs to the offices. Paul Woods was sitting in a small, bare room, a few brass offering plates at the side of the table, a few stacks of bills and checks, and a tally sheet sitting in front of him. When Jay entered the room, Paul was ready with a question.

"Father, do you know anyone named George Meyer?" Jay shook his head. "Neither do we. But I thought you might find this interesting." He handed Jay a check and Jay's eyes opened wide, with a big smile.

"Ten grand! Well, that'll help fill that budget gap nicely!" he said, beaming. "Happy Easter to us!" Paul and James exchanged looks.

"Well, that's not all," said Paul. He handed Jay another check. Jay looked at it and laughed out loud. It was another check from George, this one made out to Project Hope for the sum of fifty thousand dollars. And on the check's memo line, he had left a little note:

Zin's BMW.

31

Zin left the church with no idea of how to find Henry. About a block down the street, she started to hear the final hymn wafting out of the front doors of the church. It only took seconds after that for her to remember her first meeting with Henry and what she had told him. She knew where she had to go; she needed to go to the cathedral.

Zin arrived at her house, grabbed her keys, ran out of the house to her car, and headed downtown. Once there, she drove around the streets surrounding the cathedral until she finally found a parking spot three blocks away. She guessed that the church service had started over forty minutes ago and it looked like half of the city was there. Zin scampered up the wide stairs in the front of the church, huffing by the time she reached the landing at the top. She pulled the handle on the huge wooden doors and the sound of a trumpet fanfare burst forth. Inside, the church that had seemed so dark only a few days ago was now radiant, with bright morning light streaming through a kaleidoscope of stained-glass windows and the chalices on the altar all reflecting light. Zin made her way to the rear of the center aisle and took a few moments to take in the scene. She soon remembered why she was there and started scanning the nearby pews. She began walking around the back of the church, popping into every doorway to check the nearby rows for signs of the disheveled blonde head. She completed a quarter circle counterclockwise and then circled back to cover the other side of the church, but still saw no sign of Henry.

Zin decided her best chance was to look down from above, and she climbed the stairs to the balcony to get the necessary view. A few people were sitting up there, but she skirted across to an empty side where she wouldn't block anyone's view and stood at the railing, looking down on the crowd, scanning it systematically from front to back, left to right. Still, she saw no sign of him.

The final hymn had ended, and the priest was giving a benediction. Zin plopped back down into the pew behind her and watched as the service wound down and the attendees started filing out to the sounds of the brass ensemble. She sat and fretted as a few robed bodies straightened the altar and a few ushers picked up debris left in the pews. And then it was silent.

Zin put her face in her hands, closing her eyes, berating herself for messing things up, for letting him go like that without a decent goodbye. She admonished herself for how she had treated Henry, and how she had let him down. Was she really so indifferent, or worse, cynical? Henry had exposed her pessimistic outlook on life, but she had blamed her situation on Rick and the divorce, never thinking that those traits might just be who she was.

"Zin?" The familiar voice called to her from the other side of the balcony. She sat up and there he was, again in his baby blue suit, untamed hair, and Converse sneakers, but this time with a flower in his lapel and a look of concern on his face. Relief flooded through her.

"Hello, Henry," she said. "It is good to see you."

Henry came forward and Zin rose to meet him.

"Are you okay?" he asked, looking at Zin. Zin nodded. "I am surprised to see you today," he said. "I was just about to leave for the next leg of my journey."

"I wanted to see you before you left," she answered. "I

wanted to talk to you. I feel like I let you down."

"You did not let me down. You were kind to a stranger. Most people talk about helping others, but when the opportunity arises, they will do little more than give you the time of day. You actually did something about it." Zin looked up at Henry with a half-smile and paused to consider what she wanted to say.

"I...I want you to know that I might come across as pretty jaded, as someone who thinks people are generally mean or selfish. But deep down, I know that isn't true," she offered. "I don't think I could get up in the morning if I thought otherwise." She paused again but then continued. "I don't know why, but it was important that I let you know. I guess I don't want to ruin your report," she said, smiling. "I might be cynical at times, but I think, well, we—humanity—we were worth it."

Henry reached out and took Zin's hands, a proud look on his face. "I know," he said, and added with a wink, "And so are you."

Zin laughed and pulled him into a hug.

32

Zin approached her car, digging in her purse for her keys. As her hand-picked around the items in her purse, her fingers passed over a small metal ball. Zin pulled it out and laughed quietly. She looked around, as if half expecting Henry to appear out of nowhere. She found her keys, unlocked the car, slipped in behind the wheel, and then scanned the rest of the parking lot before sending a text message. A couple of minutes later, a long-legged teenager appeared in the parking lot heading towards her, headphones covering his ears, baggy shorts falling well below his knobby knees, the hood of his gray hoodie covering as much of his face as possible. He glanced around a couple of times as he went, and then hopped into the car quickly, throwing his backpack into the back seat and slinking low.

"You should have parked farther away. Anyone see me?" asked the boy, sliding lower, head below the window.

"I didn't know I'd have to take you home today," replied Zin. "But no. Everyone is gone." She made a mental note to park at the back of the parking lot every day from now on, just in case she needed to give him a ride. She steered her little Ford out of the school parking lot. As they hit the main highway and she picked up speed, the boy cautiously scooted back to an upright position.

"Well, only one more week of this, then school's out," she said. The boy didn't reply. They drove in silence for a while. Zin had learned to not be offended by this; he was a teen in an awkward situation, after all, and there was no reason he'd want to make idle chit-chat when he could be listening to his music. Zin waited a few minutes before throwing out an idea that had been on her mind. "So, I was thinking. You know, if you ever want to have friends over or something, just let me know, and I can, like, stay out for the evening or something." The boy, annoyed, pulled an earbud out of one ear.

"What?"

Zin rolled her eyes and started again. "I was saying, if you ever want to have friends over, just let me know. I can get lost, go out for the evening or something so I'm not around. We can have a signal, so I can slip upstairs when you're down in the rec room. I'm just saying that we can figure something out. You shouldn't have to be in hiding."

"Yeah, maybe," said the boy, putting his earbud back in his ear and checking his phone.

"And I was also thinking about taking a trip for a couple weeks this summer." Again, the earbud.

"What?"

"I was thinking of taking a trip this summer. Maybe a road trip. My husband never wanted to do that, but I do, and Kim says she might go with me for some of it. Anyway, I'd be out of the house for a while. You could definitely have friends over then and not worry."

"Yeah."

Zin let it go for a bit. Adrian was a good kid, but desperately afraid of anyone finding out about this situation.

"Do you have plans tonight?" she asked.

"I dunno," the boy answered.

"Well, it's my turn to cook tonight, but I'm not in the mood. I thought I'd treat for pizza. Just wanted a head count." She stole another glance at her passenger who kept looking out his window, his expression forlorn and almost pained.

"That's cool," he mumbled, still looking out the window. Zin was satisfied. She knew it was tough for Adrian to have a second mother figure around, especially one that was his teacher to boot, so she tried not to step too far into their space. It wasn't easy—teenage boys can drive any parent crazy—so when she found him playing a video game when she knew he had homework, it took all her will to walk on by and bite her tongue. And she tried not to talk about her class at the house unless Adrian asked about it.

When she originally conceived of the idea to have them move in with her, she was going to have the conversation solely with Adrian's mom. It seemed like the adult's decision to make. But then she thought better of it; she didn't want any chance for him to feel that this was imposed on him, and she wanted to address any concerns he might have. She invited them to a meeting at a neutral place, knowing the school setting wouldn't be good if the conversation was intended to be among peers, and she told them to think on it, that they shouldn't respond right away. Zin was painfully anxious that night, pacing around the house, knowing she had overstepped the boundary she should have with a student, wondering if they would find it insulting. Zin had asked them to help with the rent, not because she cared about the money, but because she knew that if they harbored a sense of indebtedness, it would make an awkward situation even more confusing.

Adrian sat in class the next afternoon not looking at Zin, and Zin felt sick. She knew that she had made a mistake, that she had insulted them. When class ended, Zin busied herself, trying to not make eye contact with Adrian as the class emptied. But he hung around and approached the desk, looking around to make sure no one saw them.

"Um, Miss McG. My mom and I talked about what you said last night, and we think it would be a good idea." Zin looked up at him across the desk and blinked, losing her voice for a second.

"Uhh, great!" she said. "I mean, that sounds good. Why don't you have your mom call me tonight to go over some details?" She looked at him, trying not to sound too excited, lest she scare him off.

Adrian nodded, never smiling. "Okay, umm, see ya," he muttered and lumbered out. Zin's eyes following him until the door was completely closed.

***

"Thanks for the pizza." Kim set a paper plate down on an end table and looked out onto the street. Zin put her feet up on the little wicker porch loveseat in front of her, dabbed the grease off her fingers with a paper napkin, and picked up a glass of root beer and took a drink.

"Haute cuisine," Zin replied, and then added, "didn't feel much like cooking."

"Works for me. And Adrian, from the 27 pieces he seemed to take."

"The kid can eat like a horse," said Zin, nodding her head.

"Jessica didn't seem too interested, though," observed Kim.

"You know, I think this rotating cooking thing was maybe just a little ambitious. I think we should just go back to fending for ourselves."

"It's maybe too much. They might want to keep that separation a little bit."

"Yeah," replied Zin. She looked out to the street. "I need to tread a little carefully there. It's incredibly awkward. I'm her son's teacher and her landlord. Sometimes I wonder if this wasn't a mistake. There's a reason we should have boundaries."

"What you did was to help someone out in a moment of crisis," answered Kim, sitting forward in her chair and making eye contact with Zin. Too many people express concern about situations like this but don't do anything about it. And you did. Listen, it'll just take a little time. It's only been five weeks since they moved in. I know you'd never treat her with anything but respect and kindness. I'm sure she'll open up at some point."

"Sure. You're probably right. Adrian, on the other hand. I don't think he can do that."

"Well, he's a teenage boy," answered Kim. "He's not going

to want to talk to any adult he doesn't have to, especially his teacher, especially his teacher and house-mate. That's just normal. But he probably lives in fear of being found out. Could you imagine how cruel his classmates would be if anyone found out about this situation? He'd never hear the end of it." Zin frowned and looked down at her feet. "Zin, you did the right thing. Don't beat yourself up. He appreciates you, I can see it, but expecting more from a teenager in this situation would be asking way too much."

Zin nodded and looked up at Kim, a sad, half smile on her lips. "Thanks, Kim. I appreciate it. I have to say, it makes me nervous, too. I mean, I'm pretty sure the entire school board got to know my name after that school lockdown incident. Harris let me know that I was damn lucky things played out the way they did. I know that if they got wind of this, I'd be out of a job in a heartbeat. Then what would I do?"

"No one is going to get word of this," replied Kim, giving Zin a hard look. She lightened up. "Besides, in a week, Adrian will be done with middle school, and then he'll be a high schooler at a different school, and it will be much less of an issue. Do you think they will even be living with you in the fall?"

Zin shook her head. "No idea. We'll see. I don't even know what I want to do. I probably need to wait until this divorce thing finalizes before making any housing decisions, anyway, so I'll probably stay put for now." They sat in silence for a moment, Zin's thoughts running forward to a future when she could do whatever she wanted: stay put, sell a house, even move far away and start over. She had no idea if that freedom frightened her or excited her.

33

"Well, hello!" called the figure walking quickly toward Jay down the sidewalk, greasy hair, and glasses all too familiar.

"Hello, Patrick, how are you?"

As usual, Patrick stuck to his script. "How about those Twins? They're doing pretty well."

Jay was in a good mood and didn't mind stopping to appease Patrick. "Yeah, we look pretty good so far. We've got decent pitching and some hitting to boot."

"I like Rodriguez. He's got a good curveball. I don't know how to throw a curveball. I tried but it doesn't seem to curve. He's got a good fastball, too. I bet it's hard to be a catcher with a guy like him, with the ball going everywhere. Who's your favorite player?" Jay smiled. Patrick was Patrick, and that was a good thing.

Jay and Patrick talked baseball and beards before Jay finally extricated himself from Patrick's conversational hold and headed around the corner. He bounded up the steps to Zin's porch and rapped on the door. He tried to fan himself, but he was a big guy, and the warm day combined with the black shirt, even if it was short sleeved, meant he was going to be sweating, there was no helping it. Zin opened the door after a minute, a surprised look on her face.

"Father! What brings you around?"

"I thought I'd stop by and see my favorite ex-congregant." Zin gave him a look of fake indignation.

"Not sure if I should be offended or honored by that title."

"Probably neither," answered Jay. Zin stepped back and gave a dramatic wave, directing him into the house.

"Come in, come in," she said, but as he walked into the house, she added, "that is, if you dare be seen with a floozy like me."

"Maybe we should record this meeting, for posterity's sake."

"I started recording the moment you came in," she joked. "Take a seat. Can I get you a drink?"

"No, no," he said, sitting down on the couch and waving her off. "I can't stay. I just came to check in and see how you are doing. I haven't seen you since that crazy day."

"I know," she said, sitting down on a chair across from him. She leaned in, using a quieter, mischievous voice, "I heard there was quite a fiasco at church after that. You fired your bookkeeper? And Marvin got in trouble?"

"I didn't fire her. The archdiocese did. Because she was stealing."

"That's what I heard. And Marvin was in on it, too?" Her eyes were bright.

"Yup."

"So, what did they do? If I might ask," she added, quickly."

"Well, I shouldn't be talking about it, but I trust you'll keep it on the down low."

"Of course," she said, crossing her heart.

"So, in the days before they cornered us, I was digging into the church accounting books. Something seemed strange in the annual expenses—our maintenance costs seemed way higher than they should be, so I was trying to figure it out. I looked at all the expenses we paid, and I saw something unusual; for a lot of our maintenance costs or even our purchases, there would be an initial payment, and then a little bit later, a second payment, made out to a similar name, but not identical. There'd be a note like 'final payment'. It seemed odd that we always had to pay installments. Then I looked at the numbers and saw something that struck me as odd. It's something I remember from a college course I took. I didn't remember the name, just the basic idea, but basically there is the principle that says that in a naturally occurring data set, you expect the leading number to be small. It's just statistically how it plays out. So, when I was looking at all the second payments, something must have triggered in my brain, because there were lots of sevens and eights and nines for the leading numbers. That, and all the little name differences. I called up one of the companies—a heating company—and asked them about specific invoices and payments. They had no idea about the second payments. So, I followed up with the bank where these checks were being deposited and told them about this, which started the ball rolling with an investigation. They don't have all the details, but it looks like that for each of the companies we hired to do anything, replace the boiler, redo the basement ceiling, pave the parking lot, you name it, Marvin and Miranda would set up a company with a similar sounding name and set up a checking account at a bank for that company. She always volunteered to call and get estimates for all our projects—I should have caught on to that—and she would inflate the estimates, the church would approve work based on the estimates, and then they'd write themselves a check for these overages. Marvin was doing the audits at the church, and it didn't look that suspicious, anyway. They did it for years."

"Wow," said Zin, sitting back, smiling. And now what happens to them?"

"I don't know. Ask the Ramsey County Attorney's office." Zin looked closely at Jay.

"Well, Father. I'd say you look pretty happy. Glad to have this behind you?"

"You know what, I really got into it, digging into the accounting, trying to solve the mystery. It felt good to use my accounting background and every little clue I found was more exciting. And it didn't hurt to have a motivation to find a problem in Marvin and Miranda's accounting. I just wasn't expecting that they were the cause of it!"

"Yeah, that would pretty much make my day, busting Marvin and Miranda. He's a piece of work."

"Let's just say that quite a few people have come out of the woodwork now to say something, glad to have one or both of them gone."

"Maybe you should just do the church's books?"

"No thanks. That's the last thing I need to add to my plate."

"I understand." The room was quiet for a few moments as they both contemplated what had recently transpired. Zin broke the lull. "So what else is new?"

"Well, one of the reasons I came by was to tell you some news. I'm leaving for a bit."

"Oh?"

"Yeah. I've been stuck in a rut for a while, and I think you sensed that when we were talking back in April. Just kind of questioning what I was doing, feeling like I wasn't in the right place, wasting my time. I've been thinking a lot about that, and I feel better about it, and a lot of people in the congregation reached out to me after Marvin jumped us and told me they believed me, that they appreciated what I was doing. That was very helpful. But I talked to my bishop, and he agreed that I should take a short sabbatical. It's been 15 years now, and a little time to recharge, think about things, pray, would do me good. So, I'm taking off starting tomorrow. I'll be back on the first of September to kick off the fall season."

"Good for you!" said Zin. "You deserve it. Take a vacation. Relax in the sun a bit. Think things through."

"Well, that's not the route I think I'll be taking. I don't believe people find answers just by sitting still and trying to think it through. I think I'd get bored, anyway. I'm going to be going to Guatemala, working at a mission site for a little community down there. At least for a couple months. Disconnect, work with people, build things." He paused for a moment. "I struggle with some parts of my job. Maybe I'll get a different perspective. I guess I'll see what happens after that."

Zin nodded. "That sounds like a good idea. When do you leave?"

"A week from yesterday. Yeah, I'm looking forward to it." Jay smiled at the thought, but then looked back to Zin. "Why is it that every time I come here to check on you, we just end up talking about me?"

"Maybe you're more interesting?"

"Hmmm, I don't think so. So how is Zin doing?" Zin looked out the window for a few seconds and then looked back.

"I'm doing pretty well. The divorce thing is proceeding, a little slower than I'd like, but it will happen. Rick stopped bugging me. I don't even know where he's living right now, which is weird." Jay looked around the house, noticing lots of shoes, including men's shoes, a backpack, and more stuff generally lying about.

"You have roommates now?"

"Yeah," said Zin. "A mother and her son. I met them through school—they needed a new house temporarily, and I could use the money and company. It's working out well."

"That's great. Do you think you'll stay in the house when this is all done?"

"I don't know. Probably not. It's more house than I need. I wouldn't mind moving a little bit, maybe closer to my work and my parents, they're getting on in years and I'd like to be closer to help them."

"Makes sense." A knock on the porch door interrupted them. Zin hopped out of her chair and walked over to her purse on the dining room table. "I ordered Chinese, looks like the delivery guy is here." Zin walked out to the porch and Jay stood up. Zin came back carrying a brown paper bag. "Wanna stick around for stir fry? Looks like I have extra." Jay shook his head.

"Naw, thanks, though. I've got errands to run." He started walking toward the door. Zin put down the bag and caught up with him.

"Okay, you be careful south of the border. How's your Spanish, by the way?"

"Cerveza, baño, siesta."

"That's all you need," Zin smiled. She hugged Jay, and he reached down and hugged her back. "Take care." Jay was out the door when he turned back.

"By the way, I think I met a friend of yours."

"Oh, who?"

"I can't remember his name. Funny guy. Well, I mean he talked a little funny and dressed a little unusual. Blonde hair. Anyway, he came by the church Easter Sunday as I was locking up. He said he was a friend of yours. We got talking and talked for a long time. It was his idea that I take the sabbatical. Do you know anyone like that?

Zin nodded her head. "Oh, yes. I certainly do.

34

"Watcha watchin'?" The teenager stood in the center of the room, assessing the situation. Zin had a remote control in each hand and was struggling to bring order to the screen.

"Well, nothing right now. This new service is driving me nuts." She looked up at the boy, his hair seeming to cover his eyes. She wasn't sure how he could see anything with hair like that. There were things like the hair, or when she found him lying around when he was supposed to do dishes, that made her want to step into parent mode and tell him what to do. But she was trying very hard to keep that separation. He had a mother; he didn't need another.

"Here, you try." She thrust the remotes towards him and sat back on the couch, not altogether unhappy with the arrangement. Adrian plopped down at the opposite end of the couch and quickly identified the issue.

"Oh, you had the TV on channel 5, it needs to be on 4." He offered the remote controls back to Zin, but she waved him off.

"No, you choose," she said. Unsure what to do, he shrugged, took the remotes, and started flipping through movie choices.

"How about I make some popcorn?" she said, already getting up.

"Uh, yeah. Cool." He didn't exactly sound excited, but his

response was audible and lacked the tone of dread she sometimes encountered. Zin practically tiptoed to the kitchen, never having heard him ever express any interest in spending time with her before, afraid of breaking the spell. Zin dug in the cupboard for some popcorn bags and threw them into the microwave. She threw the paper plates from the Chinese dinner in the garbage and put the leftovers in the fridge. The popcorn finished and she dumped it into two bowls.

"How about *Guardians of the Galaxy*?" he called from the other room.

"Sounds good to me," answered Zin, trying to sound something close to indifferent, not trying to scare him off. She had no idea what the movie was about, but it sounded like a space adventure, which was directly opposite her preferred genre. She walked back into the room and found Adrian still at the end of the couch, now stretched out, eyes fixed on the screen. She handed him a bowl and a napkin and sat down on the opposite end of the couch, putting her popcorn bowl between them.

"Is your mom going to watch?" asked Zin.

"No, she went to bed early," answered the boy, stuffing popcorn into his mouth.

Zin frowned. She enjoyed Jessica's company and wanted her to feel more comfortable, just hanging out as friends, less like a landlord. But maybe this was better. She had purposely kept her distance from Adrian since they moved in, not wanting to cross a line and scare him into believing his teacher was hovering around him. And Adrian had kept his distance as well, not ever being mean or disrespectful, but definitely trying to avoid her, especially when they were alone in the house. She looked across the couch at the boy. He seemed to be enjoying himself, and she realized that although she had never had children, this is probably as good as it gets when you are a parent of a teenager, simply sharing some time together without drama or tension.

Zin sat back and reflected on her situation. She was still alive. Adrian and his mom were okay. She had some people in her life now, and Rick wasn't one of them, which was a good thing. She still liked her job, and she was soon going to have her summer off. Was this bliss? No. She was still wrangling with Rick in a messy divorce, had disconnected from her friend network, and she still looked in the mirror and saw a frumpy, middle-aged single woman who had to go into the world now as a divorcée and reveal that embarrassing fact every time she reconnected with someone. But she was happy and had been for a few weeks, happier than any time in the previous couple of years. Happiness, it seems, had found her instead of the other way around. Maybe looking for happiness is a waste of time. And maybe perfection is overrated. Maybe, in the end, happiness is about finding yourself.

David L. Purcell

ACKNOWLEDGEMENTS

I would like to thank Deborah Marsh for beta reading this work and providing valuable insights, and Rachel Moulton for her terrific editorial assistance and positive feedback. Father John Hofstede took the time to provide me with an understanding of basic church administration and some of the realities of the life of a priest. I appreciate his help.

The program in my story called Project Hope is based on a program called Project Home, which is run by Interfaith Action of Greater St. Paul. Project Home has been providing overnight shelter and other services to the homeless for over twenty years. Prior to the COVID-19 pandemic, Project Home partnered with churches to provide temporary shelters, but that model has changed, and they now are able to provide services out of a more permanent location. Their director, Sara Liegl, was kind enough to provide background information for me on their program and on homelessness in general. Their program provides essential services and I encourage you to support them.

Finally, I would like to thank my wife, Kirstin, for her ongoing support, and for not complaining during the thousand times I tell her that I'm just going to disappear and do some writing.

74723609R00155